East Jesus, Nevada

The Adventures of W. W. Ronin
Book One

By Gregg Edwards Townsley
Two Bears Books Saint Helens, Oregon

Cover design by Olivia Passieux
Video book trailer(s) by Bill Fogle
Published by Two Bears Books
245 N. Vernonia Road
Saint Helens, Oregon 97051 U.S.A.
www.twobearsbooks.com
Two Bears Books, First Edition
ISBN: 0-6157-7141-6
ISBN-13: 9780615771410
Library of Congress Control Number: 2013934861
Two Bears Books, St. Helens, OR

Special discounts are available on quantity purchases by corporations,
associations and others. For details, contact the publisher at the address
above. Orders by U.S. trade bookstores and wholesalers, please contact
the publisher or visit www.twobearsbooks.com.
Printed in the United States of America

To Jared, who lived the adventure.

TABLE OF CONTENTS

My Dear Sir:
Your esteemed favor is at hand and after careful deliberation I have determined to write to you to come to Nevada. I cannot, in the brief space to which a letter must necessarily be confined, enter into details: but I can assure you that if you will come here, settle and invest your means, the final result will be most happy to you. A few brief years of existence here will prepare you to enjoy all the rest and all the beatitudes which the paradise of the blessed can bestow, and if, perchance, your soul should take the other track, hell itself can bring you no surprises. Respectfully, etc.

Charles Carroll Goodwin, The Comstock Club, Salt Lake City, Utah: The Leonard Publishing Company, 1891.

Gold Hill, Nevada
1879

Chapter 1

DUSTSUCKER

Spinning the cylinder and rocking his iron up toward the roof, Ronin ejected six spent shells from his carbon-glazed Colt. "Damn it," he shouted, feeling instantly guilty that God in heaven, who had spared his backside a second time on the Comstock, might suddenly change his or her mind, sending a bullet his way as surely as the others had missed. "I'm totally out," he murmured to no one in particular as a single loud rifle shot split the window frame above his head, instantly driving him to the floor.

He remained there, splayed like a desert gecko weighing his options. "Jesus, I've got to get out of here," he said, shaking his head.

The once-Reverend William Washington Ronin rolled slowly across the glass-strewn wooden floor toward the open doorway, fully expecting another silver-seeking hombre, or the same son of a bitch, or bitches, who had pinned him down underneath the window, to follow his flailing frame with gunfire. But none appeared.

He paused, scooting himself slowly toward the door, on one knee with his right forearm across his right thigh to help him get up and going if the shooting stopped. But a lengthy silence followed. "That's it?" he said quietly. "I get stuck in a miner's shack on the Comstock Lode, a thousand feet in the open, and a couple of ne'er-do-well brand-burners catch me with my pants down?"

He had paused to brace himself against the west wall of an abandoned house to defecate when the shooting had suddenly started. Maybe the local jackalopes had mistaken him for a claim jumper? Or perhaps someone had taken umbrage with his unleashing his explosive load against the white side of a once promising Comstock home? "Hypermotility," the doctor called it. The consequence of spending too many years in the church, he figured as he listened.

But there was only silence. The valley full of sage and rabbit weed testified in surprise, as the mining men and machinery of the Comstock rarely allowed for such a moment to exist, save for the occasional early morning groan where the yellow, mineral-laden earth wondered if its despoilment and suffering would ever end.

"It's over?" he asked himself again, not that kneeling while talking to himself didn't bring him a familiar contentment and pleasure. But just as sure as he hadn't expected a firestorm of lead, or the sudden quiet that followed, he didn't anticipate the unannounced and grinning entrance of Ormsby County Sheriff Marcus T. Slade, or "Dustsucker" as he was known to his friends.

"God, you scared me!" Ronin exclaimed when his pal suddenly burst through the doorway. "What the hell are you doing up here?" he shouted, pulling one hundred and eighty-five pounds of ex-clergyman out of a dusty corner, wiping the sweat from his eyes and forehead so that he could see.

"Whoa buddy! Put the gun down! I was sure you were dead," Dustsucker bellowed, his hands in front of him, as if flesh would shield him from a bullet, if even from a friend.

Ronin complied, leaning his 1866 Winchester Yellow Boy against the north wall of what he assumed was once a proper person's living room.

"You tell me, Dusty. I know I've had better days." Ronin was kneeling on a busted-up wooden floor, with his green-and-tan canvas riding pants still halfway down around one of his ankles. The room was bare of furniture and, judging from the sand and dust strewn throughout, hadn't been lived in since the last mining boom, four years before. Looking at his boots, he began laughing.

He tugged at his britches and caught his right pant leg on a large and broken Mexican spur.

"I have had better days, deputy; I surely have," he said, shaking his head. He took a deep breath, and grimacing in such a way as to hide his pain from his friend, pulled himself up using the jamb of a western-facing window. It was seven o'clock in the morning on the Comstock, and he could see clear up to Yellow Jacket Mine. "Jesus, it's good to see you," he said, finally getting his pants up and buttoning himself together. He grabbed his gun belt from the floor, checking to see if he had unused cartridges. He was totally out.

Dustsucker wasn't Slade's given name, not that it mattered. People picked up names as they tumbled across Nevada. Given his well-ridden and dirty appearance, the name was probably well deserved as he wasn't the kind of man to have grown up with a collar around his neck.

Dusty's loud yet friendly voice was a welcome interruption to most gatherings in the Comstock mining camps in the early days, and even into the 1870s, when mineral mining took a severe decline. He was certainly a welcome surprise given the gunfire that had punctuated Ronin's morning routine. "I heard shooting up the ravine a ways, and being no stranger to angry encounters in these parts, I thought I might investigate a bit," Dustsucker said. "I saw a few angry union men down the street before climbing the hill. I didn't expect to see you." The big guy smiled. A tin badge hung by a mere thread or two, desperately clinging to a sun-dried vest that had seen better days for dirt a half-dozen years ago. It was a perfect match to the alternately hard-packed desert clay and sand of the northern Nevada desert. And it blended well with the business of northern Nevada's mining towns.

Ronin's friend was almost two hundred pounds his senior, and dry as a weed in late September. He wheezed his way into the doorway, bumping his Kris Kringle-sized frame into place until it blocked nearly all of the light. A distracted visitor to the Comstock cabin might have considered it a solar eclipse, Ronin mused, but he welcomed it.

"Man, I thought I was a goner!" he exclaimed. "How many of them were there? I've been pinned down in this place for a couple of hours, since daybreak anyway."

Ronin reached for his hat, struggled again to his feet, slowly standing tall, turning this way and that, looking out each window to make sure his attackers were gone. It wasn't enough to look, he'd often said to soldiers, and in latter days deputies and marshals. A man's gaze needed to follow his body if he was to hit anything with his fist or shooting iron. Rifles and shotguns weren't much different.

Though Slade was a deputy sheriff in Carson City, Nevada, being a county officer didn't pay the bills. Part-time work did. And when work failed—the state's capital had seen a major depression in the late seventies with the failure of nearby mines, farms and related businesses—he liked to while away the time seventeen miles or so up the Virginia City canyons looking for gold, silver, or whatever else might strike his fancy. Ronin never asked. He was sometimes gone days at a time, an absence nobody seemed to notice in Carson City, the territory's capital, and since 1864, the capital of one of the nation's newest states. It had been more than a dozen years since the Silver State had joined Lincoln's Union, and noisy years at that. But times were turning sleepy again, and as difficult as that was for folks in Virginia City, Carson City and places in-between, both Slade and Ronin liked them that way.

"Lordy, that was a hike!" Dustsucker exclaimed as he sat down on the creaking floor a few hundred feet south of a switchback known as Greiner's Bend. Dust settled up as soon as Slade settled down, and at three hundred and fifty pounds or more, the deputy didn't exactly sit as much as fall. A good amount of sweat crossed Dustsucker's brow but was just as soon wiped away by a quick forearm swipe of dirty worn red underwear.

Dustsucker thought about his friend's question. He tapped his fingers, as if counting, and pursed his lips. With his hesitation, Ronin was certain he was being careful in his reply. "Maybe five, maybe six," he said, breathing heavily. "Seemed like they were out of cartridges when I hit the crest of the ravine though. Slapped their belts a couple of times and looked real surprised to see a bear-sized man staring down at them," he said, laughing as much at the way he told the story as Ronin's predicament in it.

"You say you were taking a dump?" he asked, hardly controlling his laughter. His eyes glistened as tears streamed down his face. "Well hell, Ronin! I haven't roared like this in years! Always was afraid that might happen to me," he said, spitting tobacco on a floor already littered with brass and nickel shells from Ronin's handguns and rifle. "Pinched off a good one, I imagine!" He bent over, trying to control a belly laugh that guffawed its way into Ronin's face anyway. Grabbing his friend by the shoulders, he shouted, "God, you're a sight for sore eyes!"

They embraced in a way that cowboys generally don't but good guys sometimes do, briefly remembering the good times, which were bad times, goddammit. But you make the best of what you've been through, and Ronin had been through a lot. And then you keep going.

"I've been up this way every couple of weeks my friend, generally steering clear of the mines, homes and business around the Crown Point and to the hills. Still, I don't believe I've seen anyone at this house in quite some time," Slade said, "though there's a tedious pack of people still living up here, some of whom are probably now wondering what is going on. What the hell were you doing here?"

"Well, that's a real story," Ronin replied, "one I'm anxious to tell. But what do you say we first get out of here, do what we can do to avoid the Gold Hill Police and grab us a beer?"

"Hell, they're not going to bother us. McLeery hasn't been around much since his deputy was killed in July. Poor son of a bitch was walking past a house where he heard a couple of folk arguing. He knocks on the door, and the next thing you know he's shot in the head."

"Jesus, I had no idea," Ronin said.

"Imagine not," Slade replied, "a lot of folks missed it. But not McLeery. Marshal took him into custody, shooting him in the arm."

"He should have shot him in the head," Ronin said.

"No kidding. Would have saved Storey County a lot of heartache. The man's trial is coming up soon. He'll likely be hanged by January."

Ronin stood quietly for a moment. He hated the cruelty he'd seen in the West. And he'd seen plenty of it, after leaving the Pinkertons. Hell, he'd seen plenty of it before joining the Pinkertons, even in the church.

"He deserved better," Dustsucker said, turning in the doorway and beginning to look for his horse.

"We all do, brother, and some of us get it."

"A lot of us don't," Dustsucker said.

"Well, what do you say we head to Virginia City? There's a real nice saloon a mile or so up the hill that I haven't seen in some time. I'm plumb thirsty. And frankly, Slade, when you hear what I've got to say, you'll be real thirsty too."

Chapter 2

BUCKET OF BLOOD

"God, I love this place!" Ronin exclaimed as he eased himself down into a well-worn wooden chair, rocking backward a little ways at the Bucket of Blood Saloon in Virginia City.

He was careful not to tip the chair over as he inched his lips forward to the first beer he'd seen in weeks. "I don't know how they do it," he said to his friend. "I get they don't ice their beer. And maybe it's my fault for getting started on those cold Philadelphia-brewed German lagers, but I do like my beer colder than warmer, if I can get it." Ronin smiled broadly, "This comes close."

Ronin turned to look at Dustsucker, expecting an argument, but the man was halfway through his first beer and on his way to a second, suffering like a regular when he got hold of the Bucket of Blood server's arm. "It's simple negligence, my friend," he said. "These people don't bother to keep their beer warm. It just sits on the back porch and brings the weather in with it. Leave it to you to find a cheap place to drink, though. This ain't no two-bit saloon like the Crystal. We could drink all night and still get out of here for less than a dollar!"

"Hell, at a nickel a beer, I would hope so. But listen, I'm telling you, someday they'll be hauling cold beer to places like this on railroad trains, packing them with ice and insulating the hell out of them. As much as I hate the railroads, and you know that I do, I'll excuse their excesses for access to a good, cold beer when I want one. I've been up the Crystal, Dusty, even had a member take me to the Washoe Club, since you mention it. It had some fine chandeliers, as I recall, a nice pool hall and a great many pretty women. But the beer was warm, just like it is everywhere else."

"As it should be, Ronin," Dustsucker said. "Senorita!" he shouted, still holding on to the Bucket of Blood's server, who was now having a difficult time smiling. "Another beer for my friend and a couple more for me," he said, laughing. He threw his head back and opened his mouth wide, finishing the beer he had in his right hand. The big man belched loudly enough that a couple of dusty, chemical-stained mill workers sitting close by laughed at the sight of the red-faced fat man, dressed a jolly woolly red on a July sun-drenched afternoon.

"Lordy, I like it here too," he said patting the barmaid's behind as she walked off. The glance back was unnerving. "Where's my beer?" he shouted, and then turning to his friend, "and where's my story, Ronin? A guy doesn't have all day you know. Not a sober one, anyway," he said, slapping his knee as if he had heard or said something extraordinarily funny.

Ronin smiled. He loved the man. Most folks did, even when they were on their way to the hoosegow. Dustsucker had that much personality. Ronin leaned forward so as to start his story when he noticed a couple of slack-jawed yahoos walking into the saloon, thirty-some feet to his right. Dusty men, covered with the kind of dirt you picked up on a long ride, not the generations of soil that Dustsucker had sticking to him, or the red dirt you might accumulate simply riding the road up from Carson City. These men had been laying in it, batwings and all. The cowboys' careful approach to the bar heightened his interest.

"See those guys?" he whispered to Dustsucker. "Ever see them before?" he asked. The men's clothes weren't just dirty, they were shredded. One man's left sleeve was in tatters and the other's right sleeve looked equally torn and bloody. They had been involved in something, and yet despite their natural hesitation and appearance, they were strutting like turkey gobblers at layin' time.

Dustsucker looked up from the row of glasses that had just been set before him. "No, can't say that I have." He eyed the well-worn gun rigs slung low on their hips underneath their riding coats. "I find it interesting, however, that there isn't a single cartridge on their belts." There were poor folks and rich folks in the Queen City of the Comstock, as Virginia City was sometimes called. But poor folks didn't carry six-guns and ride horses. "What do you make of that, Ronin?" he asked, pushing his chair out from the table and turning business-like. He peered around the post through the large plate glass window to Ronin's right, so as to gander at the horses they had ridden in on.

"Healthy-looking Mustangs," he said. "Can't say much by that, 'cept that somebody's feeding them. These might be two of the boys I saw skedaddling up the ravine in Gold Hill." He looked at Ronin, who had tipped his hat forward and slid down in his seat, and wondered what was up. "What's going on, my friend?" he asked, turning to face his pal while keeping an eye on the saloon's newest guests.

"I'm glad you're here," Ronin breathed, placing both hands on the table, as if he was getting ready to rise his chair. "You can watch me kill these cow punchers," he said. His weight shifted, but he didn't get up, because Dustsucker's hand weighed him down. Ronin knew that if he stood he'd surely need his gun hand free.

"Let go, friend," Ronin said, his generally kindly eyes turning steely bright.

"Not before we talk about this, Ronin. We're close enough to Carson City that I'm going to have to answer to whatever you're thinking of doing. And Marshal Ash, the law up this way, isn't the kindest of men. I want to know the whole story."

Ronin settled back into his chair, grabbing his beer with his left hand as the barmaid removed a couple of empties. "Alright, so maybe I'm not sure," he replied. Dustsucker settled back too, anxious not to push the friendship beyond its limits, or the story's slow unfolding, or the occasional grace that enveloped them both.

"If you don't know ..." Dustsucker continued.

"I know, don't show." Ronin hated Slade's occasional attempts at rhyme, given that his own experiences with violence were so much more severe. But he listened, knowing Slade to be a good man, and not because he was a lawman, but because he was a genuinely honorable man. There were so few of them on the Comstock. Silver and gold lined many a pocket, particularly when it came to men involved with the banks, mills and mines. True enough, what didn't jingle didn't count for shit on the Comstock, except for the occasional heart of a genuinely good man. And Dustsucker was that.

"Tell your story, partner," he smiled, lifting his paw off of Ronin's gun hand, "and we'll figure out what to do after that. And if it's a good enough story, I may make the play with you," Dustsucker winked as he swallowed a little more beer.

No, Dustsucker wasn't a good man because he was a lawman. He was a good man because he knew what was right and wrong. And he wasn't afraid to make things right when it was only him, or him and a friend, standing between right and wrong. He looked at the deputy and grinned, his eyes still taking in the two strangers at the bar. He doubted he had ever felt closer to anyone.

"Alright, I didn't see the guys in the gulch. I was ... busy with other things, you might remember. And I never got a clean shot at anyone, given the smoke in the room, though I kept up a decent rate of fire, if you know what I mean. But listen, do you remember Kuon?" Ronin asked his ragged friend, who was looking about for some oysters and crackers.

"Sure," Dustsucker nodded, shifting his chair a bit and placing his back against the wall so he could keep his eyes on the long riders at the bar, locate a server, and still listen to Ronin. "I always thought that was a dumb name for a dog."

"It's the Bible word for 'dog,' Dusty. I've told you that before, as in 'a dog returns to its own vomit?'"

"Whatever. You know I don't read that stuff."

"Yeah, well Kuon and I were camping in Washoe valley a week back, doing some trading with some of the Indians there before heading out to hunt some. I was there maybe a couple of days." Ronin took a sip of beer and allowed it to sit in his mouth and appreciating its natural coolness before he swallowed. He had heard lake ice was stored underneath some of the boardwalks in Virginia City for use in the mines, and wondered briefly if any of it might have lasted through the summer months. It would be nice if some of it had. The beer might be colder and Dustsucker might appreciate his earlier point. "Well," Ronin said, continuing his story, "I liked this group, and had seen them up the mountain a ways when the weather was warmer, so we were catching up when these cowboys rode hard into camp."

"These fellows?" Dustsucker asked, lifting his chin in a simple nod toward the dusty boys at the bar, who by this time had noticed Ronin's intermittent gaze.

"Those men, I do believe," Ronin said, lowering his hat in a quick nod. "I can't say they were the hustlers shooting at me in Gold Hill," he added, taking his eyes off them for just a moment when both he and Dusty noted that the one closest to the door began to repeatedly touch his leg and fidget. "But if they're the hombres I'm thinking of, they showed an unusual interest in Kuon and some of the kids in the camp."

Dustsucker turned his eyes toward them and stared. The cowboy that was previously tapping on the bar was now playing with his vest, patting it as if he were pacing himself. Both men were clearly agitated. They were aware that they were being talked about. Ronin sat quietly, his right hand resting beneath the table, where he always kept it when sitting down, but a certain restlessness began to crowd into his head.

"So these fellows didn't dismount," he continued, "which I thought was odd, given that they towered over my Washoe friends, who were sitting on the ground. And not being a mean dog, but an observant one, Kuon was acting real nervous. Australian Shepherds are like that, you know. "

"He always seemed to know what was up, Ronin."

"Yeah, he did. And the Washoe do, too. I mean, as passive as the tribes are, and given that they've only known white men since Fremont surveyed the mountains thirty-some years ago, they don't cotton to being talked down to. So when one of these guys mentions a little girl—I wasn't part of the conversation at first so I didn't catch everything that was said—suddenly everyone is super animated, jumping up and down like a cat on a hot tin roof! Kuon starts barking, and there's a whole lot of angry swagger on everybody's part. And these guys ride out yelling at each other and the Indians they're talking to.

"These guys?" Dustsucker asked again, rolling the toothpick in his mouth from one side to the other, pondering what Ronin was saying while still watching the guy closest to the door, his friend now turning toward Ronin as well.

"Yeah, these guys. Turns out they had asked about a little girl." he said raising his voice.

The men at the bar reached for their guns! Maybe to communicate their displeasure, perhaps they thought they needed to protect themselves, having misunderstood the two friends' attention. But Ronin, never inclined to be someone's fool, didn't wait for an explanation. Considering gunplay a rather poor way of beginning a conversation, he dumped the heavy wooden table forward and dropped to his knees. The former minister-turned-man tracker thumb-cocked one and then fanned two additional .45 caliber slugs into each man, twice. Six shots cleared leather, but sounded like two, before Dustsucker dropped the toothpick from his lips.

There was a sudden and unexpected stillness in the Bucket of Blood Saloon. Had there been a sudden, mid-morning noise, no one could have heard it over the still-lingering sound wave of Ronin's angry Colt. No one moved. No one breathed. No one questioned.

Ronin took a deep breath. "Kuon turned up dead a couple of days later," he said, slowly turning his head toward his friend. "I'm guessing he followed them from the camp."

"I'll be damned," Dustsucker said, his mouth still open.

"Not likely," Ronin said after a moment. "Not like these guys."

Chapter 3
TAKING OUT THE TRASH

As sure as nighttime always gives way to morning, it didn't take too long for the piano player at the Bucket of Blood to realize that the joint was losing money with people just sitting there with their mouths agape. It took even less time for the gaming manager to motion to the barkeep to get a couple of guys to move the bodies—two fingers up and an index finger pointing in the general direction of the bloody mess. Moments later, two large men exited a room to Ronin's left, parting both the curtains and the saloon's lingering stillness with anxious breathing and mumbled expletives.

Ronin was as startled seeing them as they were seeing him, the smoke from his shortened Colt Peacemaker still clearing. The gun was not quite back in its holster.

"Jesus," one of the men said as they passed by, brushing Ronin's linen duster and pausing to apologize profusely. "Did you see that?" he asked his friend, regaining only a portion of his composure. "I don't think I've ever seen anyone shoot that fast!" The other nodded in quick agreement while glancing backward to see if their passing so close had riled the shooter any. No one had seen Ronin draw and only Dustsucker, if anyone at all, knew that his six-shooter was already pointed at the men under the table. The two barmen were as anxious to take to care of business as to avoid the continued gaze of Ronin, who had returned their table to the upright position and was considering what to do next.

The mere presence of a badge on a big man who did nothing about something kept the peace of the place. No additional sheriff was called. No town constable was sent for. And no U.S. Marshal was summoned. Dustsucker's badge carried an apparent and appropriate amount of weight. It didn't take long for the curious chaos of girls and gambling to return to Virginia City's most important watering hole. A killing or two a day didn't keep business away, as neither patrons nor employees questioned the sudden rattling of Ronin's gun. The large men from the back room moved as if it was a practiced pace. Ronin wondered how vulgar a saloon's activities could get before there was a significant interruption to the city's business. It had been worse in earlier days.

"Listen Ronin," Dustsucker said, breaking the silence, "I'm all about your doing what you do. Lord knows that some people in this world need it. Someone has to take out the trash and these boomtowns on both sides of the Sierras seem to generate a fair bit of it. But I'm uncomfortable with what your business is doing to you." Dustsucker paused. Ronin looked up. "You look tired," he said, looking at his friend, "I mean bone tired, my friend."

Ronin sat for a moment, wondering if he could share his heart. If not with his friend, he thought, then who?

"It's been hard," he said, thinking of the years he had been collecting bounties by bringing bad men back to justice. But he wondered how two men could have appeared so suddenly behind him without his noticing. He'd heard that Hickok had been killed while playing poker in Deadwood, shot from behind. He never saw it coming. But gunfights were like that, not that he was new to the business. His father's untimely death a decade or so before had contributed to Ronin's taking up a new mission in life, leaving the ministry and his mother's good pleasure in order to deal with men a great deal more angry and far less capable of expressing it than the people he had ministered to in church. Still, it would be a sorry way to die.

He looked at his friend and appreciated the risks he took every day as an Ormsby County sheriff. Most of Ronin's experience at shooting folks—those, he observed, "who needed shooting" anyway—had been at some distance. Wyatt Earp could take the close ones, he figured, though the Earps were better known for simply banging people on their heads. Or maybe one of the Masterson brothers, or Dustsucker, he didn't care. He simply didn't want the emotional bother and complications, if he could avoid them, of shooting people up close. It was too intimate, too overwhelming, too disruptive to business. He looked around the saloon and felt immediate relief that the incessant clamor of the Comstock, inside the saloon and out, had resumed without more than a moment's pause. Still, he hated it.

Looking over at the barkeep, Ronin remembered why he hadn't been to the Bucket of Blood in years. Senators or no senators—the establishment occasionally made a big deal of the legislators and other clientele who drank there; he didn't know if Twain had ever had a beer at the bar, but still—he hated crowds. He hated the busyness of places where crowds congregated. He pushed his handgun back into his strong-side holster. If nature abhorred a vacuum, as one of his favorite New England essayists had written, he hated whatever the opposite of a vacuum was. People-filled rooms, busy train stations and stage stops, churches filled with goofy, grinning people waiting for something important to happen, as if important stuff could ever happen when people weren't alone. Groups made him feel uncomfortable and were generally a waste of his time.

Maybe it was a control thing? He wasn't about to let life take him anywhere again, as his father's anywhere had turned out to be so damn pitiful. And his own experience in the church, or later riding with the Pinkertons as a guard and then investigator had not been much better. In the end, that's what had ended his ministry as a Protestant clergyman: a disdain for people. The constant tug of responsibility. The lack of options. The unending sack full of folk hoping to get their petulant needs met. The thought that a Great Spirit of some kind, certainly not loving, never loquacious, was going to take him somewhere, somewhere maybe that he didn't want to go? Anymore, it made his stomach turn.

Gulping down the end of his beer, he swiveled to stare more intently at the back room from which the two men had exited. A slight gap in the saloon's ornate green velvet panels didn't allow much of a view. He'd have to be more careful next time, or the next couple of guests out of sight or hearing may be the most painful or terminating.

"You wondering about the drapes?" Dustsucker asked, still surprised that Ronin hadn't been aware of the men standing behind them. "You didn't hear or see those guys, did you?" Dustsucker had noticed them, and he was staring in the opposite direction.

"Yeah," Ronin whispered, thinking of the last few moments when his attention had been so riveted elsewhere that he hadn't heard or seen anything other than the men at the bar. "It'll cost me big time if I'm not more careful," he said. "It will cost me good. But what I'm doing is what I need to do, Dusty, right now anyway. And there's seemingly no end to it, brother. It's that important."

W. W. Ronin and Dustsucker sat for a few moments, maybe as many as ten moments before Ronin spoke again.

"Take that Washoe thing, for instance," Ronin said, his eyes moistening. "I tracked those sons of bitches for at least a week, losing them, finding them, losing them again. Until you came along, I didn't know where they were, save that maybe the people shooting at me were them. Then you invited me for a drink."

"Invited you for a drink?" Dustsucker exclaimed, laughing at his oldest living friend. "You invited me, compadre!"

God, he hated it when his friend attempted to speak Spanish.

"Don't be hanging this silver dollar bar tab on me, Ronin! I can't afford it on a deputy's salary. And I've certainly not found enough metal in these parts to make up the difference!" Dustsucker squirmed in his chair as if to emphasize his point. "You were about to tell me a story, Ronin," he said. "Was that it?"

The man was patient to a fault, and was probably not a good guy to play poker with, he thought. Ronin took out a deck of cards from his vest and then, returning them to their box, placed them in the pocket opposite his father's New Testament and watch. Dustsucker knew he hadn't heard the whole story. Ronin's face flushed and gave it away.

"Well, there's more," Ronin said. "And I don't imagine that I can fix it alone."

Chapter 4
SILVER CITY

About a half mile out of town, Dustsucker couldn't stand the silence any longer. Ronin was ruminating quietly when Dustsucker cleared his throat. "Ronin," he said.

"Just give me a couple of moments," he replied.

The former Reverend W. W. Ronin didn't really believe in a heaven or hell anymore. Not since seminary, when the college deans had quizzed their young starlings on the finer points of Christian thus-and-so. But he still pondered such things after killing someone. Reading here and there, or simply wondering in the same way that the great bards and prophets of old had done, he hadn't found a whole lot of comfort in the church's teachings.

It seemed to him that if there was a hell—and the West was surely it, at least the parts he had seen, places where no crop or crazy could put down roots long enough to make a life or a living—then there certainly had to be an end to the labors that had defined him these last many years. And a future as well, he hoped.

Ronin had left the Episcopal mission in Wichita without saying a word. He was sick of cows, cowboys and the girls who needed them. Surprisingly, the congregation didn't seem to mind. Maybe his East Coast ways where just a little too toney, or maybe his outspokenness was the problem, as folks there seemed a little too enamored with the railroad. Unable or unwilling to see the down side of growth and the human garbage the railroad had brought with it, Ronin had decided to move on. Three years after the town incorporated, it wasn't his kind of town anymore.

Despite the traveling—he had lingered a bit in places here and there to catch a crook or two, the way he now made his money, "a detective" he sometimes called it, a "bounty hunter" some had said with a condemnatory look or a sneer—he had never gotten used to the bleakness of the West until he arrived in Carson City. That's where he'd met Dustsucker, or Marcus Slade, his real name though few friends ever called him that. Despite the sheer economy of his new calling in life—a hundred bucks now and then, sometimes more, never less—he never did get comfortable with killing even the baddest of men, no matter what they had done.

Some people deserve to be killed, one of the Earp brothers had told him. He liked that, but he preferred, when given the opportunity, to use his brain instead of his brawn, his guts instead of his gun, though he wasn't against pushing people into a wall or two along the way when things got difficult. And if he had to shoot the son of a bitch—it was so much easier to objectify the men he killed than to get too personal—he preferred to do it at a distance, a great distance, the kind of distance that a rifle would take neatly and nicely.

Meanness didn't need to be messy.

Given that the district marshal was gone, according to folks at the Bucket of Blood, they might want to head back to town the next day to square things up before heading back to Carson City. Augustus Ash had been appointed to the District of Nevada in 1876, and while Ronin had never met him, he'd heard that Ash might have been involved with the rest of the Marshal Service in rooting out Confederate spies at one time, though he couldn't imagine the man to be that old. Whatever the case, it sounded as if the local constabulary would take an interest in the shootings. While folks were generally reasonable on the Comstock regarding the dispatching of hooligans, they planned to camp just a few miles outside of town to make sure.

They rode slowly, kicking up dried yellow and red clumps of earth as they weaved west over the mountains, picking their way between the abandoned homes and hovels that overlooked

Virginia City's finer housing. The Virginia City economy had crashed again in the mid-seventies. Ronin wondered if there'd ever be people in some of the houses they were passing. Many families had left the Comstock for places north, south, east and west. The railroad in Reno had drawn folks north; a mineral bonanza in Bodie had seen some of the younger men head south. And there was always Butte, Montana or San Francisco, California if you were looking to see what had happened to your Comstock neighbors.

Coming to the crest of Mount Davidson, they paused long enough to see the beginning of what promised to be a surplus of folks heading up Greiner's Bend from Silver City and the capital to see Ulysses S. Grant. The former President of the United States was due to speak from the balcony of one of the more prominent downtown buildings on Monday. Ronin noted the date, October 27, 1879. A former Confederate cavalryman, he was unimpressed and anxious. Tennessee's 19th Calvary Regiment was among the last of the troops east of the Mississippi to lay down its arms. Despite significant efforts to ameliorate his hostile feelings toward the general, the hoopla over Grant's visit—the last leg of a "world tour" of all things, as if celebrating the end of the Civil War could be any more distasteful than burying the Union's war dead in General Lee's Arlington estate and gardens—running into more of the generally unionist crowds of the Comstock would certainly feed his already angry and anxious insides.

"Ronin! I'm trying to get your attention," Dustsucker groaned, as he fidgeted uncomfortably, just a few hundred feet from the top of Mount Davidson, overlooking the Comstock. It was a hundred mile view.

"How far does a man got to ride before his buddy starts talking to him? I'm simply plumb out of patience to hear the rest of your story!"

Ronin looked up, glancing at his friend and then back to the dusty path over which their horses were moving, Dustsucker's gaze was too intent for Ronin to keep the scattered thoughts he was thinking and feeling.

"I'm sorry," he said. The deputy sheriff's looming and careless appearance always brought a smile to his lips, no matter what was on his mind. His friend could attend a Philadelphia wedding (not that he'd ever been East), looking dirty and disheveled, and not ever be aware that he was desperately out of place. A man's got to love being that comfortable with himself, and a couple of dead guys could certainly wait given the story he was about to tell his friend.

The former reverend took a deep breath, his respiration labored as much by the winding trail as the day's precipitous events. "So I was saying, before those two trail busters came to their comeuppance … I was in Washoe Valley doing some trading, just east of the lake bed north of Carson City, when these guys galloped up. There was something about the two of them that just didn't sit right. The boy I call Little Wolf saw them first. He's one of the kids in the tribe, lives with his mother part of the time and with his father, at the edge of Washoe City, the rest of the time."

Dustsucker shifted in his saddle and looked like he was growing impatient, so Ronin picked up the pace.

"Well, the kid's got a sixth sense about him."

"Sixth sense?"

"Yeah, he knows things that other people don't, him and his father; I can't account for it. He sees them riding toward the camp from the north, skirting the western shadows as the sun was going down. It was the time of day when a rider wants to decide whether he's coming or going, it's getting that kind of dark. Kuon starts growling and, well, pretty much everybody in the camp gets agitated before I figure out anything is going on. "

"You're normally a pretty observant person, Ronin."

"Well, I had my head stirred in another direction, if you know what I mean, not that the lady noticed. So these two cowpokes ride in, just as suddenly and as quickly as they can, and moments later, ride out. Kuon is jumping up and down, along with every other crazy heathen."

"Heathen?"

"You know I don't mean that. But I pretty much kept to myself during the whole thing, until the next morning when I noticed that Kuon is missing."

"It's not like that dog to wander off," Dustsucker interjected, "except maybe to wonder if he might find a normal name."

Ronin shot him a glance. He'd been with the dog since he was a pup, and had appreciated how close they had become. Even in his ministerial days, Kuon was constantly by his side. The dog had been with him so long, he could probably read Latin or Greek.

"No, it's not," Ronin responded, skipping Dustsucker's remark. "Or wasn't, anyway."

"Wasn't? I'm not following."

"*Wasn't*," Ronin said coldly, looking directly at his lawman friend as they rode side-by-side into a protected ravine near the top of Mount Davidson, on the mountain's western slope.

"I found him about mid-morning, his throat slashed, lying up against some rocks. He was likely trying to stay cool as he fell into his last sleep."

"Damn," Dustsucker said, wincing. "Coyote get him?"

"No, that's my point. It was as thin and as biting a cut as I've ever seen."

"Jesus."

"Yup."

Ronin was quiet for a moment as the two dismounted, hobbling their horses in brush to camp for the night. They gathered their bedrolls, a pile of sage and headed toward a quiet clump of trees.

"Knifed, my friend. And Kuon must have taken a big chunk out of one or both of them, given the blood on the fabric scattered about. And that's when I got to thinking about the Washoe thing."

"The Washoe thing?"

"They didn't want to talk about it at the time," Ronin continued. "And it wasn't my business, they said. Generally I don't mind keeping things that way when folks are real decided. But it didn't take more than a couple of hours to loop back, check in with my Washoe friends and compare stories to understand."

"Understand what?" Dustsucker asked.

"I lost a dog," Ronin practically whispered, his eyes moist again, though it might have been the sagebrush fire. "But these folks, these people apparently lost something far more valuable."

"What are you talking about, Ronin?" Slade wanted to be patient, but Ronin's measured words were just simply not Slade's style. It was late, he hadn't had a lot to eat and he wasn't thinking too clearly anyway. Besides, the fire likely wouldn't last long enough to fry up some beans.

"I'm talking about their kids," Ronin growled angrily, his eyes wide and as wild as any mountain bear or wolf Dustsucker had ever seen. "I'm saying, someone's been taking their kids."

Chapter 5

AMERICAN GOSPEL MISSION

The American Gospel Mission entered Nevada's Great Basin in 1868. You might say it started out as a Presbyterian churchman's wet dream, if Presbyterian churchmen had such things, which they generally don't.

Emma and Henry Nauman had left a nameless backwater town along the Ohio River just outside of Pittsburgh in hopes of finding something more meaningful. "And less wet," Emma used to say, given the river's propensity for flooding each springtime in their little farm town in the southern West Virginia shadow of Steubenville, Ohio.

Emma and Henry were hoping for a new life in the fast-expanding West and took one of the first missionary assignments in that direction in order to establish something "God-honoring, soul-saving and Christ-rich."

Henry was agreeable with Emma's missionary vision, more or less, until a day or so after they had reached the Sierra Nevada Mountains. The mission was quite a ways from any other Protestant missionary's effort, and might be promising, to Henry's way of thinking, for those who might also want to make a profit.

"I'll not stay another day," the spindle-framed pseudo Presbyterian cleric told his wife when they had reached the area outside Carson City. They had rented a carriage for a couple of hours to look over a home site near Genoa and paused a few miles south of Nevada's capital to survey the Carson Valley's expanse. "Not another day of whining about Jennie. Not another hour listening to you talk about how things might have been different if we had stayed in Pittsburgh. And not another minute of hearing you tell me how you wished you had done this or done that, but never had the gol-darned chutzpah to do anything about it!"

Henry was referring to his wife's insatiable desire to live a meaningful Christian life among the Indians out West, winning "the heathen to Christ"—not something he was entirely against if there was money to be made—while somehow retaining a full set of china and other social accoutrements in hopes of a finding a similarly civilized city like Pittsburgh.

Nauman was amazed that anybody could hold two so very opposite desires together, and he was finished with his personal efforts, however involuntary, to do so.

Their journey west hadn't been easy, overland by joining multiple wagon trains through Iowa, Nebraska, Wyoming, Utah (where they had seen Mormons for the first time in their other-wise sheltered lives), and finally taking the California Trail toward Sacramento. Hitting the Sierras just before winter had finished Henry Nauman's quest to please his wife and whatever God she worshiped, and had provoked an uncommon come-to-Jesus discussion of the couple's future.

"You can't have both," he said, measuring his words so as to be firm but hoping to circumvent his wife's cyclic expressions of wrath. Her madness had driven them to the very edge of the American West, but had pretty much played out his limited supply of compassion and patience.

Nauman loved his wife, in the same sense that he appreciated food and water, but whatever abiding passion he'd once had for Emma was long gone. The ups and downs of their relationship had been too much, or not enough, depending on whom he was talking to and how frustrated he was with Emma's driving desire to do something different with their lives while holding on to all of the civilized accessories of their previous life outside of Pittsburgh. And it wasn't like they lived in Pittsburgh proper, he often mumbled. Steubenville's social registry didn't include their small burg, and it was a big step backward from the emerging titans of Pittsburgh's manufacturing and business community, where he had originally hoped to build a meaningful career.

Stepping out of the carriage, Emma touched his shoulder.

The romantic feelings were long gone in Henry's mind, given the back and forth of Emma's crazy moods. Their sexual life had become a train wreck and any intimacies approaching their being together had been real difficult for him after their daughter's death. But he stepped carefully as he wanted her happiness and, more so, was intent on escaping her wrath.

It was the anger that provoked his occasional thoughts of fleeing.

"You can't minister to the Indians, who have gol-darned nothing in this gol-darned valley of denial and still live among the civilized denizens of Carson City," he said.

Henry liked the word "denizens," and couldn't recall ever having used it among his friends and family, though he occasionally snuck it into a Bible lesson at their small church, which had blessed their journey and whose regulars hoped they'd stay in touch now that they were members of the church's official missionary role.

He understood his wife's desire to move beyond the passing of their little girl, who had died by drowning at just two years old in a West Virginia lake near their home during a church picnic.

He agreed that a new life was in order and had hoped to find a place to settle down where they could put down roots and have their ministry, but still make a little bit of money. He didn't care about having socially prominent or powerful friends, except where they served his business interests. But the farther west the couple journeyed and the more his wife desired "to live a life worthy of their calling in Jesus Christ" (whatever that meant, save that preaching to the Indians seemed to be a significant part of his wife's ideations), the more of a hindrance this great Gospel dream of his wife's appeared to be in Henry's unfolding business plan.

"Look at this place," he said, gesturing to the land just south of Carson City, a brownish plain east of the verdant foothills of the Sierra Mountain chain. "Nobody lives here," he said, hoping to provoke a moment of reality in Emma's religious outlook. "At least there are churches in Carson City."

He looked over at her, he kicking the sandy soil of the Carson Valley, she sitting smugly serene in the buckboard. Was that happiness on her face? God, the woman would follow Christ into hell fire, if he asked her to and she deemed it necessary.

"You can't live in the goddamned wilderness!"

There, he said it, he thought. Henry never cursed. A lay preacher in the Presbyterian denomination would never do such a thing, there being so few of them, but more of them than before in the quickly expanding American mission fields after the Civil War.

"Henry!" Emma turned and scolded. "I will not have this moment marred by your negative mindedness. And you, almost a clergyman! Watch your tongue! It's led many a man to even worse sins than your attitude and will surely ruin our chances of achieving something meaningful in this Valley of Desire. "Ye shall go out with joy, and be led forth with peace: the mountains and the hills shall break forth before you into singing, and all the trees of the field shall clap their hands!" Her lips were trembling as she remembered the prophet's words. She was in ecstasy.

Nauman didn't know what his wife was speaking about, except that he should be more careful with his talking if he wanted his wife to come around to a reasonable way of thinking.

"I'm simply saying, dear," he revisited in a quieter way, "there's no place for us here, working with the Indians while trying to set up a civilized household."

He thought that was what she would want to hear, given her desire to keep heart and home together, and home containing so much, not to speak of his own preference to be closer to business contacts and an ever-increasing population of people who would need his services, or wares, or whatever he decided to do or be.

Nauman straightened his black vest and tie, an outfit he thought doubled nicely for a businessman or a clergyman, though he was neither, despite a last-minute ordination of sorts that had been performed to satisfy Emma's desire that he be her religious equal or overseer.

Emma clasped her hands in her lap, after gathering a golden brown, hand-crocheted wrap around her favorite maroon long-sleeved housedress. She pulled it tight around her shoulders. "Then we'll leave some of that behind," she said to him, smiling.

What?

Henry's eyes imperceptibly widened and his heart just as quickly felt trapped in his own familiar despair.

"Yes, Emma," the scrawny would-be businessman replied, realizing that they had just picked a home site, which would become, within a few months' time, the great American Gospel Mission.

Chapter 6

MARSHAL AUGUSTUS ASH

Ronin hadn't expected the marshal to catch up to him. He had hoped to catch up to the marshal, who had been out of town, according to Versal McBride, the owner of the Bucket of Blood Saloon, who seemed to have an unusual handle on things. McBride was a likable guy, but the constant flitting of his eyes left Ronin somewhat annoyed. He had seen the same behavior in gossipy church folk in Kansas so he knew it wasn't as criminal as much as it was creepy. It was his opinion that there was something about human commerce that should lead a person to expect that the talkee will focus on the talker, as there could be an economic reward for doing so.

Whether the reward was affection, sex or money, Ronin thought it behooved civilized folk to pay attention to those speaking to them. He had learned that some people, however, despite protestations to the contrary, were more interested in what's happening *around* them than what's being said *to* them, despite the sometimes negative outcome of being so occupied.

In any case, the Bucket of Blood Saloon owner was probably just a friendly guy who was keeping his options open in the quickly booming business world of Virginia City. And knowing where the marshal was on any particular day might prove to be a handy trait. It certainly established him as the "go-to guy" for things both immediate and serious.

Ronin was surprised to find himself awakened by the characteristic three clicks of a Colt single-action revolver being pressed to his head, and even more surprised to see that Dustsucker, his occasional friend and traveling companion, had already packed up and left.

Ronin didn't all that much like the hard stuff. He could handle his beer all right, but whiskey brought with it an unusual bang. Fact is, Ronin had never been drunk. But rolling over on his side and staring into the face of the handgun-heeled man now towering over him—a man he assumed to be the District Marshal by the fact that he was wearing a newly minted Carson City silver dollar-sized badge on his chest that said so—he remembered throwing down a few shots of something Dustsucker had said would surely "do him good and not evil all the days of your life."

Dustsucker's sudden religiosity—he didn't normally give a whit about such things, Bible quotations included—left Ronin wondering, as the late night sharing of an unmarked bottle certainly hadn't done him any good, he thought as he propped himself up on one elbow and asked, "What the hell?"

His reaction caught him as insanely funny, given that he didn't believe in hell, accentuated as it was by the heavy hurt of a headache, which now beat in increasing tempo to the gravely bleating which was his morning voice.

"What the hell!?" he bellowed again even more loudly, pushing himself to a fully seated position looking around for his hat and handgun, which he saw laying just a few feet away under the horse blanket he must have tossed off during the night.

"The Reverend W. W. Ronin, I presume?" the towering man asked slowly, framed by the eastern sun.

"At one time," he responded, managing an embarrassed smile and remembering he hadn't paused long enough in his nighttime victuals to empty his bladder, instead heading only to the bottle Dustsucker had extended him. "Three-months aged," he said when he removed the bottle's cap.

Payment for his sins, he figured as he blinked and began to focus his eyes in the mid-morning sun, trying to make some sense of the situation. Where was Dustsucker?

"Put your hands on your head if you would sir, and roll over on to your side," the man asked, placing his left foot on Ronin's hat and pistol. He hated it when somebody put his hands, or feet for that matter, on his hat.

"Not that side," the marshal said, noticing Ronin's glance to his right where his revolver laid, "the other side."

Ronin rolled, as he was instructed, catching the toe of his left boot behind the marshal's right heel and suddenly popping his right boot against the man's knee joint, toppling the marshal backward. It set off the marshal's gun prior to his letting loose of it, leaving the weapon to fly two or three feet behind the now downed man's grasp. Ronin was on top of the camp invader before the man knew he'd fallen, throwing himself forward despite his headache and the sheer insult of it all.

Digging his heels under the man's hips and crossing the man's arms across the neck of what appeared to be a duly sworn U.S. Marshal, judging by the heavy silver badge, he growled. "What do you say we have a chat before too much more happens? I need to head into the weeds to piss a bit, and you're holding me up." Ronin continued to exhale, grinding his right forearm into the man's jaw and poking his left thumb in the marshal's eye socket, just next to his nose as a violent warning of what might come next if he didn't comply or conform.

The marshal struggled a bit but found quickly that he couldn't move, his elbows now covering his mouth, both arms trapped beneath Ronin's keen attention and weight and his right eye suddenly experiencing tremendous pain.

The marshal had never found himself in this position before, certainly never had someone's thumb in his eye, and never before discovered that his arms—normally numbered among the more powerful arms in Virginia City—had no room to move, except to create a small pocket of air so he could breathe a few official words despite his practically hopeless situation.

"You're under arrest," Marshal Augustus Ash wheezed, protesting the position he found himself in. "Get off me and I won't beat the shit out of you when you let me up." It took a moment, but both men began laughing at the absurdity of the marshal's weak-kneed attempt to bring a commanding voice to the situation, the marshal a little more slowly than his intended prey.

Ronin rolled over the marshal's head like a seasoned circus freak, picking up his revolver and the marshal's gun as well before he landed on one knee and foot and turned around. "Sit up against the log," he barked, both eyes now wide open, his full bladder still directing the morning's business.

"No sudden movements or you're a dead man breathing."

W. W. Ronin was, for the most part, a law-abiding man. It was his experience, however, that the average western lawmen was wanted somewhere, and had found their jobs in the course of escaping someone or something. There was no telling who this man was or what he was capable of doing if given a chance.

"Why don't we begin by your telling me who you are and why you're attempting to pistol whip me?" Ronin said, as he unbuttoned his fly and looked around for some cover.

By the shine of his badge, Ronin assumed he was from Virginia City. Silver was cheap in the Sierras and lawmen elsewhere sported tin if they sported a badge at all. A badge could get you killed if you wore it in the wrong places.

"I'm Augustus Ash," the man responded, rubbing his neck then moving his arms a bit to make sure they still worked. "I'm the U.S. Marshal for the District of Nevada, and I'm assuming you're the Reverend W. W. Ronin, judging by the Bible there." Ronin nodded, thinking that correcting the marshal as to his current occupation was generally irrelevant.

"Despite what looked to be a righteous shoot a day or so back in the Bucket of Blood Saloon, I'd like to ask you a few questions. Mind lowering the gun?" he said, checking his silver star for bruises or scrapes and, finding it unscathed, straightening his shirt's starched collar and cuffs. "You sure know how to handle yourself," he smiled wryly, as if giving Ronin respect. "I mean, for a preacher."

"I'm not a preacher," Ronin said, not missing a beat while shaking himself dry and buttoning up his fly. "And I'm asking you again," his eyes drilling down on the man, "why were you rolling your gun up against my head?"

Ronin didn't sit for making hash out of a man's head if he didn't deserve it, and he knew he didn't deserve it from *this* man, no matter who he was.

"My apologies, Mister Ronin," Ash nearly whispered, checking the ribs on his left side where Ronin's right knee had landed, Ronin being careful not to puncture a lung given the guy's star. "I don't tend to take much shit from folks I'm arresting," he postured, "and I guess I just assumed I was going to be arresting you."

Ronin nodded.

"Versal McBride, the owner of the Bucket of Blood saloon, said it all happened pretty quickly but that it was hard to see who drew first. And you and the big guy, who I am assuming was Deputy Slade from Carson City, didn't exactly hang around for commentary."

Ronin loved an educated man. The word "commentary" struck him as a little out of synch with other men he had met on the Comstock Lode. Cracking a smile, Ronin relaxed a bit, dropping his pistol to his knee so as to encourage further conversation.

"No, we didn't hang around to talk," he quipped, suggesting that lesser men talked while others went about more important things, an inference missed by the marshal. "It was getting late," he continued, "and we didn't need any more company."

Chapter 7

COMPANY OF MEN

Ronin found the West, particularly Nevada, to be an awkward place to make friends. The sheer geography of the state declared that a person would be lonesome and that life would be, at its best, difficult and challenging. Sagebrush and desert practically defined the land, save for ridges and ripples near the Sierras, the occasional desert stream or the unavoidable cacophony of the Comstock Lode, even in its decline.

Ronin had spent the last six or so years in Nevada. He had left Kansas in 1873, the year the Colt Patent Firearms Manufacturing Company designed their great equalizer, the Single Action Army. His parting gift from the congregation was a nickel engraved custom-tuned Colt 45. Despite the pain the congregation and he had shared—the result of his wanting the church to be more than it apparently desired to be—some members of the church had great affection for him. Sensing the extreme shift his life was taking, Bill Hutchinson, a local printer known for his "eccentric mentality" and "erratic temperament," as one church member put it, thought a Frontier Peacemaker would be a profoundly appreciative way of expressing their gratitude. Other members, notably attorneys William Baldwin and James McCulloch, agreed.

He loved it.

Finding friends in Wichita's East Jesus Church, as he now called the congregation more formally known as St. John's Episcopal, had been difficult. He'd had great expectations for the church, but arriving without a purse or a wife, or an economy to provide him with either, the ecclesiastical union was an awkward one.

The St. John's congregation was only eighteen members large when he left, meeting in a home before they built their first log building at the confluence of two great rivers. It was a primitive little log church by anyone's standards. Four years later, he left wondering if things would ever get better.

Nevada hadn't been much of an improvement.

Still a territory when compared to his home state of Pennsylvania, the Silver State had been suckered, as far as he was concerned, into Lincoln's Union because of its metal and mineral wealth. The federal government needed silver and gold to support its emerging monetary standards. Nevada's entrance into the Union, in 1861 as a territory and later as a state in 1864, secured the prominence of east coast currency and ultimately its politics, but not the eastern way of doing things.

Ronin was always at odds, whether in the church as a pastor and "fisher of men"—a term Jesus had made popular and one that his church people had liked—or with the dusty tramps and troublemakers who now made up his congregation. Ronin hunted men still, even after leaving the church. It's just that their names were different. Most of them (not all of them, for sure) were rougher and less redeemed than the ones who used to sit in his pews. But the journey was still not what he had hoped for, as finding family or friends wasn't any easier. He often wondered if he would have turned out any differently had he simply stayed put on the east coast and done something other than ministry for a living.

The sort of man who came west was an independent, solitary cuss of a man. What good man would prefer a country covered with scrub pine, juniper and rocks to the civilized, prosperous cities, towns and farms of the nation's eastern coast? Few, it would seem.

Ronin built a morning fire, picking up scattered sage and cottonwood branches from around the camp, still wondering about Dustsucker.

"Say, you didn't see my rather large friend, did you?" he asked the marshal, who was now on his knees trying to set sage shavings and cottonwood twigs aflame.

Ronin dropped an armload of kindling at the marshal's feet. "We intended to head up your way after breakfast," Ronin said, not really knowing what their intent was, except to clear things up in Virginia City before heading back down to the valley, where he was sure Dustsucker was headed, if he wasn't sitting out in the rocks a little ways with an old newspaper. Ronin glanced a small ways up a rocky hill, an area that Dustsucker and he had designated a latrine before retiring for the night.

Of course the marshal's accidental discharge would have alerted his friend that something had happened, if he was still within range. Looking at the sun barely cracking the mountain's shadows, Ronin assumed the time to be about 9 a.m., more than enough daylight for Dustsucker to have reached the valley below if he was headed to Carson City instead.

"Never saw him," the marshal replied, setting a coffee pot on the fire. It didn't appear that Ronin was intending to brew coffee. He had already dug into a bag of biscuits. Ronin joined the marshal by the fire and told him the story he had told Dustsucker the day before.

"What do you think is going on?" Ash asked, struck by the ex-preacher's compassion. He didn't care one way or the other what happened to the Washoe, and considered them generally lazy compared to the Paiutes he knew. Depressive by nature, he was generally unmoved by anyone's troubles and suspicious of people different than him.

Ash didn't like the Chinese, and approved of their segregation from the rest of folks in the towns he'd visited. Despite their significant contribution—the Chinese he knew worked as cooks, merchants, laborers and laundry workers—he was supportive of Comstock union efforts to keep Chinamen out of the mines and off the Virginia and Truckee Railroad.

He didn't like Negroes much either, though an African American man in Virginia City cut his hair and another shoed his horses. Ash thought all races probably had their place in the economy of a growing nation, but like most people he knew, he preferred to keep to his own kind. Hell, he didn't even like children much.

Ronin tried the coffee, spitting it out as quickly as sipping it in. God, he hated coffee. Most coffee tasted like dirt. Ash's effort—no doubt, he was used to hurriedly heating his grounds in a pot—was particularly suspect.

"I don't know," Ronin said, grabbing a hard biscuit from a bag he assumed Dustsucker had forgotten. "But this I do know," he replied, looking at the marshal directly so as to signal the seriousness of the matter. "There's more than one child missing, and more than two people doing the missing. That raises more than my interest," he said, lifting his left eyebrow. "It raises my ire."

Ronin bit off a piece of bacon, taking it from the pan with his fingers and pushing it into his mouth, having not eaten in a couple of days. He paused for a bit and then said, "Look, I'm sorry for having to kill those two men, and I probably should have hung around. But they drew first and their intention was nothing but bad. From what the Washoe were telling me a couple of days ago," he added, relishing the bacon's gristle (he didn't much care for the burnt parts), "there are a dozen or so kids missing. I don't know what to think, except to say that something awful is going on here. Those two men weren't the end of it," Ronin added, casting a burnt piece of bacon into the fire. "But this I do know," Ronin said settling his gaze even more intently toward Augustus Ash, who was listening with interest. "When I find out what's happening, I'll put an end to it. I hope you'll agree."

Chapter 8

A CUP OF COMSTOCK TEA

Augustus Ash and Versal McBride had breakfast together every Thursday morning. McBride's Bucket of Blood Saloon died a missionary's death on Wednesday nights—not because of Wednesday night prayer meetings, which despite the number of churches in the valley didn't exactly amount to much on the Comstock Lode—business died because of the Wednesday night discounts on D Street, Virginia City's red light district.

Gold had been discovered in 1859 by a couple of Virginia City miners who probably should have kept their mouths shut, as it didn't take long for their tiny mining operation in the Sierra foothills to come under the control of others. In just a dozen years, there were thirty thousand people in the hills, most of them wanting somewhere to go and something to do other than wiping the gray mud off of freshly bought mining boots and shovels. The resulting boom—or booms, as Ash and McBride had weathered the best and the worst of the Comstock's history—not only provided financial fuel for Lincoln's Union, but turned the otherwise nondescript desert crags and ravines of northern Nevada's Virginia Range into a millionaire's milieu of hastily built mansions and outhouses.

Virginia City was, when everything was considered, a rich person's shantytown, and Ash and McBride enjoyed it that way. The Bucket of Blood Saloon wasn't the biggest edifice in town, but from its front room you could see some of the bigger houses and hotels, and from its back room you could see a hundred miles or so. The saloon was a drinking man's paradise.

In Virginia City, a working man didn't need to brace his back against a tree to take a shit, all the while wondering when someone might cut it down to make a mining shack or desert slough. The trees were long gone, most of the mining shacks as well. Despite the recent downturn in mining activity, Augustus Ash and Versal McBride believed Comstock living to be real desert luxury, a marketable watering hole that would outlast the silver and gold booms. And they intended to keep it that way.

At breakfast, on the Thursday morning following the sheriff's discovery of the Reverend W. W. Ronin sleeping behind a house a short ways up Mount Davidson, Ash remarked that he thought there might be a darker side to the town's underbelly than either of them thought.

Like most Nevadans, they liked the town's prostitutes circled close by. "Can't have them traipsing up and down C street," the Bucket of Blood's owner liked to say, "boobies hanging out where the kids can see them," missing the fact that women's breasts and children had more in common than the female physical feature had with the miners, who had a equal but more lascivious interest in the swag of the Comstock Lode's imported entertainment.

The town's opium dens weren't a problem either, as long as they were kept lassoed by strong municipal codes and active enforcement. No, everyone needed somewhere to go and something to do when the sun went down and the lights went up. Virginia City offered what everyone seemed to need or want. "So if there's something worse going on," Marshal Ash said to his friend, "something we don't know about," he added with some pause.

"Something we haven't thought about," McBride interrupted, his chair leaning against the Bucket of Blood's west porch wall so he could see the six-mile canyon's entire expanse, his favorite seat in the house.

"Right," said Ash, "then everything we do here is in jeopardy."

Despite being an U.S. Marshal, Augustus Ash was concerned about increasing federal interference within the city's limits, where he lived and had mining interests and investments. "The best government is local government," Ash liked to say, shining his engraved badge with his blue neckerchief, a gift from McBride and other Virginia City merchants a couple of years back when the town christened a new courthouse and jail. Federal marshals were not reimbursed for office space, so Ash much appreciated the friendly relationship he had with Storey County and the local merchants who were more than willing to lend space to the marshal as he needed it.

"You're goddamned right," McBride interrupted. "If you gotta have government, it's best to keep everything local." McBride smiled, nodding his head in that funny way, eyeing the saloon's customers on his left and right to make sure they heard what he was saying.

Augustus Ash and Versal McBride understood what each other meant without having to say too much to each other, which is the way some men like it. And they didn't like the thought that somebody was stirring shit into everyone's cup of coffee or tea.

Chapter 9

AN ORMSBY STREET SALOON

Henry Nauman took a seat by one of the windows along the back of a saloon on Ormsby Street in Carson City and began to ponder his options. The director of the American Gospel Mission didn't think people recognized him in the saloon, given that most of his work was among Indians and the mission was a good half-hour carriage ride from the downtown. But the growth of the mission, as well as his gambling and whoring habits, were the talk of the town.

Nauman sat in his usual seat. His usual server handed him his usual beer and he took his usual first big gulp. (He liked to sip his beer after that, as too many beers interfered with his in-town sexual habits). As the afternoon sun began to fall behind the Sierra foothills, he sat there wondering how things had gotten so out of hand.

Construction had proceeded so quickly at the mission site overlooking the Carson Valley that he'd hardly had an opportunity to investigate business opportunities in the capital city. By the time the first building had been finished—colored native stones set by Indian masons, a nice gift to his wife, he thought—the first of the kids sent his way by act of the Nevada legislature were already there, building a coal shed, laundry and a 10,000-gallon water tower. More students were expected from tribes throughout the West as few other options were available to assimilate young Indians into mainstream Christian culture.

Nevada's forward-thinking legislative action had an unexpected and profound effect on the gospel mission as no other option existed for Nevada-based Washoe and Paiute tribes. Hopi, Apache, Pima, Mohave and other groups throughout southern Nevada were expected to begin placing their children there also, as soon as space allowed.

Emma's dream had turned into Henry's nightmare, and there seemed to be no way out.

Looking up, he noticed that Ally, one of the bigger-breasted saloon girls, was bouncing his way. Nauman uncharacteristically waved her off as he settled into what he hoped would be a long afternoon's consideration of the problem.

The Naumans had agreed to journey westward after a week-long revival at their home church, west of Steubenville, Ohio. They had left a moderately successful farm, successful in the sense that they were rarely hungry, and had been able to put a little money away from the sales of chickens and other livestock to farmers decimated by flooding in the area.

Henry had grudgingly agreed to journey westward, not because he'd been moved by the meetings held under the big top by a big shot Pittsburgh minister-for-hire, as much as there might be money to be made in the American West.

What little they had earned with poultry sales was mere chicken-feed, Henry liked to joke, though few church members liked to listen, to the kinds of dollars he and Emma might dig out of the hills, or those living in the hills along the Comstock Lode. And while he wasn't at all sure what he was going to do when he got there to make such money, he was certain that he'd have to do something, given his wife's fixation on "winning Indian souls to the Lord Jesus Christ."

West Virginia religious meetings weren't known by their intellectual content, so Emma's meeting-born vision was bare of anything other than emotional vitality, and that liveliness had gotten old before they had crested the first hill out of Ohio on their way West.

Henry was incredulous that Emma's efforts had brought such little fruit financially. But he felt he couldn't be blamed, though no one was doing the blaming save himself, for his own lack of success. He was counting on time to do what he wanted to do, let alone figure out what he wanted to do. And despite the generally open business climate in Carson City, it seemed as if his time to do either was running out.

Ally intersected the server, taking a second bottle of beer from the tray and, scooping up a dish of peanuts, sashayed a bit more brazenly toward her friend's table. "Henry!" she yelled in a high-pitched whistle. "Yo, Henry!" she repeated, practically squeaking as she hopped and skipped across the near-empty Carson City saloon.

Henry had reminded her many times to keep her voice down as some people in Carson City might know who he was. Should his afternoon libations and liberties get back to Emma at the mission, there'd surely be hell to pay. "Sit down, Ally," he said, shushing her with his hand flapping as if were patting a dog or waving to a baby. "Hell, missy! Are you trying to ruin my life with all that blabbering?"

At four feet, six inches tall, brunette when others were blond or redhead, and having to stuff her corset to achieve bigger than ample bumps in all the right places, tiny Ally Washburn didn't think she could ruin anybody's life. Henry seemed to pay her attention, however, so she had gotten used to the scrawny man's cravings for friendship and had even grown fond of his awkward sexual advances. In fact, she had grown fond of him and was hoping her friendship with Henry would serve to finish her trip west to San Francisco. She had been looking forward to seeing him all week.

"I'm sorry baby," she said, sitting down. One hand soothed his arms and another touched his forehead to wipe away his worry. Few women had touched Henry in such a way.

"I didn't mean to make so much noise, honey. I just missed you," she said, smiling, pushing her bodice up with both hands while bumping into place with her behind and beginning to squeak again. "You make me so hap-p-py," she giggled, extending the word way beyond its normal length and in a way that made Nauman wonder if he could ever listen to her the way he listened to his wife Emma.

Probably not.

"Are you thinking of our little trip-ee, again?" she asked, now making up words which was always irritating to him, especially since he was tutoring the Indians to speak and behave in a more appropriate fashion than they were used to. In a Christian fashion, or at least a civilized fashion he thought, though encouraging either was probably as hopeless as planting crops on their West Virginia farm that would survive the occasional flooding.

Some things simply can't be changed, he thought, or maybe shouldn't be. He signaled the server to head his way.

"Ally, you want something to eat?" he asked. "I'm real hungry, and I'm real tired of eating the sorry gruel we serve at the mission."

Henry grimaced when he thought of the Indian beef, and bread with bugs. And tomatoes that tasted ... well, so different from what he had tasted in Pittsburgh or Philadelphia, or any of the big cities he had been to. Hell, the kind of tomatoes they were growing at the mission might well be poison, he thought, remembering a story he had heard about a man in Salem County, New Jersey who had stood on the courthouse steps, consuming a basket-full of the damn things to prove that the fruit wasn't as dangerous as people thought it to be.

"Well sure, baby," Ally answered, looking at him and then turning to the server who was now standing behind her, a tall, gaunt man who was better suited to undertaking, she thought. She'd been in his employ no more than a couple of weeks. "What's good, Jack?"

Jack visibly flinched. Henry managed a nervous and hopeful smile. "The quail is nice," he said, a presumptuous word for the birds that skittered along Carson City's streets.

"I'll have the quail," they said simultaneously. Jack paused as Henry and Ally looked at each other with embarrassed smiles.

"We'll have the quail," they added, and then, laughing, took turns drinking from two full glasses of beer on the table, their hearts empty while grasping each other's hands across the table.

Chapter 10

DRIED BISCUITS AND BEEF

Slade stirred earlier than usual, his habit being to rise well after sunbreak or whatever hour was best tolerated by his boss or boarding house matron.

The son of a well-known Iowa pioneer family, Slade had fled the dust bowl state when he was sixteen, having given what he figured to be more than fair warning to his father that he didn't see his future gathering corn cobs and cow droppings for the family's fuel supply.

He felt a certain amount of guilt over abandoning his parents, brothers and sisters to what appeared to him to be the drudgeries of prairie life. But his dad had been generous, remarking that "a man needs to find his own way in the world," and he recalled his mother's reaction as equally as gracious as her son boarded a train heading to Council Creek.

Slade still remembered leaving as if it were yesterday, though it had been a dozen or so years previous. He often replayed the scene in his mind. It gave him comfort when he traveled the similarly bleak landscape of the Silver State. He much appreciated the Eagle Valley's soaring green mountains and the rocky foothills that leaned up against them, prior to their deforestation by the Washoe Valley mills. Towering clubs of juniper, rabbit weed and sagebrush grew in their place. He wondered what it would have been like to grow up there, playing among the rocks and trees.

The last time he saw his family, his father's strong right arm had gathered his mother to his side as if they were joined at the hip, a posture the two of them often assumed, she loving him as much as he loved her. His mother had dabbed at her eyes with a red-checkered apron Slade often thought would have made a better tablecloth than a smock. Both his mother and father swatted at his youngest sisters, twins who were often, and carelessly, swaddled around his mother's legs and feet. His older brothers and sisters stood nearby.

"You'll do well, Marcus," his mother had said, wishing him godspeed and pressing a cloth filled with warm biscuits and dried beef into his hands, having assumed he'd made no provision for food for the train trip west.

Slade had always planned his meals well. Even as a young boy he had counted the final minutes of a day in the family's fields, until the hour they would sit together in the timber (not sod like many of their neighbors) home they had harvested and built themselves. He was proud that he had come from such people—a family that had worked together, even sacrificed together—as folks he was acquainted with in the Sierra Nevada foothills often seemed as if they had come from lesser stock.

Slade's family had constructed one of Iowa's first successful farmsteads. They had carved their home from the tall grass and occasional timber stands, built their own wooden furniture when wood and work allowed, and fought, practically alone as there were few neighbors in those days, the prairie's fires, loneliness and disease.

People slept with "one eye open," it was often said, as there were good years and bad years, and a bad year could start without a moment's notice.

Slade's time in Iowa had been mostly positive, he thought, as his folks had weathered the economic highs and lows, never losing a child, never losing their house to fire, and never really being threatened by serious disease. They had even benefited in the brief profits encouraged by five years of conflict with the southern states. Iowa was the "bread basket" of the Union. Iowa's grain and beef had fed the nation, both North and South.

His family had lived comfortably in Iowa, owning a large swath of land both south and north of the Eight Mile Prairie, providing him a small sum of money when he left, and continuing to deliver a stipend now that he was settled.

Despite the river's influence, the area had been lonely and isolating for the young man, now a full-grown man and Ormsby County deputy sheriff. Given that he left before his brothers and sisters had grown, Slade had missed the occasional laughter that now filled his family's Iowa home. He was happy to hear they had continued to prosper in the correspondence that came from his brothers and sisters, and the regular check and letter that arrived from his mother and dad. His room in a small hotel on East Fifth Street in Carson City was littered with their letters.

Slade rooted around in one of his rear saddlebags with his right hand to see if he had brought any letters with him as the giant mare he was riding continued to make its way down the final hill into Washoe Valley.

Suddenly bewildered, he noticed he didn't seem to have brought enough biscuits for the trip into Washoe Valley. Glancing to his right and wondering if he had dropped a bag, he saw a lone Indian standing a hundred yards or so away in a small stand of aspen, silently watching.

"Friend, talk out," he yelled in a Paiute dialect, as he hadn't managed to learn the Washoe language, their being so private about their ways even when working for whites, and his being so busy operating an occasional coyote hole along the Comstock Lode.

Closer now, he noticed the Indian man was actually a boy, not quite a teenager he guessed.

"Do you speak English?" the Indian child asked. Slade, called "Dustsucker" by his friends, smiled.

Chapter 11

WASHOE LAKE

"How is it that you're standing so far from your settlement?" Slade asked, not meaning to infer that Indians should stay in their colonies or on their reservations. It was a thought commonly held by many of the deputies who served with Slade, but not one he generally shared given the Indian's usefulness on ranches in the valley, and the beauty of their women if Slade was being honest.

The three hundred and some-pound man rarely had little luck with women, even Indian women. But he kept his eyes open to the possibilities, though generally Slade's more exciting moments were limited to the softening of a ranch matron's gaze or an occasional finger or two on his arm when ordering a glass of wine or a Comstock oyster.

"I mean, how is it that you're way out here, little one?" hoping that rephrasing the question would make up for any possible previous offense. The young boy seemed friendly, but Slade still wondered how a young boy would find his way up into the hills without friends or family.

"I'm waiting for *you,* my friend," the Indian boy responded, grinning.

The Indian's eyes were clear, his skin unusually clean except for the dust that lightly clung to his legs and chest from climbing a thousand or so feet up from the valley floor. His smile was contagious, and Dustsucker wanted to join him in his joy.

The deputy drew up his horse's reins and sat them in his lap as he came to a stop ten yards from the young man, his right hand drifting toward his gun belt while still wanting to appear friendly.

Thirty feet is the blink of an eye, Slade had discovered in altercations with drunken men in the Carson City Indian colonies. And while the boy seemed friendly enough, and oddly compelling for an Indian, he wasn't yet satisfied that he and the Indian were alone.

Dustsucker paused, as if to drink in the scenery appreciatively, but looked about to determine if anyone was watching. He'd seen full-grown Indians hide in mountain shrubbery before, or hadn't as the case had been.

One time, he had actually watched a rabbit weed bush stand straight up as if it had had legs, only to find that a white man was wearing it as a headdress and waving a huge Colt Dragoon. The man had meant to hurt him.

On another occasion, he'd seen dirt-covered bodies sit straight up like the Lord Jesus did on that first Easter morning. He was not a religious man and only assumed the tale was true. It was an amazing sight, especially when they began walking, throwing stone spears and war clubs his way.

Seeing a single Indian standing, albeit serenely, in a juniper bush didn't do his heart any good.

"I mean you no harm," the boy smiled as if he had been reading Dustsucker's mind. He moved closer. Slade inexplicably relaxed his grasp on his Colt Peacemaker but stayed erect in his saddle, the horse pitching a bit so that Slade had to pull more leather in order to hold him still.

"You don't mean me any harm?" Slade said, chuckling. "How is it a young Indian boy finds his way up into the mountains, to stand in front of a bear-sized man and not mean him any harm?" he asked, playing to the clear difference in size between the two of them.

He observed the boy's hands. They were empty, and no sudden movements were occurring in his steady yet peripheral vision.

"How is it that you were waiting for *me?*" he asked, looking down from his towering mare at a small boy who couldn't be more than four and a half feet tall, if he was four feet at all.

"You are the reverend's friend?" the boy asked, still smiling. "I saw you in a dream last night, laughing."

Once a minister, always a minister, Dustsucker thought to himself, smiling. Even the Indians think he is still a priest.

"I am he," he chuckled. "But that doesn't answer my question." He pulled on his horse's reins so as to keep the beast's attention. "How is it that you have found me here?"

The boy lowered his head, still staring at the large and dirty man. For a moment, the boy lost his smile, but fixing his eyes on the Reverend Ronin's friend, said, "You would have to be an Indian to know that."

A moment passed, and they both began to laugh. Such nonsense, when spoken by two men, is often acknowledged as such if both men are honest.

"Can we sit a while?" the boy inquired. Dustsucker let up the reins and lifted his right leg over the mare's head, dropping to the sand between them. Looping the leather over some sage, he folded his buckskin-covered legs and sat down on the ground. If it wasn't for his brown, beehive-shaped hat, a passerby might have thought that there were two Indians sitting in the brush.

"Let's do that," Dustsucker said, interested in making this young man's acquaintance. The boy seemed kind, especially when he laughed. They sat talking for a couple of hours, before the boy named Little Wolf led his new friend a couple of miles down a canyon into a ring of huts along the valley floor.

The Washoe generally stayed in the mountains near Lake Tahoe, during the summer months in order to catch fish, pick nuts and harvest various berries. They would dry them so as to store food for the winter months that were spent in the valley, just north of Carson City. Slade had noticed that it took the Washoe longer to secure the annual food supply, given the decimation of the Washoe's traditional hunting grounds by the lake's lumber mills. The Pinyon groves east of the valley were long gone, having fed the hungry mines and mills in Virginia City. Slade was surprised to see any Indians in the Valley, given it was September. A small group of women and a couple of older Washoe men were gathered by an old railroad tie, sorting pine nuts and other seeds. A young boy was skinning a rabbit nearby.

Dustsucker and his young friend gestured a greeting, and sliding off his horse, went up to a man he believed to be the tribe's elder.

"I am sorry that your family has suffered so much this season," Dustsucker said to the old, sun-wizened Indian who stood to greet him. He offered his hand to the man who, in return, squeezed his own hands together in front of his chest and then, touching Dustsucker's hand, gestured that they should sit down on a blanket strewn outside one of the lodges.

Dustsucker asked the young boy to translate. The older man spoke first.

"You've come from the city," he said. "I have seen you there. You are a sheriff, I presume?"

Slade nodded, and looked down at his torn and dirty brown corduroy vest, which was a slightly lighter shade than his hat. He had folded the flap of his breast pocket into his vest. Over the years, he had learned to keep his badge hidden. He once had a very short man shoot at him for looking too much like a deputy, which in fact he was. No amount of shouting at the man could convince him that shooting at a deputy was a bad idea, but shooting back did cool the man's temper.

He pulled the material up and out, letting a small circular badge with a star in its center fall out onto the left side of his chest. A handkerchief and some biscuit crumbs from a couple days before fell onto his chest as well.

"I am a deputy sheriff," he replied. "Have I seen you before?" he asked, cocking his head to one side.

Slade meant no disrespect, of course, but the directness of his question seemed too forward, too accusatory, and he instantly wished he had phrased it differently. Looking at Little Wolf, he whispered an apology and signaled with his eyes that he should offer some help. Little Wolf did nothing. Instead, he sat there smiling.

"Tell the elder I meant no disrespect. I meet so many people." Dustsucker's voice trailed off as he waited for a response.

The boy laughed.

It was not a habit Dustsucker tolerated in taller men, but he waited.

Little Wolf burst out laughing. "He is not offended and he is not the tribal elder. He is my father. He is simply asking if you are a sheriff because he wants to make a report about my sister, who was taken."

Dustsucker blushed. He had no idea he had been talking to the young brave about his sister. They had sat together for a couple of hours conversing about missing children at the colony. He didn't know how he could have missed the relationship.

"Little Wolf has told me that you sent your daughter to the American Gospel Mission in Carson City." He paused, waiting for the young man to translate. The father nodded. "You wanted her to learn the white man's skills?" The father nodded again, but said something to Little Wolf.

"The white *woman's* skills, my father says. It is not appropriate for a woman to want to be a man."

Smiling again, Dustsucker replied, "Of course," though he didn't care what a woman wanted to be as long as she was respectful and kind. And he knew of Washoe men who didn't feel so fiercely about the role of their women. His mother had been a virtuous woman in every respect but had certainly pulled a man's weight on their Iowa farm.

"Have you attempted to visit your daughter?"

"Yes," he replied. "We go to the great American Mission every week when we are allowed to visit. Many things are said. But our little one is not there."

Little Wolf placed his hand on his father's shoulders. The older man's head was now bent forward into his lap. His sun-baked hands were clasped behind his well-oiled hair, and his entire body was now shaking.

"We do not know," he said weeping, and looking up, asked "Would you please help us?"

Dustsucker had met a great many people since leaving his family on their Iowa farm. But none had reminded him so of his family until now.

Chapter 12

THE INDIAN SCHOOL

Ronin didn't learn to be a man hunter by going to school. No Western detective or lawman worth his weight learned his trade that way. He learned to do what he did—finding people, collecting a bounty or reward and occasionally solving a crime or two—the way everyone else did, by simply doing it.

Not that what he was doing with his life could be considered "police work," he told his mother in a heated discussion some years back. "The basic mission of the police is to prevent crime and disorder," he said, referring to the work of a British statesman, who had helped to create the Metropolitan Police Force in London, England. Not that he had ever been there.

Policing wasn't his calling. A curious man with a heightened sense of how things might be if he followed things to their end, Ronin believed the people skills he'd learned as a priest could be put to better use living in a wider and more public arena. As a private detective and occasional bounty hunter, he simply looked into things. When the dust settled and things became clear, well, people paid him money.

After leaving the Episcopal parish in Kansas, Ronin's Pinkerton work had taken him to the New Mexican, Nevada and Oregon territories, and a few other American states along the way. He hadn't yet been to California, though he knew he'd get there sooner or later. One time he'd taken the day-long ride up to Lake Tahoe—whether in Nevada or California he didn't know which—and he liked that. Folks there said the other side of the Sierras was the place he ought to go, where grassy plains led to a clear blue ocean and a special kind of quiet blanketed a promised, golden land. It sounded beautiful, but Ronin's heart wasn't generally given to things golden. The special kind of yellow that had made California so attractive to so many wasn't something he cared about at all.

When multiple mineral rushes transfigured the Golden State, adding hundreds of thousands of people, roads, churches and schools, it didn't make Ronin happy. It reminded him of Kansas and everything that was wrong with the world. And while he wasn't an Indian lover per se, the harm it had caused the natives? Well, it just reminded him of what well-meaning but equally cruel and thoughtless people had done to Chinese Americans, or African Americans before that. More than a hundred thousand Native Americans died in the multiple mineral fevers that changed America's westernmost state. Golden State? Ronin wanted none of it.

Not everything that glistens is gold, he'd often say, though occasionally the former priest and Pinkerton detective wondered about other directions his life might have taken had he not been so well connected to his inner convictions. Decisions that might have kept him out of the church, gotten him married, gained him kids, made him some money. Meaningful work was what really mattered, most of the time, though he was occasionally bothered by the question of what he might have done if he hadn't done what he did.

W. W. Ronin was headed to Carson City because he agreed to look into a situation suggested by his friend Dustsucker, whose suspicions were raised when he told the Ormsby County deputy sheriff that children were missing from the Indian settlements at Washoe Lake. His friend had suggested he talk to the people at the American Gospel Mission just south of the city, as they had been placing Indian children with church-going families for a number of years. And while "their motivations were high and mighty," as Dustsucker put it, Ronin didn't necessarily share such ideals, had a hard time understanding how they might motivate someone to get out of bed in the morning and at times made him wonder what economic benefit there might be to keeping the supply of Indian children flowing.

"Follow the money," his district manager said while he was employed with the Pinkertons. "The money will never steer you wrong."

Dustsucker's sense of how bad church people were was way stronger than Ronin's experience of folks growing up in Pennsylvania, or while serving his parish in Kansas. They'd have to have a conversation about that someday, though he doubted it would hold Dustsucker's interest or amount to much.

As an almost-graduate of a small religious school in western Pennsylvania, the Reverend William Washington Ronin had taken a train west to catch the opening of the American frontier. It was just a small step to go to the Ohio River towns, where settlements were popping up everywhere. But when nothing looked particularly interesting, he was happy to select a small Episcopal mission in Kansas that was willing to take a single man in his thirties, however motivated.

His first and only, Wichita's "East Jesus" Temple of God, Light of the Healing Savior church—though it wasn't located in the east, didn't resemble much of a temple, and everything considered, didn't turn out to be all that healing—hadn't been all that bad. Well, not bad for a church anyway. And while he was hardly a religious virgin anymore, he found the American West a hell of a lot more interesting than Pennsylvania, and Nevada, not to mention a great deal more engaging than Wichita, Kansas.

He arrived at the American Gospel mission a little after five in the evening. Greeted by a comely woman working in the home of the mission director, he apologized for the lateness of the hour and asked if the master of the house would see him. Learning that he had been gone for a few days, he made excuses to gain entrance to the director's office anyway.

"W. H. Nauman," he said, smiling, noticing the man's use of initials, a habit he had picked up while pastoring his first church, as it added a certain stature to his work, even if it was sometimes undeserved. Ronin smiled and wondered if the director's name was also William.

The woman, an otherwise attractive lady despite her disposition, was in her early thirties. She let him into the director's office when he identified himself as coming from the Ormsby County sheriff's office. Not that he had, but he figured he'd be going there later that evening to see what had happened to his friend Slade.

The room was larger than he expected. A heavy wooden desk sat in the middle of the office, its top bearing a large Celtic-shaped cross. Two small, brown pine-back chairs perched in front of the desk were likely student chairs. He turned around to see the whole room and wondered where the housekeeper had disappeared to.

Ronin liked to get the feel of something or someone before he engaged the more rational side of his mind. If there was anything to the supernatural in life, a fact that he very much doubted after his experience as a Pinkerton investigating a certain medium, it was found in a person's intuition. Let a man relax, and all kinds of impressions were liable to flood his understanding. Some of the impressions, he found, were worth holding on to.

The room was messy.

Ronin had anticipated it to look cleaner, more professional, squared away. Instead, papers were stacked and strewn everywhere. And there was nary a book to be seen. Odd, he thought, as religious people typically lived in their tomes and pamphlets, preferring the voices of the dead to any that might emanate from a still-living voice or divine.

Ronin yanked on a nearby filing cabinet, and, finding it empty was suddenly surprised when someone gently touched his right arm. "Jesus!" he exclaimed, looking behind him and finding the housekeeper who had let him into the building.

"I'm sorry. I didn't mean to scare you," she said.

He smiled. "Is the room usually like this?" He stuttered when he asked, not wanting to give any offense. But the room's appearance could hardly have been its norm.

Waiting for the woman's response, he remembered a seminary classroom, similarly disposed. He was listening to the Reverend Culbert Rutenber, his religion professor perched on his shoulder, as only a Baptist preacher could be, lecturing on how to be a godly man and a perfect pastor. But he was no longer a pastor, he thought. He was a bounty hunter, a detective. How was it that the professions seemed at times so similar?

"Try to read the story in the same voice," Rutenber used to say when turning to a story in the Christian scriptures. "Read it with the same intent as the original writer might have intended. See what the story's actors see. Listen to the way they speak to each other. Watch for things that seem odd or out of place, for the story teller is trying to make a point by what he's saying and how he says it."

Ronin's mind flooded with classroom memories of the quirky, gray-haired man, sitting on a wooden chair, balanced on top of a classroom table in a Pennsylvania seminary. "So as to see everyone," he'd explain when asked why, and he was asked often.

Ronin shook his head, clearing his mind so he could better think about what he was doing. He continued to examine the office, as the woman stood quietly by an empty bookcase. A dark blue woolen suit coat hung on a hook by the door. Papers were scattered everywhere, some lying crumpled on the desk or the floor, like a man writing a speech or a sermon. Not satisfied with one thing, he'd discarded it so as to start again on a clean sheet of paper, and the process repeated itself over and over. The papers were so widely strewn about, it was as if the actor or writer was struggling with something.

Yes, that's for goddamn sure. The man was struggling.

"A story doesn't always begin at the beginning," he said to himself, rifling through another stack of papers on the director's desk. "Sometimes a story begins mid-way," he said to himself.

"I'm sorry, what were you saying?" the woman asked. There she was again. What beautiful hair, he thought, noticing her backlit silhouette against a western-facing window.

Standing behind the desk, he straightened up and stood with his hands on his hips, his right hand reflexively falling to his leather belt and gun. He liked the heft of the Peacemaker. It wasn't as heavy as the Paterson revolver he had carried in the war. And it was a nice to receive something so substantial from a well-meaning congregation. As easily as his hand slid around the Colt, it knocked a piece of paper off the desk and on to the floor. He bent to pick it up. There were so many pieces of paper scattered about, and what an odd size, the size of a playing card, small pieces of paper with even smaller writing on them.

He felt the woman's eyes upon him and remembered that he wasn't alone.. "I'm sorry," he said to the woman. "What was it that you asked?"

How odd. Nauman was said to be a fastidious individual. More than one person had said so, and yet the room was so disturbed. That's the word, disturbed. Like a man trying to decide something.

"A double-minded man is unstable in all of his ways," the brother of Jesus was reputed to have said. Ronin wondered why the *Epistle of James* would dwell on such things as wrong-hearted men making immoral decisions.

"Excuse me, sir? I can hardly hear you," the woman interrupted. He turned slowly, trying to hold on to the connection between an old Jerusalem scripture and a double-minded director in charge of Indian children in Carson City.

"Is it always like this?" he asked again, gesturing toward the small scraps of paper scattered throughout the room. "I don't mean to offend. It just seems so unusual to keep one's office this way..."

Picking up the paper he had knocked to the floor, he noticed some writing on it. "Can you read this?" he asked. "It appears to have a name on it."

"What's to tell you, sir?" she said, taking it from his hand. "It's the name of one of our students." Picking up a couple of other pieces off of the director's desk, she remarked, "They're all names, though this isn't his usual handwriting. Creighton here, he's a very tender child. He's perhaps three or four years old." She smiled with her head tilted to the side.

"And Grace, she's probably six. And this says 'Sophia.'" She held the paper as if considering it. "It means 'wisdom,' though she had some other name when she came to us. They all did." She turned it over in her hand. "She's a pretty little girl, and bright! She's maybe nine or ten," she said.

The woman paused, as if concerned or perhaps confused. "I'm guessing Mister Nauman was praying for the children," she offered, "though I haven't seen the office like this in a very long time."

It was a possibility. Ronin had often made lists of the members and friends of his parish to assist him in his daily devotions. Everyone needed prayer. Some people need more prayer than others, though praying for the people in his Wichita church generally left him with a headache. But it didn't explain why papers were tossed everywhere, some crumpled beyond recognition.

"I notice you paused a bit when you looked at that last one," he asked. "Tell me more." Ronin nudged gently, hoping not to pry. The Pinkertons had developed a procedure for investigations. While it had been a couple of years since he had been in their employ, and he had only been involved in a couple of cases before leaving, he knew that gaining more information and not less, was important to his conducting a thorough investigation.

Questions were a good thing, though he personally didn't care for them. When pressed on a personal issue by people in his church, he preferred to keep his mouth shut rather than react. Good people could be so difficult. And there was always the issue of his temper.

"Well," she said with some pause. "About a week or so ago, she left us." He noticed the small scar above the woman's left eye when she flushed. Even when agitated, she was an attractive individual. He could imagine kissing her, though it hardly seemed appropriate. The color of her hair and the slenderness of her waist made him want to try.

"The point is she's gone. That's all I know. Mister Nauman never shared the specifics of a child's placement with me. I assume she's happier where she is," she added, pulling at her blouse and smoothing her skirt.

She put the papers back on the desk and looked at Ronin. She suddenly grew stern. "The American Gospel Mission isn't always the happiest place," she stated forcefully, "but it's a great deal better than some of the places these children have come from."

"Indeed," W. W. Ronin interrupted. "What with everything you all are doing for these children..."

His voice trailed off, a sure sign he wasn't being totally honest. It was a habit he had developed in his parish work, hoping that folks who ought to know better might pick up on the irony. Ancient Greek and Roman philosophers used the same device, contributing a certain clarity and poetry to the lives of people around them. He hadn't had much luck with it in his own life, though it didn't stop him from trying. Dim is as dim acts. What the hell.

"How long has Sophia been gone?" he asked gently.

"About a week," she replied. "I assume she left with the other children."

"She left with the other children?" replied Ronin. "There were other children who left at the same time?" It was if someone had kicked him in the stomach or knocked him upside the head. How had he missed it? The man was choosing, maybe fretting because he was choosing. But the emotion was clear, given the crumpled paper strewn around the room.

"How many others are we talking about?"

The woman folded her hands across her bosom, growing even more uncomfortable. Perhaps the interview was over.

"You'd have to talk to Henry," she said, pulling at her skirt again. "Three or four days, too many for sure." She picked up some of the paper scraps as her voice trailed off. "I just know the dinner count is down. He should be back soon and you can ask him about it."

"Not likely," Ronin thought to himself as he glanced a final time around the office. It was time to find his friend Dustsucker.

Chapter 13

ALLY'S FUTURE

"So there's no chance at all that you and I are going to be together?" Ally asked in her best inside voice, as Henry had little tolerance for anything "squeaky" or loud.

Ally believed herself to be the best and most popular saloon girl in the house on Ormsby Street. She was friendly and she had what men wanted. She was incredulous that this man, with whom she had spent so much time over the last nine months, was simply going to walk out of her life unattached, save perhaps to his wife, she huffed, or some other woman, she thought, shaking her head. The point was, if she was hearing correctly, Henry Nauman was not going to take her to wherever it was he was going. And their trade—his cash and promises for sexual affection—weren't adding up to anything permanent.

Ally hesitated for a moment and then brushed the crumbs from her best red velvet corset, which Jack, the saloon's owner, had laced up earlier that morning despite her disdain for the favors he demanded in order for her to work there.

Henry watched with interest, as she pushed back the tears and looked out onto Ormsby Street. There was talk that they would rename it Curry Street, after the founder of Carson City. She didn't care.

She didn't do well with tall, thin men, she figured, looking into the eyes of the almost-a-cleric sitting across from her, who had promised her a ride off of the Comstock to parts more civilized. She had believed him when he'd talked about their making a life together in San Francisco or Sacramento even, though she thought she'd prefer the bigger city for its climate and charm.

She'd sat or cuddled dreaming with him of such places, of the businesses they'd start, the cultural events they'd attend and the parties they'd host, inviting the best known entertainers, legislators and businessmen.

It wasn't as if Henry was the only one taking chances.

Jack had explained to her that the county was cracking down on prostitution in the capital city. He'd said there was an exception for places on Ormsby Street, located between Second and Fifth streets, but that the ordinance was likely the city fathers' way of saying that saloon girls wouldn't be long tolerated. She'd begun looking for a way out then, for a gentleman, or group of gentlemen even, who would help her move from the Eastern Slope.

Sure enough, Carson City tightened up the regulations. Penalties were now in play for house girls and whore-haulers, even for those who merely advertised such services. The risk of relating to men like Henry was now real, Jack said. She was lucky to have a job, he'd told her. Henry didn't seem to understand any of that.

No matter how much she adjusted her expectations, the money wasn't enough. The point of the trade, as far as she was concerned—and she thought she had explained this to Henry— was getting off the Comstock. And it now seemed that all Henry cared about was getting off.

She looked around the house. The saloon had seen better years, to be sure. The large mirror behind the bar was no longer as clear as it used to be, the purveyances not nearly as many or as popular. Some mornings, she'd look down from her window above Jack's business and wonder if it wasn't just the saloon, but all of Carson City, that was doing so poorly. In the last two years, she'd seen some of her favorite shops close on Carson Street, their owners she had been told, had relocated their businesses to Portland, Denver or San Francisco. A friend of hers in Gold Hill told her that the Comstock was hurting, too. The younger miners, her friend had said, were moving to the next gold rush, in Bodie, California, where 10,000 people were clawing through the hills for gold, or setting up saloons, opium dens, gambling houses and brothels to take the money away. A younger woman would head there, she thought. But I'm done.

It used to be that Carson City's streets were filled with Jews, Germans, Russians and Chinese. Now it was a rarity that she saw a person different from her, someone who wasn't struggling. Her life had become simple white bread, when the meal she wanted was something more substantial.

Jack looked over to see what the matter was. He pointed to the floor, suggesting that she get busy. Nobody was earning any money otherwise. Despite a colorful vest and tie, he looked like an undertaker, his sunken cheeks, thin skin and eyes so pale that their blue color seemed gray, even ghostly. And Henry, a much handsomer and better-dressed man to whom she had given everything despite his being so goddamned scrawny and religious, had begun to look the same way.

Ally made a nice pile of crumbs with her fingers curled like a brush, sweeping toward the center of the table like her employer had taught her. Jack would be happy with that, she thought, beginning to smile, the dumb-ass. But a bird in hand was probably better than one about to leave the bush. The dreams she had for this Christian John Henry were definitely gone, if the missionary's words were to be believed.

Her eyes flashed. Picking up Henry's unused napkin across the table from her, Ally wiped a small piece of food from the corner of her mouth. Keeping her voice in as low a tone and measured beat as she possibly could, she said smugly, "You didn't seem so goddamned independent a moment ago when I had my hand on your Jimmy."

Nauman squirmed. The act had been pleasurable enough, but the mention of it was inappropriate. He had told her that many times. Each time he had talked to her about speaking in such an uncouth manner further confirmed his decision to cut things off. There would be no future. There could be no future together, if he was going to be successful. As much as he appreciated their frequent trysts and expressions of affection, he didn't favor talking about them. He sighed.

Ally sat straight up in the chair, smiling, and felt for a moment that she was doing the right thing, not needing the two-timing, self-righteous kind of man she thought she did. And who's doing the whoring anyway, she wondered—mister "I'm going to build a big business someday" or herself, having a small trade of regular customers and a great deal more if she wanted.

She adjusted her bodice with a subtle shift and lift, and, looking Henry Nauman straight in the eyes, pursed her lips together in a half-upturned smile.

The two of them sat quietly in the southeastern corner of the Ormsby Street saloon, looking at each other, by Henry's usual window, with Henry's usual beer, and two well-eaten California quail dinners. Ally figured that the almost-important man in front of her was probably done with Carson City. And likely the goddamned mission as well, whatever that was except that it involved Indian children, which she didn't particularly cotton to given that they were so dark and all.

And as she sat figuring, she realized that maybe she didn't need Jack the saloon owner, or the goddamned saloon she was working in, or the goddamned dream she'd had that she might actually get out of this place to find a better place, wherever that place might be.

And as she sat there, quietly detached from her expectations that life would get better or be better if only this changed or that man changed or something inside her changed, everything was right with the world. For just a moment, everything was as it should be.

And the director of the American Gospel Mission sat there as well, though not as peaceably or as deeply. He held his breath, because he didn't know what to say or do. Even though it was uncomfortable to do so, he held it until she blinked.

Then Ally, who had stayed so long in the Silver State that she remembered when it was a territory, said to her corset-tying friend behind the bar, "Jack, I think I'm done for the day."

She stood straight up, and looking at Henry Nauman, the almost-a-cleric sent westward by his very supportive and proud church in the West Virginia shadow of Steubenville, Ohio, the biggest-busted and best call girl in all of Carson City simply said, "Good day."

Exiting the saloon, she left Henry Nauman alone. That is, until a large Carson City deputy sheriff sauntered in.

Chapter 14

CARSON CITY

Dustsucker had gotten back to the Ormsby County sheriff's office sometime after 7 p.m., he figured, given that most of the capital's shops were closed and his stomach was growling. The lawman didn't wear a watch—it got in the way of his "gun work," he liked to say. He could generally keep track of time simply by knowing when it was time to eat.

Carson City's largest deputy sheriff didn't like to miss a meal; three or four meals were his daily maximum. But he did need to keep his weight from exceeding the Ormsby County Sheriff's arbitrary, and unofficial, standards. And though it took some doing to get what he needed in only four sit-downs a day, one of Carson City's most capable deputy sheriffs was able to monitor his intake in such a way so as to keep his distant mother proud, his large stomach satisfied and his firm but sometimes furious employer off his back.

He liked the Warm Springs Hotel because it was a mile or so east of town, had a decent restaurant without an inordinate need for personal cleanliness on the part of its patrons, and featured what he considered to be a reasonable, short wait.

Occasionally servicing the state's legislators when the more prominent and proximate rooms were unavailable, one of the capital's oldest hotels was far enough out of town that Slade had his privacy, but housed enough of the city's movers and shakers that news of the city's goings-on was never more than a couple chairs away.

There were rumblings that the hotel would soon transition to a much-needed state prison, a change Slade thought wasn't much of a change at all, given that it sheltered so many lying legislators. But the upcoming renovation would necessitate his moving closer to town into better known houses and hotels that preferred a generally cleaner clientele than he was used to.

Personal hygiene was too much of a bother for someone just as comfortable sitting down in a stream or river if the need for a bath arose. Which it generally didn't in Dustsucker's life, save to occasionally substitute for the sheriff when his employer had business out-of-town.

Dustsucker didn't like that Nevada was now a state. He preferred life as it once was. The city's streets and shops, though fewer than a couple of years ago, looked cleaner now, he figured, with surplus Chinese railroad workers providing street and sidewalk services. And capital city businesses catered to a more upscale group of citizens than he recalled when Carson City was governed more by mining interests than commercial developers. A branch of the new United States Mint meant that federal employees were now better acquainted with the city—but with that came some insistence that America's newest and smallest capital keep in step with the fast trot of civilization experienced by other cities in the Union, particularly those east of the Sierras.

Despite being tolerant of the Chinese neighborhoods Dustsucker had to pass through to get to his home, the deputy felt a slight irritation toward people who cleaned for a living or, more to the point, had something to do with his having to be clean. But it never kept him from doing what he needed to do. Few people knew about his feelings, or the palest prejudice he held against the more civilized folks who employed them. And neither bias stole his joy over a big, delicious meal, which, of course, was the point.

He was sitting in a Carson City saloon when W. W. Ronin found him eating a mid-afternoon snack of biscuits and gravy. "Hi, friend," Ronin called when he saw Dustsucker seated across a crowded saloon on Ormsby Street, near Ronin's boarding house.

Dustsucker liked to enjoy his breakfast no matter what time of the day it was or how many times he had it. And so he was not at all happy that Ronin had found him.

It had taken about an hour for the former Reverend W. W. Ronin to get back to the capital from the American Gospel Mission southeast of town, and another hour to locate his friend after having first stopped by the St. Charles Hotel and then the Ormsby County sheriff's office.

"Your friends didn't know *where* you were, let alone *who* you were," he said as he pulled a chair a ways out from the table and sat himself down, with his back, uncharacteristically, to the door. Ronin took off his hat, a tan-colored slouch hat that had seen better days, having been worn with Biffle's 19th Tennessee Calvary, drawing more of its fair share of fire in Alabama, the Carolinas, Georgia and Mississippi. Uniforms had improved some during Lincoln's War, though not for the Confederacy. Ronin was still wearing his original issue hat: one hundred percent wool, with a faded tan belt instead of worsted cord. He's once used it to secure a fugitive in New Mexico.

"What are you talking about, didn't know who I was?" Dustsucker responded, pushing his friend's hat away from his food and closer to the chair Ronin was sitting in.

"I'm saying when I went to the office to look for you, I asked for Dustsucker, and no one knew who you were until I uttered the name Slade."

Dustsucker laughed in a way that only department store Santas laughed back east. A half-dozen biscuits smothered in white, greasy bacon gravy waited on his plate. A few moist crumbs spilled from the side of his mouth. Rich, dark San Francisco coffee, from the J. A. Folgers Company, sat at one o'clock.

"Mind if I grab a cup and join you?" Ronin asked.

"Golden Gate Coffee," his friend said.

"Doesn't matter," Ronin replied. He never sat for a meal he didn't have permission for—something left over from the more genteel moments in his life, a habit that had served him well in the church and more recently had helped him keep track of who his real friends were and weren't. He waited until Slade nodded.

The latter group of people, a consistently expanding group of folks given Ronin's success in finding wanted men and women who had escaped the law's more recent grasp, always gave Ronin a slight stomachache, the kind a person gets when he or she has eaten rich foods or had too much to drink.

The former minister turned man tracker was careful who he ate with, given that bad guys often had family—bad brothers, dads or mothers who were just as likely to give a good man heartburn if he didn't stay alert. The policy kept him out of trouble, or at least allowed him to sleep better at night.

Dustsucker had been a deputy sheriff in Ormsby County since 1861, when William Marley replaced John L. Blackburn, who had been killed in the line of duty. He hadn't served in the national conflict that had so dominated the eastern and western states. In fact, he had remained totally immersed in the Ormsby County sheriff's office's reorganization, even as many of his friends had journeyed one way or the other to take part in the hostilities. As the sheriff's office grew larger and more active, Dustsucker had taken to grabbing assignments that pushed him further out into the bush. It meant greater travel and freedom, and allowed him to ignore the larger context of government and goings on, except when it served him most.

It also meant missing a few meals, a fact he was making up for when Ronin pulled out a chair and sat down.

"Yeah, the city guys still know me by my given name," he said, eyes twinkling, "not by my scent or appearance ... I much prefer it that way, to be frank. You might as well pull up a cup of coffee," he laughed, "now that you've got a chair. You can tell me what you found out at the Gospel Mission."

The deputy wiped his salt-and-pepper beard on his red forearm sleeve, dabbing his mouth when he was finished with the gray, faded cotton shirt he wore underneath his corduroy vest. "I'm real interested, given a discussion I had yesterday at Washoe Lake with an Indian chief."

"Figured as such," Ronin remarked, as he had imagined Dustsucker leaving their camp outside of Gold Hill for the Indian encampment around Washoe Lake.

Dustsucker laughed. He didn't know whether Little Wolf's father was an Indian chief or not. He said it simply to be funny, and it struck him so.

Chapter 15

A TABLE OR TWO AWAY

Ronin had never given any real thought to working for a city police or county sheriff's office. Western sheriffs followed the British model and were entrusted with "the maintenance of law and order and the preservation of domestic tranquility." But since everyone had a history in the West, and some folks were more given to domestic tranquility than others, the maintenance of a peaceful society, like the daily tasks he found himself about as a priest in an Episcopal church, didn't really interest him. A man is going to be who a man is going to be, no matter how many times the man (or woman) is introduced to the county hoosegow. Gender being what it was, Ronin figured, there were a great many more women acting out in the church than there were men doing the same outside the church. And he wasn't about to lock them all up. It simply was what it was.

"Damn Dustsucker, you eat a lot," Ronin said as he sat down, moving his shooter to the side so as not to impede his leaning forward a bit.

He found Dustsucker, or Deputy Sheriff Marcus T. Slade, an unusual oasis in a sea of usual creatures. Despite his desire at times to settle down or to fit in, usual was boring.

If people in Nevada had anything in common with those he knew in Wichita, it was their ability to say one thing and mean another. It was not a trait the once-Reverend Ronin could easily abide, but the sheer numbers of people acting that way made it something he worked at, whether he liked it or not.

Dustsucker, despite his rough and tumble appearance, gave Ronin the opportunity to occasionally relax and trust people again. He was who he said he was, and didn't spend a whole lot of time pretending.

"You likely don't know the rest of the story out of Virginia City, do you? I mean, given that you were up and gone by the time I woke up," he said, grabbing a cup from the center of the table and glancing at a coffee pot at a table nearby.

His friend interrupted, "I do, actually. Saw a telegram this evening sitting on my desk before I came here. Says you and Ash worked things out, more or less." Dustsucker looked up from his meal and smiled, remembering Ash's brief description of Ronin's resistance to being arrested.

He liked that Ronin wasn't afraid to mix it up with law enforcement types. He had enjoyed their friendship over the last three years. And he found him a principled man.

Whereas local sheriffs were sometimes all that stood between those whose histories were more colorful and those whose were less, there were shades of gray within lawmen living on the Comstock. One could think oneself to be facing one thing only to find out that he or she was, in fact, facing something or someone else. Ronin didn't seem to care. He was motivated by the same clear set of ideals that kept Dustsucker going, didn't assume much, from what Dustsucker could see and both knew it.

The two of them were friends, as much as men made friends. They had each other's back, which was wonderful, as far as either of them was concerned. Dustsucker had never thought of being a pastor, and it had never occurred to Ronin to become a lawman. Still, their lives crossed occasionally when the former priest's work as a man-tracker or detective brought Ronin to Reno or nearby Carson City.

"You sat with an Indian family?" Ronin asked. "One who had lost a kid?"

"I did, W.," the deputy said, sliding his chair backward and reaching for the coffee that sat at another man's table. "Excuse me," he whispered, barely looking up.

"I found the young'un you mentioned. Actually, he found me. And we found the father and, I guess, the young'un's sisters who testified that his very comely 12 year-old girl was missing. Other kids are missing, as well."

"Uh-huh," Ronin replied, untying his neckerchief to dab at the coffee he had spilled while pouring his own cup. He was tired. And he was distracted by the well-dressed man at the table whose coffee Dustsucker had borrowed.

"I'm sorry," he said, placing the coffee back on the table where it obviously belonged, a fact suggested by the man's momentary glare.

When the man looked over, Ronin held his gaze for a moment to give him an opportunity to respond. The former reverend didn't take to being stared at. A scrawny-looking businessman in a good-looking vest and a very nice tie, the man's eyes softened and he nodded. "You bet. I didn't mean to seem upset. You're welcome to it, gentlemen."

"So ... we already knew that," Ronin said, turning back to his friend, a number of kids from the tribe are missing. I get that," he said. "What else?"

"Well there's a connection of some sort, it seems, to the mission outside of town, or might be anyway, as the father has had some difficulty in seeing his daughter and now suspects she's missing along with the others. It's our first lead, so to speak, given that the girl has a name."

"Okay ..." Ronin paused, remembering that Dustsucker had already wondered about a possible connection. He briefly glanced at the man with the coffee, who seemed to be leaving.

Appearing haggard as he stood up, he put a Carson City silver dollar down on the table, dusted himself off and went to gather up a large gripsack and satchel. "Mind if we borrow your coffee again, mister?" Ronin asked, this time waiting to reach for the porcelain pitcher until he heard a response.

"Sure thing, cowboy," he responded. Ronin ignored the comment as he had been riding all day and was likely looking and smelling pretty ripe. But turning to leave, the man paused for a minute, stood there and then asked, "I'm sorry gents, but I over-heard you mention the American Gospel Mission a moment or so ago." He adjusted his hat and baggage, moving both bags into his left hand. "I've not been there in years. How do things seem out there?" he asked, his voice turning more animated.

Ronin looked at his buddy and looked back, surprised. "Well fine, I guess. Why do you ask, if I may inquire?"

"You sure may," he said, smiling. "I buy and sell, mostly. And I always thought that was a piss-poor piece of property," he said, straightening his tie. An odd man, Ronin thought. Not a small man, but an odd one and scrawny nonetheless.

Ronin noted his freshly shined shoes. "I never imagined that anything might come of that place." The man turned toward the doorway, and sticking a newspaper under his arm said, "Well, good day, gentlemen."

"Good day," Ronin said.

And with that, Henry Nauman left the saloon and boarded a Carson City stagecoach for Placerville, California, where he purchased a ticket for San Francisco and was never heard from again.

Chapter 16

HOME ALONE

Emma looked at her husband's office as soon as her unexpected visitor left. A much taller and stronger man than her husband, who looked more like a minister than someone associated with the Ormsby County sheriff's office, she took Ronin's early evening appearance there as timely, though she wasn't yet ready to speak her suspicions to others. Especially to someone she didn't know.

Her visitor had indicated he had come from the capitol city in order to speak with her the mission's director. But watching Ronin, "damn dusty from riding from Virginia City, ma'am. I'm sorry, I can leave my boots outside," he had said apologetically, she'd noticed his quick-minded curiosity, piercing blue eyes and apparent candor. Emma wondered if her fear that something was amiss at the mission was well founded.

She looked around the room, amazed at how unkempt it appeared and surprised by the desk's disorder and the names of students strewn on the floor. She'd often written students' names on the back of worn playing cards—anything less than a full deck was generally considered useless, she had heard in the area's saloons, so she hadn't been shy in asking for them—and it kept the mission's children foremost in her mind. But she had never considered crumpling them during prayer.

Fact is, up until that afternoon, she had stayed out of her husband's office at his request. "I like to pray aloud," he said, "about the children in our care. And there are moments that I'm deep in scripture study and meditation," he explained. She respected his privacy and prayed that his quiet afternoons alone in the office were helping to shape Henry's character into the man she hoped God was making him to be. But if the tone of Ronin's voice caused her to wonder again if something might be wrong at the mission, his sudden leave-taking confirmed it.

She had talked to Henry many times about missing children, and the record keeping in particular, noting that at some point that state or federal government would be attentive enough that Henry's poor record keeping would get them into trouble.

"You keep the kitchen," he'd say, wincing at her inferences that he couldn't handle so simple a task as making sure all of the children were in for the night. "And I'll take care of the rest. A man doesn't count his joys," he often said, "only his troubles," as if quoting a famous writer or educator.

Discipline was sometimes needed to make the children conform to their training and "Christianization," a word she wasn't entirely comfortable with and one she hadn't heard before Henry had used it. Correction was a man's job, Henry maintained, whether kids were slipping away or not. "And why would they? This is such a happy place."

Despite Henry's protestations and without his knowledge, Emma had instructed the kitchen staff to keep a simple count of the children at breakfast and dinner, allegedly for meal planning. She was being more than careful, she was being curious. She had begun to worry.

"I don't understand why there's such a variance in the number of children at dinner," she remarked to her husband, who pointed out that federal Indian agents were constantly bringing new children in and sending others back.

"It's a necessary part of our discipline," he said. "You know the saying. 'One bad apple spoils the bunch,'" he added, pointing out that the words were in the biblical book of *Proverbs*, something Emma knew was not true but didn't care to argue for fear she'd crush her husband's new-found enthusiasm for things spiritual.

But with the continued and often pronounced swing of the weekly meal counts, Henry's lengthier moments alone in his office, the light streaming through large, partially covered windows on the south side of their home and the occasions when she'd discover that he wasn't in the office but had gone walking or on an errand, Emma had begun to wonder if something horrible was happening at the mission. And given her commitment to God "to build a mighty Christian work in the capitol city," she couldn't ignore her fears any longer.

It took her a couple of hours to put things back in order before her husband returned for a late-night supper. She could ask him about the piles of papers she'd made in his office during dinner, she figured. Surely there would be an easy explanation to what had caused the stranger to leave so suddenly, and for her husband's increasingly frequent unexplained absences from the mission.

She summoned the kitchen help when she saw her husband's carriage bumping up the road outside the mission gates, framed by the dusty, snow-blown Sierra foothills a dozen or so miles to the west. It had grown cold earlier in October than she had anticipated, so Emma has asked the kitchen staff to keep the stove lit to provide some warmth around the table should Henry return in time for a private supper.

Moving a pie tin of her husband's favorite beef and beans to the stove's center, she waited with her hands folded on the table for what she knew would be a very important conversation.

Chapter 17

THE GLOBE SALOON

Ronin and Dustsucker stayed at the Ormsby Street saloon until about 10 p.m., talking about the American Gospel Mission. He mentioned the odd scattering of children's names throughout the room and the fact that at least one, if not many, of their children were missing.

Dustsucker listened with interest and indicated that a couple of deputies would ride out to the mission in the morning to investigate. Given that they had confirmed that Washoe children were missing from the valley, both friends were perplexed enough that they decided they'd think about it again over breakfast in the morning.

Ronin was tired. It had been a long day of riding, but he agreed to accompany his friend back to his office to make some very important notes. It was dark as they headed north on Ormsby Street past the Globe Saloon.

The Globe was a source of color and consternation for Carson City lawmen, and Dustsucker liked to drop by on his way to anywhere in order to check on things. Ronin knew the way. He often walked north of his rooming house on Carson Street and then west to Saint Peters Episcopal Church, where he'd stop in to pray.

He didn't think himself a particularly religious man—spiritual, maybe, but he found himself drawn to Saint Peters as it represented what his life might have been had it not turned into something else. And the space seemed, when it was empty at least, sacred.

They were walking along listening to the sounds of the city when the Crestwell brothers fell out of a doorway south of the Globe Saloon, arguing about who was going to get back up on his horse and "get the fuck out of town," and who was going to get another beer and "think things over."

The brothers collided with Dustsucker, whose mass was not about to be moved, and drew down on the deputy without seeing who he was or wondering what had happened. The deputy was just turning toward the Crestwells when Ronin caught one of the brothers mid-bounce and, continuing the man's awkward momentum, had spun him face-first into a sandstone wall.

Remy Crestwell crumpled after rebounding alongside a brown commercial edifice. He sank like a stone to the street, taking just long enough that his brother Clem stood there with his mouth agape, eyes blinking.

Seizing the moment with Dustsucker just beginning to move, Ronin dropped his left foot behind his right, skipping a well-heeled Texas-style spur and boot into Clem Crestwell's chest, knocking both of his legs out from beneath him and sending an intoxicated and clearly agitated elder Crestwell brother ass-first into the building's doorway. The impact broke both the door and frame.

Dustsucker turned to his friend and, just beginning to figure out what had happened, said with a chuckle, "You don't … uh, give folks much of a second chance, do you? I mean for a reverend and all that?"

"I'm not much for gun play," Ronin responded, watching the two men now crawling toward each other on Ormsby Street, his hands still up by his face ready for an additional assault if one were needed.

"No," Dustsucker responded, "of course not. I've never seen you draw down on anyone," he said, laughing, remembering Virginia City. "Perhaps these guys didn't mean anything by coming at me that way. They might have just been startled," Dustsucker chuckled.

"You've got to be kidding," Ronin replied, wondering if his friend's new-found gift for gab was evidence of his thinking of running for political office. He picked the younger man up off the street, grabbing the back of his vest, and leaned him into the wall so as to get a better look at him. "Take the other one, would you?"

Ronin was irritated. Dustsucker's prissy attitude was reason number one why he'd never tolerate a job with a city police force or county sheriff's agency. Dustsucker grabbed the older man from the doorframe, a well-muscled mouth breather who looked as if he had been riding for a while, and instantly recognized him in the faint light given off by a twenty-year old lantern hanging outside the saloon.

"Well, looky here, Dustsucker exclaimed, "if it isn't one of the Crestwell brothers!" Ronin cocked his head with curiosity. "The ones I was telling you about, W. These boys have been making a lot of trips to the bank recently, if you know what I mean, spending money here and there as if it was going out of style."

One of the Crestwells muttered, "Leave us the fuck alone, fatso!" Ronin didn't know which as he was dusting off his pants. He had stirred up some gravel with his step-behind rear kick and it had dirtied the inside of his trousers. W. W. Ronin was still a very neat man, despite his having left parish work nearly ten years previous. There was always the possibility that he'd need to sit with someone important, he figured, or the possibility that an attractive woman might turn his head. He lifted his face at about the same moment that Slade jacked three pounds of iron from his holster backwards, hitting the elder Crestwell across the side of his head and knocking him into the doorway again.

Dustsucker carried a brace of guns, Hickok-style across his front belt. He spent most of his time riding, and the strong-side carry favored by Ronin and many others only caused his forty-fives to fall out. It was not a pretty sight to see a fat deputy bending over.

"You talk about me!" Ronin said, shaking his head and smiling. "How are we going to talk to these boys if you keep knocking them out?"

Ronin dragged both Crestwells into a standing pile of street scum and gestured to a looky-loo who was staring their way, to grab another deputy off of Carson Street, just around the corner.

"Looks like we've got a passel of bad guys to sort through, deputy," Ronin said to his friend. "I mean, assuming you don't mind."

Chapter 18

SAVATE

Dustsucker pushed the Crestwells' guns into the sides of his belt, given that his midsection wouldn't permit their secure carry if lodged by the front buckle. Tossing their gun belts over his head, their gun pouches trailing to the middle of his back, he looked around for their horses.

The portly Ormsby County deputy sheriff looked the part of an out-of-breath but happy pirate, with multiple belts and braces of pistols hanging on his side. Fortunately, he didn't have to go far to pack up the Crestwells' gear in order to move them over to the County Jail, a couple of blocks south of Eighth Street.

"A nice cutlass might complete your pirate outfit look, Dusty," Ronin said, given that his friend had taken to keeping his left eye closed and was rolling an "R'" at the back of his throat as he exerted himself.

"You're lucky I've got all of this stuff in my hands, reverend, as I'd be happy to drag you to the jail as well, given all the scrapes you've gotten me into these last couple of days."

Ronin knew his friend was kidding, but the threat didn't sit well as he had long given up his capacity to act one way when he was feeling another. "I'll not go there with you," he said generously, knowing that Dustsucker's bulk wouldn't stand up to Ronin's capacity for speed and violence. "And I'll assume you're kidding, though I don't like it." Ronin had spent a few days in jail one time for disorderly conduct, while working a Pinkerton case. Though it had been a generally relaxing time—he had beaten two men within an inch of their lives, a fate he was certain they deserved, though a Santa Fe marshal disagreed—he wasn't about to lose his life or liberty to a part-time policeman again. As the capitol city fathers hadn't yet seen the wisdom of financing a permanent and more pleasant lock-up, he figured he'd skip the opportunity to visit a Comstock blockhouse, whether it was in Virginia City or located in the Carson City hinterlands near the end of town

W. W. Ronin's hand-to-hand work had turned into a serious hobby when he was in seminary, with him initially imitating Irish boxers he'd known back in Greensboro, Pennsylvania. The Monongahela River town settled primarily by Germans, Greensboro had been a trading center for early travelers heading north to Pittsburgh and to parts farther west. While the settlement soon became a place known for glassmaking and German stoneware, Ronin's exposure to the Irish and English fist arts had given the seminary student an unusual way to work off steam.

Ronin loved combat, and understood it, given his middle child status was firmly fixed, no matter how hard he tried to rise to the top of the family order. Somehow the church, or rather his ten years in the church as a pastor and missionary, hadn't pacified that. "You've never been to a church meeting out West," his bishop had counseled him early on. "You'll be surprised how they sometimes settle things."

He assumed the Right Reverend James O'Reilly, episcopal bishop of the Diocese of Pittsburgh, was referring to the Christian virtues of patience and prayer when faced with his suggestion that the then almost-a-reverend W. W. Ronin still had some learning to do before heading to Wichita. After the surly man picked him up by the front of his clergy shirt and vest and held him fist-firm to a vestry wall, he understood that church meetings in Wichita might not be as he expected.

"You'll appreciate your fist arts," his bishop said as he unclenched his left hand and allowed Ronin to touch the floor again with his shoes. "Get yourself a good hat and some boots before you're ordained. And a sturdy pair of gloves might serve you well also," he winked, glancing at Ronin's well-worn bag gloves sitting on a table in the college gymnasium where he exercised, sparring with other seminarians. "You'll appreciate the hand protection. Things can get kind of dicey out there, from what I hear."

Bishop O'Reilly was speaking about the American frontier, a few hundred miles west of the St. John's Episcopal Church in Wichita that Ronin served prior to resigning his small pastorate for parts and future unknown.

An old French fur trader had completed his martial education, introducing him to the foot arts favored by French sailors from the port of Marseilles. The sport known as "Chausson," later known as "Savate," had become something of a rage among the French in later years. The French were explorers and seamen, and given such, had been exposed to many cultures including those in the East. And being a passionate but practical people, the French had turned English boxing into a devastating hybrid system of hand and foot fighting. Ronin had spent many a Monday, after Sunday services, with the old fur trader, who lived in a log cabin just south of the church in a trapped-out river. He initially thought of it as parish work, "caring for the lost," on his day off. The grizzled old Frenchman was quite the unconverted soul, but it didn't take Ronin long to realize who was schooling whom, and in what.

Ronin grabbed the Crestwell brothers by the backs of their collars, twisted his hands so as to achieve a firmer grip and, kneeing each of them in the back and behind, propelled them aggressively across the street toward his friend who waited by the horses. Tossing one, and then the other, up over their saddles, he laughed.

"I'm not near tough or foolish enough to be mixing it up with you, my friend," he winked. Dustsucker knew, of course, that he was lying as Ronin repositioned the younger Crestwell so that he could sit straight up in the saddle. He tied the young man's reins around the horse's saddle horn, pinching him briefly on the inner thigh so that he'd sit upright and hold on. "But if you've got some concerns," Ronin said, "we should talk about them."

Dustsucker put his hand to his forehead and sighed. "Well, since you mention it ... I'm good with what happened up in the Virginia City, and with whatever happened between you and the marshal afterward. But what's bugging me is this. What the hell was that skipping thing you did a minute or so ago?"

Ronin was silent for a moment, tightening a strap on the older Crestwell's saddle. It was hard to tell if his friend was serious. "The guy who taught it to me called it a *chasse marche croise*," he said, scrunching up his nose and lips in his best attempt to mimic a proper French pronunciation. "I call it a cross-behind rear kick, because it engages the gluteal muscles and allows for a more forceful kick."

"Whatever," Dustsucker said. He slid a steel-framed 1873 Winchester into the scabbard on the younger Crestwell's horse and draped the Crestwell boys' gun belts on to the saddle horn of his own horse. "I'd tell you that you looked like a girl doing that skipping thing except that the result wasn't all that ladylike," Dustsucker laughed. "I am, incidentally, grateful for that."

"Yup," is all Ronin replied, checking the heavy iron handcuffs Dustsucker had placed on each brother. They were still secure. Looking past their prisoners, Ronin smiled and said, "I figure we're even then." Dustsucker nodded.

Truth was, Ronin didn't care whether they were even or not. And more so, he sometimes wondered what the deal was with his violent streak. A job was a job, he figured, having given up a "calling" to pursue his detective work. These particular skills, however violent they were, seemed to come quite naturally to him. Moreover, they served him well.

Chapter 19

CARSON CITY JAIL

The four of them soon arrived at the Ormsby County Jail. An unpretentious block building a few doorways south from the center of government, the jail housed half a dozen prisoners on a good day and great deal more if needed, though the conditions were always crowded and the jail's deputies were never accused of offering kind or Christian hospitality.

The Crestwells were taken to the front desk, where the night man took down their names, secured their valuables, tagged and threw their guns and gun leather into a trunk underneath a full sheriff's rack of well-used rifles and shotguns. Dustsucker walked the Crestwell boys through two locked doors and placed them into a cell with a window that overlooked a short, narrow alley. Then he returned to the office, where a much younger deputy was talking with his friend. A picture of Judge Orson Hyde, the organizer of Carson County (now named Ormsby) and of law enforcement efforts in the county, hung on a wall behind the desk.

"So, my understanding is that you *used* to be a minister, but *now* you're not," the deputy was saying when Dustsucker entered the room. Another deputy stood quietly over by a window and had pulled his hat down to hide his face. He was clearly amused at the younger deputy's agitation.

Ronin was irritated by the man's tone and was about to launch into a severe dressing down when Dustsucker, the senior of the three, interrupted the hapless inquisition by laughing.

"Jack, you're an ass," he said. "You don't even know the man and you want to question his credentials."

"I have no credentials," Ronin said quietly. "Don't need them. It's still a free country, last time I noticed anyway," he said, poking ever so slightly at the man's desk with the toe of his boot.

"Not when you knock down a duly-appointed officer of the law, steal his gun and threaten his life," the younger man said. "What I hear is that you've been a general son of a bitch, reverend!" he exclaimed, raising his voice without skipping a beat while grinning.

Jack had obviously heard about Ronin's man-handling of the U.S. Marshal, who had turned out to be a gentleman and was simply doing his duty in a careful and respectful way, Ronin had concluded after kicking the man's legs out from under him and holding him at gunpoint.

Ronin exhaled through his nose, his upper body just a little bit tense. "I really don't think you need to take that tone with me," he said, turning a steely glance to the deputy and then to his friend Dustsucker, who was now locking the door between the sheriff's office and the secured area of the jail. Dustsucker was focused exclusively on the pimply-faced loudmouth behind the desk. He did not meet his friend's eyes. Midstream in forming a mental list of inappropriate ways of educating the young lawman, Ronin was about to speak when Dustsucker interrupted.

"I'll not get in between the two of you if you're really set on seeing this man's less-than-friendly face," he said, hardly smiling. "But what you do need to know before you turn into a complete jackass, Jack, is that this man likely saved my life a couple of minutes ago and would just as quickly take yours if it meant protecting mine again."

"He did *what?*" the deputized youngster bellowed. Dustsucker winced.

"You heard me," he said. "Sit down. Shut your mouth and open up your ears," he said, barking orders in an uncharacteristically unfriendly way. "We've got some work to do, and it might be helpful to all of us if you were still alive to do it."

A sudden moment of silence descended upon the room as the man looked back and forth a couple of times at the senior deputy. And then, noting Ronin's large, well-worn, gloved hands and his angled, well-traveled sidearm and gun belt, he realized he was so clearly owned that it was embarrassing. Ronin didn't seem to be breathing; his focus was unnerving.

Jack glanced at his mentor, who had raised both of his bushy white eyebrows and pushed his red sleeves up until they practically had disappeared under his woolen checkered shirt. Seeing that Slade was clearly waiting on a response to his words, which were not so much a request but a demand, he placed both hands on his desk chair, slid back into its grasp, slid his feet onto the floor and shut his mouth.

A moment passed before the young man spoke again.

"My apologies, Mr. Ronin. I didn't know you were," he paused, "about the Lord's business," he said, smirking, eyes lit up like a born loser.

Dustsucker snorted, shaking his head. He did not believe what he was watching. Holding his breath, he hoped it wouldn't erupt into something awful when he was surprised to hear his friend speak.

"Apology accepted, my friend," Ronin replied barely smiling, while looking at the man by the window. "Frankly, I didn't think it was appropriate yet to introduce you to the baby Jesus. He's not always in such a good mood, you understand. Nor am I." Ronin rested his eyes on the deputy's chest as if he was "going to punch the man's heart out," his bishop used to say when they sparred. His hands were clasped across his vest and stomach, resting six inches or so above his gun belt in preparation for what might happen next. But then, relaxing his arms, Ronin raised his eyes to meet the deputy's glance, and said simply and slowly, "Thank you, friend."

Dustsucker exploded in laughter, in part to gasp for breath but also to break the tension in the room. He could not believe the ignorance and inexperience of his fellow lawman. "Ronin, you sure are a hoot!" he guffawed, glaring at the young deputy who was finally sitting quietly at the desk. The other deputy by the window visibly relaxed as well, lifting his hand from his revolver, having wondered which man he'd shoot if shooting became necessary. "Both of you sit down for a minute," Dustsucker said. "We've got some business to attend to."

And the four men did just that: One large lawman, big enough to do the job and a lifetime of experience to ensure that he did it right. A former priest, French kick-boxing, Irish pugilist, who knew when he had control of an audience, big or small, and now held the rapt attention of everyone in the room. A nameless night man, who was suddenly more curious about what was happening inside the sheriff's office than just outside his window. And a small German-like wiener of a boy, who was old enough to wear a badge but not yet wise enough to wield it and who now needed to change his pants.

Chapter 20

MY HENRY

Emma stood at the front window of their single level stone home at the American Gospel Mission just south of Carson City. She thought it odd that Henry hadn't entered the house and come looking for her, given that she had seen his carriage coming up the road. Because it was dark she had gotten up to see if he was delayed, perhaps by talking to some of the mission children, or maybe chatting with some of the ranch hands. Emma moved from the window to the door so as to step out on to the porch, but paused to grab a sweater because the night air was so chilly.

The mission she and Henry had carved from the Carson Valley foothills over the last couple of years employed many of its own Indian children and adults to grow crops, care for cattle and to keep the hundred and some acres of surprisingly fertile land in good order and production.

Neither Emma nor her husband wanted the ranch to be anything less than perfect, which explained her surprise earlier that evening to find Henry's office in such disarray. Emma figured this was the safer of topics for the two of them to discuss, since they agreed that tidiness was next to godliness. She hoped Henry would pause long enough in the conversation to realize that her involvement in the mission's goings-on, and particularly the care of the mission's children, was terribly important to her. She hoped, too, that there might be an opening to discuss the many other things that were beginning to bother her.

As she stood at the front of the house wondering where her husband was, she reviewed a mental list of children she hadn't seen in recent weeks. Emma figured there were a dozen or so that had disappeared in such a way as to arouse her suspicions. And while she didn't know where the children were, her husband's explanations—that some had been sent home for disciplinary reasons and others had been employed elsewhere as good fortune had permitted—seemed hollow and untrue. She needed to ask also why he had been increasingly more absent from the mission's properties and business. And why he had been so resistant to keeping better track of who was where and when.

Emma was rehearsing her side of the conversation when there was a knock at the back door adjacent to the house's personal storehouse and stable.

"Ma'am?" A voice she didn't recognize called from the kitchen. "Mrs. Nauman? Are you here?" The voice sounded like a Negro man, she thought, though none were employed by the mission and they had none as friends. Henry had been adamant about making a careful selection of entries to their social circle, and given that there were so few black families on the Comstock and its environs, they would want "to keep to themselves," he said. Emma was scared for a moment, but "girding up her loins,"—she whispered the biblical phrase to herself as if to take strength from it—she "took Jesus as her Captain and Protector" and ventured a few careful steps back toward the kitchen.

"Hello?" she said tentatively. "I'm Mrs. Nauman," she acknowledged, peering around the doorframe into the large service kitchen used by both the house and the mission's staff and children. "Can I help you?" she asked, facing one of the largest men she had ever set her eyes on.

A black man stood tentatively in the mission kitchen doorway. He seemed nearly seven feet tall, with a robust chest and large arms and shoulders, though in the darkness he appeared taller and stronger than he really was. The mission's unexpected nighttime guest, however, was a handsome man and, given the size of his hands, clearly used to hard physical labor.

The door was still open when one of the Washoe house servants came into view under the covered porch between the house and stable, where the wood was stored for the kitchen stove and parlor heaters. Both Emma and the black man relaxed with the Indian's sudden appearance, though Emma remained in the kitchen doorway.

"Mrs. Nauman," the Indian asked, "Are you okay?"

"I am, Rupert," Emma replied, nodding slowly. "Won't you come in and sit down, sir?" she asked of the large Negro, who had now entered the kitchen. "What can we do for you?"

"Thank you ma'am," he replied, "but I've got to soon ride back to the city. My missus and children are waiting for me so as to be sure I'm okay."

Emma pushed away from the doorframe and entered the kitchen. Pulling out a chair so that it was facing the table but was nearer the door, she addressed the stranger again. "Please sir, sit. I'll not let a guest in my kitchen stand," she said, forcing a smile. "What brings you to our door tonight?"

Spying an unfamiliar horse tethered to the back porch, Emma was now more than curious and began to suspect that something was wrong. Her house servant was putting her husband's carriage into the barn and she had yet to see Henry. "Where's my husband?" she asked. "Is everything alright with my Henry?" Silence was the only response. "My husband," she pleaded. "Do you where he is?" Her voice cracked, despite her intentions to remain calm as she stood with her hand on a chair facing the unexpected stranger. The man sat down, but did not move the chair closer to the table. He extended his hand toward the table, however, as if to brace himself.

Emma held her breath. She felt warm. Steadying herself with the chair, she reached for a cloth napkin on the table in order to fan herself and was surprised that she had to reach for it twice before she was able to touch it to her face, wiping at small beads of perspiration around her mouth, nose and neck.

"Where is my husband?" she insisted, even more emotionally than the last time. Her arms felt heavy. Her breathing became more profound. She labored to listen and felt as if she were unable to speak.

"Ma'am, I assume your husband is fine," the man said. "Please calm down." Emma looked at him blankly. "Your mister gave me this carriage and a coin."

He displayed a silver dollar in his right hand. His left hand lay flat on the table. His feet began to shift underneath the chair. "He instructed me to take the carriage here to the mission." Emma continued to look at him uncomprehendingly. "The carriage, ma'am," he repeated. "He told me to take the carriage here."

The man seemed honest, Emma thought, though it had been a long time since she had gazed so intently at a black man. Not since West Virginia, she remembered, when she and Henry as newlyweds had gone up to Steubenville for farm seed and stayed over at their cousin's house and attended a church meeting. Negroes had taken care of their horses, she remembered. They listened at the church's windows to the Word of the Lord as it was preached and experienced by all who fell under the itinerant preacher's spell. It had been an amazing night, she remembered. It had changed their lives. Now they were here in Carson City. She and Henry were doing such a good work, caring for the children and enjoying their church's blessing and support, though it was never enough. It was never enough. Culling the thorns from the land, she liked to think, they were planting good seeds for the Lord Jesus Christ and his children.

How is it that her husband was not here with her? Where was he if he wasn't here and why had he paid a man to return their carriage? Whose horse was that tied to the back porch? Where was Henry? She looked at the door, now closed, and glanced at the two east-facing windows that faced the storehouse and barn.

Emma's questions began to tumble when she noticed that her stomach was turning sour and her bowels were suddenly cramping. Looking about for a cloth napkin on their large wooden table that had seated so many of the mission's children, though it always seemed necessary to feed the children in multiple shifts so as to accommodate them all, Emma swallowed and tasted acid.

She wondered if her kitchen had turned into a "groanin' cart," what the cowboys sometimes called their food wagons. Had she had too many frijoles, she speculated? She should really learn to cook better, she thought. Why was she feeling so sick?

The kitchen was suddenly chilly.

She stood there in her housedress and hastily combed hair, her arms crossed around her waist, holding her elbows, perseverating and staring, unblinking, at her guest. She began to shake. She gathered the gold-colored woolen shawl around her shoulders, the shawl that Henry had given her when they had started their journey west "to do an amazing work for the Lord Jesus," her husband had said. She met her guest's eyes, her head slowly turning from side to side as if to say no.

"Why would my husband give you his carriage? And how is it he paid you a dollar to bring it here?" she asked, confused over what was going on. "I don't understand," she sighed. She waited uncomfortably for what seemed like an unholy moment where even the angels in heaven feared to utter aloud a single sentiment or word.

Turning her head slightly to the right, her left eye now fixed on her hesitant guest, she listened intently and incredulously as she heard the stranger speak. "He gave it to me ma'am. Before he got on the stage, ma'am. The stage to the mountains, ma'am. To California, ma'am. He said I should return the carriage to you, ma'am."

Hearing those words, Emma sat down and wondered what had become of her Henry.

Chapter 21

JAIL BREAK

The explosion was deafening. It sounded as if the back of the jailhouse had blown away from the rest of the building, which is in fact what the blast had done. Knocking a hole through two of the building's walls, the unexpected explosion left cell doors swinging and prisoners scrambling toward the street, gasping for the clean night air.

Ronin reached the still-secure inner door of the office first, having been partially shielded from sure concussion by the large oak desk and the mouthy deputy he had been arguing with earlier. A twelve-inch piece of glass and the metal screen that contained and reinforced it were missing from the door, its pieces embedded in a series of white oak cabinets across the front of the office. Peering through the window opening, Ronin realized he could see very little except smoke. He assumed the worst.

Given that no one else was moving, he reflexively drew his right knee up to his chest and stomped hard at the middle of the door. The force of the piston-like blow broke the door's lower hinge so that it almost swung free. A second, more powerful kick dropped the gate like a gang plank into the dark and dust-filled space that had been the Ormsby County Jail.

Ronin lived to regret it, because without pausing to think or to look, he bolted through the dusky opening like a prairie rabbit, assuming the jail flooring would catch his feet. But the boards were no longer there and his left foot dropped a foot and a half into the building's rubble foundation.

Unable to move, he squatted precariously amidst a pile of men attempting to flee through the doorway in which he was situated.

He could hear the muffled shouts of deputies behind him when a large, well-muscled forearm swung hard at his neck. It knocked him nearly unconscious and twisted his body to the right, wrenching his right knee. He cried out in pain. Still woozy from the blow and hearing someone call his name, he turned the opposite way and was hit again by a large piece of timber seized from what was left of the jail's construction. It caught him square on the side of the head and hurt like a bastard.

Ronin raised his fists to cover up, but seeing the legs of the man who hit him, he instead fixed his fingers firmly around both ankles as Dustsucker and another deputy slammed into the attacker's chest and face, driving him forcefully to the ground. The inmate lay there unable to move, the breath knocked out of him, blood oozing from one of his ears.

"I tried to warn you!" Dustsucker screamed above the other voices. Ronin was wiping furiously at his eyes and ears hoping to regain his focus when he saw yet another man come stumbling toward him.

Given that his leg was still stuck—the hole he was standing in was now up to the bottom of his behind—and his knee was badly wrenched, Ronin could do little to escape or evade. Grabbing the man's belt and buckle with both of his hands and rolling backward, he tucked his chin so that his head would not be any more damaged than it already was and yanked the hard-charging inmate up and over the left side of his body, driving his assailant's head into the broken rock and flooring behind him. Both men were screaming. Instantly, his attacker went limp, collapsing beneath him. Unable to breathe or move, Ronin was whispering a call for help when help arrived.

Dustsucker and the other deputy fell to their knees, pushing the large man over onto his side. They shook their heads smartly when they noted the odd angle to the attacker's head and neck. Ronin took a deep breath.

"Jesus," he said, still struggling to see. "Get me out of this hole," he wheezed. Pausing to look at his assailant, he remarked, "He looks dead, doesn't he?"

Dustsucker laughed. Ronin could take the worst of circumstances and turn them into something funny.

"That he does, reverend," Dustsucker whistled, smiling. Bracing his knee to stand up, he remarked, "That's the older Crestwell brother. Imagine you'll recognize him once your eyes clear. He's the one you drop-kicked through the door frame at the Old Globe Saloon a few hours ago."

"I can see that now."

"He looks real bad," Dustsucker remarked. "I don't imagine he's going to make it."

"He looks real dead is what he looks like," Ronin corrected, smiling back at his friends. "Well?"

They turned their attention toward the former reverend, pinned his elbows to his side and lifted him up and on to the remaining floorboards. Unable to support his weight with his injured right leg, Ronin crumpled.

"I think it's broken," he said, beginning to faint.

"Yeah, a lot of things are broken back here," Dustsucker said, catching his breath and looking around. "It would also appear that every one of our prisoners is gone as well. That will keep us busy, I guess." He grabbed his friend by the back of his shirt and, nodding toward the other deputy, dragged the bounty hunter back in the direction of the office.

Chapter 22

THE DOCTOR

Emma hadn't intended to go to the doctor's office. She had ridden into town at first light to see what she could find out about her husband's leaving. Still unsteady from hearing the news the night before, she had fallen off her horse in front of the Ormsby County sheriff's office. Two deputies found her there, having just returned from Dr. Amos Quinn's office on Carson Street.

"Whoa, partner," the big one shouted to his smaller friend, bending over her. Emma was still very much confused from both the fall and the previous night's revelation that her husband had apparently left her for parts even farther west.. Still, she thought she heard the larger deputy say to the other, "Looks like we're famous!" ... when in fact the larger deputy, a three-hundred-fifty pound bear of a man if there ever was one, had simply said, "Looks like we're headed back to Amos' office."

We have two ears and one mouth so as to listen twice as much as we speak, Emma reminded herself before she felt the deputies lifting her up and placing her across her horse. Fainting again, the last thing she remembered prior to waking up in the doctor's office was that the Stoic philosopher was right. "Epictetus," she said, looking up into Dr. Quinn's crystal clear blue eyes.

"Excuse me, ma'am?" the doctor asked. Emma remained silent, a practiced trait given that her religious visions and "prayer language," as she called it, had been grossly misunderstood by well-meaning folks before.

"Nothing," she replied smiling, her right hand reaching toward her forehead, as if searching for the source of her pounding headache. She looked around the room and, figuring it to be a doctor's office given the instruments on the table, noticed the unconscious man lying on a door beside her.

A bill had been passed by the state legislature in 1875 prohibiting individuals from practicing medicine who had not received a medical education. Fines and imprisonment were imposed if a copy of a diploma or certificate from a "regularly chartered medical school" wasn't found hanging in the physician's office. Emma didn't see one, but had heard that Governor "Broadhorns" Bradley had accomplished a slight change to the law, given that during its enactment, he was lying in bed with an attack of paralysis, surrounded by several older physicians who maintained that uneducated doctors, who had certain experience in the state, were at least equal to if not better than inexperienced physicians who had no education.

Quinn was both experienced and educated. He had been a doctor all of his life, he liked to answer when asked. He was still a young man, though "not a day over twenty," most had mistakenly concluded in the capitol city. But as that the nation's doctor mills didn't ask for much more than a year or two of training, it was understandable that he wasn't as old as some of the other doctors in town. A physician father had trained the boy in the ways of allopathic medicine, and ticketed lectures at a nearby medical school had accomplished the rest.

The "go-to" man as he was known for gunshot wounds and the like, Ormsby County law enforcement types typically headed his way when a someone turned up full of holes. Though corpse and cartridge occasions generally deserved more than a teenager just out of barber school, folks liked to tease, Quinn was quick about his work and didn't hit the already-underfunded sheriff's office up for much when he was needed.

"Why am I here?" Emma asked. "And why is he here?" she inquired, noting that her unfortunate neighbor looked "practically dead," an easy conclusion given that he man was reclining on an old door.

Quinn laughed. "You're here, ma'am, because you fell off a horse and bounced your head off a hitching post. That's my guess, anyway."

He smiled. He sure is striking, she thought when she heard him say, "How are you feeling?"

"I'm fine, except for a headache," she said, still touching her forehead but not failing to notice his beautiful eyes. Quinn caught her hand.

"It's still bleeding; don't touch it," he said, noticing that her pupils were dilated, a sure sign that she was in shock or suffering from a concussion. It was awkward, but he wondered how to ask her to allow him to examine her further. If she was bleeding elsewhere, the good doctor would need to know.

"And him?" Emma asked again, gesturing to the man on the table beside her, "May I ask why he's here?"

The former Reverend W. W. Ronin was unconscious, with one leg buckled strangely up underneath the other. He was breathing, and there was a strong smell of alcohol.

"Him? Well, not that it's any of your business," the doctor said, smiling. "But it turns out our hero fell into a hole," he remarked, "and the hole didn't like his left leg one bit. He's fine."

Emma scrunched up her nose. "Smells like he's had a bit too much 'tornado juice,' if you ask me," she said.

Quinn laughed, and pulling a clean sheet from a counter, unfolded it so as to cover Emma's legs and torso. "Where'd you hear words like that ma'am? You appear to be a good Christian woman. I don't know that I've heard words like that except outside a saloon."

Emma propped herself up on one elbow to see what the doctor was doing, and finding that she couldn't support herself, fell backward, her eyes beginning to close. "Epictetus has never been in a saloon …"

Quinn worked quickly to ascertain if his unconscious female patient was bleeding anywhere else, and finding nothing of note, bandaged her head wound so that he could turn his attention to the man the deputies had brought in an hour or so before.

Ronin was beginning to stir when Quinn looked his way.

"I don't know that I've had so much to drink in a long time," he said, opening his eyes and noticing there was a woman in the room. "Who's she?" he asked with a slightly inebriated grin, wondering if the doctor had set his leg yet.

"That's Emma Nauman, I'm told, the director's wife out at the American Gospel Mission. The deputies brought her here about twenty minutes after they delivered you. Sounds like she fell off her horse early this morning just outside the sheriff's office."

"It's raining saints then," Ronin quipped, still grinning. "I believe I might know her," he said, blinking his eyes. "Though you've got her turned the other way, I want to point out."

He paused for a moment, admiring her form. "She's a good looking lady," he said.

Ronin liked thin, and though most folks thought thin meant hungry, he appreciated a man or woman who might practice a little bit of discipline around the table. He liked Thomas Jefferson's thought that "One never has to repent if one eats too little," though he had never figured out a way to share the insight with a portly man or woman. He had gained weight in his religious work, but lost it when he rode west, given that the Pinkertons paid too little to overeat and his independent work didn't pay him much either.

"A small scar above her left eye?" he whispered to the doctor, wincing as he was in some pain.

"Why yes, how did you know?" Quinn asked. A ruddy youthful face looked down at Ronin, framed by brown unkempt hair punctuated by brilliant blue eyes.

"I met her at the mission, though I thought by the way she was hovering over me that she was a housekeeper."

Grimacing again, Ronin attempted to prop himself up on one elbow, but found he was unable to accomplish the movement due to the amount of alcohol the doctor had given him, and his friends an hour or so before that. Looking at his one leg bent precariously underneath the other, he said to anyone who might be listening, "Goddamn, that looks bad."

Quinn grabbed an unopened bottle of whiskey from the shelf and, breaking the seal, refilled the former reverend's glass. "You're still conscious, my friend. That tells me you haven't yet had enough to drink."

"I'm something of a bar rag, doc. You don't need to pour me so much ..." And with that, the former priest, later detective, now hero nodded back onto the table. "I don't much imbibe," he said, hitting his head with an audible bump.

"An old habit for sure," Quinn said, noticing the small Bible in the man's vest pocket, "except this morning, dear Christian, I want you to be good and ready for what I have to do."

Chapter 23

BONE SETTING

The anesthesia choices by physicians and dentists were generally rich in Carson City. Nitrous oxide was preferred by the city's dentists. Chloroform was more often used by the city's doctors. But alcohol was certainly the oldest and best known of the sedatives available. A certain percentage of Doc Quinn's patients not only preferred the drug, but came to his office thoughtfully premedicated.

Given that Ronin had arrived with whiskey on his breath, Quinn was reticent to prescribe anything else.

The boys at the sheriff's office had done their best to alleviate the former minister's pain after they pulled him from the rubble of the jailhouse. Setting him in a wooden chair, they examined his leg. The hole he had stepped in hadn't been that deep, Dustsucker reasoned. Nor had the prisoner who collided with his friend been that heavy, he figured, so it was hard to understand why his friend couldn't support himself without whining. But when Ronin buckled under his own weight a second, and then third, time trying to get up from the chair, both deputies figured it was time for some doctoring, and Quinn came immediately to mind.

Quinn had grown up in the Philadelphia area, where his father had lectured in the medical department of the University of Pennsylvania, the nation's first medical school. He had attended his father's lectures as a boy and had found a youthful passion in understanding human anatomy, physiology and pathology.

Given his father's disdain for some of the medical substances used in healing—Quinn's dad thought most medications to be quackery at best, and damn near poisonous at worst—the son had developed a more eclectic bent, combining botanical remedies with physical adjustment and other non-traditional therapies. Amos Quinn's scorn for medicines was troubling to other physicians in the city, who consequently thought of the boy-doctor as naïve or untrained. But in fact, Quinn was as well educated as other doctors in Carson City, and was a great deal more talented than some.

For instance, the young doctor held to an interesting theory of modern medical practice and disease. He believed that most of what bothered men and women on the western frontier was due to living organisms. Unclean organisms, for the most part, unseen organisms. He thought the transferable seed-like entities, when inhaled, imbibed or embedded in or upon a human body, could cause fever, small pox, measles and malaria.

Other physicians in the city thought Quinn's theories were rubbish. They had even less respect for his antiseptic preparations before treatment or surgery.

But Quinn believed that British, Italian and Viennese doctors were on to something when they found that patients treated by physicians who washed their hands lived longer, or that maintaining a rigorous degree of cleanliness about an operating table, or instruments used on an operating table, resulted in a higher percentage of successful surgeries.

"I can't see the microorganisms that cause you to have a disease or infection, Reverend Ronin, but I know they are there."

"Former reverend."

"I stand corrected," Quinn said.

"But as sure as you are that a God lives in heaven," the doctor said to his patient, lying before him on a covered, chemically-treated antiseptic table, "I am certain that your future suffering and even subsequent survival will be determined by the cleanliness of this operating stage."

"What is it you're going to do, Quinn?" Ronin asked. "I've grown rather accustomed to this leg. I'd hate to see you remove it."

"Yours is a simple fracture, sir. The skin is intact and I see no blood anywhere. But some angulation has occurred, likely from your trying to stand on it or struggling to get free. That displacement will need some manipulation to get it back in place. I don't think I'll need to remove it."

"You're a confident young man," Ronin whispered to the brown-haired boy-doctor in front of him. "I saw quite a few legs removed during the war, doctor. I'd hate to lose one of my own, particularly that being such a religious leg, sir," he said, winking.

Quinn used his sleeve to brush his hair up off of his forehead and back on top of his head. He appeared to be sweating. It was not an observation that left Ronin feeling confident about outcomes.

"Ronin, to tell you the truth, I'm not going to know what I'm looking at until I get in there. Generally, when the tibia is involved the fibula is involved, too, because the force is transmitted along the membrane to the non-weight-bearing bone."

"But what I do know is this, you've been very lucky so far. Most fractures of this sort aren't closed. They're open and quite messy."

Ronin groaned. The boy-doctor continued.

"Once I open the leg, I'm going to try to put the pieces of your leg as close together as I can. Then I'm going to sew the opening shut. When I'm finished, I'm going to tie a splint to your leg. And you're going to take it easy for a good three months. It will take that long before you're able to move again."

"We'll see about the three months, doc, once I'm up. Tell me again why you're wearing a mask?" Ronin had never gotten used to men wearing masks after his experience with highway men as a Pinkerton detective. "And the young woman beside you, doctor." Ronin nodded to Emma Nauman to indicate that he recognized her. "I'm glad you're doing fine, ma'am. But don't you have work to do at the mission?"

"I'm still a little woozy, Mister Ronin, thank you. But the doctor tells me his nurse is out of town, and that he is unprepared to perform surgery today without her. I'll do fine," she said, handing the doctor a sponge and a small, blue vile of chloroform.

"I'm sure you will, Mrs. Nauman. The first time I met you, ma'am, you impressed me as a strong woman." Ronin paused and then continued, "Your husband can spare you?" he asked, hoping to ascertain whether her husband had returned, or fled as he had suspected.

"Apparently," Emma replied.

Their eyes met in such a way as to communicate the rest of that story, though the details might have to wait until both of them were of clearer minds.

"What's on the sponge, doc?" the patient asked. Ronin was aware that his chattiness indicated some anxiety on his part, but he didn't know what to do to control it. After all, it was a perfectly good leg.

"A little bit of anesthetic," Quinn replied. "The alcohol doesn't seem to be enough to take care of your pain and I'm going to need some time to work. The masks are to inhibit infection," he said. "I'm sorry for how they appear."

He busied himself with a set of surgical restraints for Ronin's arms and legs that didn't look at all dissimilar to the restraints hanging in the Ormsby County sheriff's office. He groaned.

"Doctor," the former reverend whispered as the chloroform neared his face. "I'm not sure that I believe in God anymore. I hope you're not counting on his help."

Quinn's eyebrows arched over his white mask. "Let's just hope he believes in you."

Ronin put his head to the pillow, drifting into a lazy sleep, when he recalled to his lips the words of the Old Testament prophet Ezekiel, and mumbled:

"The hand of the Lord is upon me, and carried me out in spirit of the LORD, and set me down in a valley which was full of bones. So I prophesied as I was commanded, and there was a noise, and behold a shaking, and the bones came together, bone to his bone ... and the breath came into them and they lived ..."

Amos Quinn and Emma Nauman looked at each other, surprised by the gunman's recitation. But even more that they answered his prayer in tandem with a hearty, "Amen."

Chapter 24

A SECOND CUP OF TEA

The Pacific Coast Pioneer Society held its annual Admission Day dinner on October 31st, in the evening, despite it being a Sunday. The announcement of their "grand celebration," as the *Gold Hill News* referred to it, set quite a few churches in Virginia City on edge, particularly those that had evening services. But come the date of the gathering, churched and un-churched folks sat down together and had exactly that. "It was a sumptuous banquet," people said afterward. The good members of the Pioneer Society were happy as always to hear that their Admission Day event had been so well received.

"It was cold!" Marshal Augustus Ash told Versal McBride the following Thursday when they sat for breakfast at McBride's Bucket of Blood Saloon.

"Cold enough to freeze the tits off ..."

"There are children present!" McBride interrupted, looking around the already crowded saloon, where proper Christian families were gathered, only because it was breakfast time.

"... the belly of a prize winning hog is what I was going to say," Ash continued, managing a look of pretend surprise for his friend.

"I don't know why you think I'm going to act or say something inappropriate all the time," the marshal complained, slapping at his chest and fidgeting in his chair. "I may track shit in here, McBride, but I'll sure as shit never be inappropriate!"

"Alright," the saloon owner said, elongating the word as he knew the marshal was having fun with him. Both of the men broke out laughing.

Their Thursday morning gatherings predated the Pacific Coast Pioneer Society's Admission Day dinners, not that anyone had noticed. The fact that they shared a cup of tea instead of an early morning beer or bourbon was nobody's business either. They were there to get their work done, which needed to be everybody's work if Virginia City was going to stay strong and healthy.

A devastating fire in 1875 had destroyed nearly three-quarters of the town. The nation's newspaper, the *New York Times,* led with the headline, "Nevada's Principal City Almost Entirely Destroyed." The story couldn't have been more true, as significant business, mining and residential structures were lost. Ten thousand people had been left homeless, and churches, county buildings, newspapers and hotels were just as suddenly put out of business.

Given that the fire began in a lodging house during a drunken brawl, folks were a little sensitive that similar conduct might once again set the town ablaze. While the eighteen months after the fire had brought a frenzy of rebuilding, new roofs and walls hadn't rid Virginia City's residents of their fear that cold and darkness could come again, and was always, for the non-vigilant anyway, a quick step away.

While a district marshal, Augustus Ash had a residence and business in Virginia City. Ash and McBride, the owner of one of the city's favorite saloons, sat as they did every Thursday morning discussing the day's events and tending the positions and points of view that might benefit their town or businesses.

"The Admission Day event went fine. There were a lot of good people there. Some speech-making and very little drinking from what I could see."

"You might be interested to hear that there was some talk that they might try to get Mark Twain to give a dinner speech next year."

"Doubt that he'd come," McBride said. "The boy hasn't been back since the fire. And things have changed so much that I can't imagine that he'd be interested anyway! And incidentally, it's Clemens, Samuel Clemens. What's with still calling him Mark Twain?"

Ash went on, speaking at length about how Clemens had continued to use his Virginia City "nom de plume" since leaving town, and that "Twain" was the name on his best-selling news and magazine articles. And that if he had wanted to be known by Clemens, he would have signed that name to his newest book, *Roughing It.* "Which, if you've read it," the marshal continued, "It's all about his Nevada experiences, and ..."

"Augustus," McBride interrupted, "do you speak French?"

Ash stopped abruptly in his explanation of the famous Virginia City newspaper man's writings, and replied, "No, why?"

"Well, how about you put a rag in it then? Nobody likes the French and even fewer people like people pretending to be French! Nom de plume, my ass! God ..."

McBride shook his head. Virginia City might be, or might have been, he didn't really know at this point, the largest city in Nevada. But it sure as hell wasn't New York. "Wanna tell me instead what happened the last couple of nights? I sure as hell don't need to hear about some no good, boom and bust, yellow-bellied newspaper man who got lucky and wrote a couple of books."

Ash took a long sip of tea, remembering that lots of townsfolk had taken it hard when Twain left town after being challenged to a duel. Setting his tea on the table, he folded his hands and then said quietly, "Okay."

"I talked with the sheriff and a couple of the police chiefs yesterday. It's been the usual number of liquored-up fist fights and public whoring the last couple of nights. There's a new business the south end of C street, but I imagine you've seen it," the lawman paused. "I don't think there's anything that might be useful, Versal. Whoa!" he suddenly remembered. "You might be interested in the fact that the back end of the jail house down in Carson City got blown up."

"Jesus, really? Anybody hurt?"

"I heard a minister got his leg broken, but that's it. No loss there." Ash laughed. McBride smiled.

"I'm asking about prisoners, Augustus. Were any of our friends or employees in the jail at that time?" McBride asked.

"Nobody but the usual riff-raff, according to Slade, though he did say the Crestwell brothers were there and got away. He was out looking for them. They thought the bigger guy was dead, but apparently he slipped out of there with the rest of them."

"The rest of them?" McBride asked.

"Yeah, they lost the whole bunch."

"Jesus," McBride said, sipping at his tea. "I saw the Crestwells a week or so back. They were here at the bar and I was heading over to them to tell them to keep it down. They tipped their hats before I needed to say anything and snuck off to the quiet side of the room to meet with a man in a dark business suit. They seemed pretty embarrassed about my seeing them, to be frank."

"Embarrassed? Remy and Clem? I don't know that I've ever seen them embarrassed! What do you figure that was about?"

"I don't know. But I do know this," McBride responded. "The Crestwells are scum. And if they're fishing around with folks up this way, it's not a good thing."

"Not if they're wearing suits, Versal."

"Exactly," McBride said, looking at his friend.

Chapter 25

THE CRESTWELL BROTHERS

The first thing Clem and Remy Crestwell did when they escaped from the rubble of the Carson City jail was to thank the Clancy brothers. Waiting with horses a few blocks east on Stewart Street, the Clancys had planted charges along the building's southern wall, next to an alley thought to be too narrow to be used as an avenue of escape and just out of sight of the nighttime deputy's observation.

The Clancy brothers were quick fisted, banty-legged boys from County Clare, Ireland. Stunted by the potato famine but large enough to become a pain in the ass to Cornish mining superintendents on the Comstock, the Clancys exploited certain other opportunities available to lesser men who were no longer welcome to live among their own kind. Burglary, for instance, or in the case of the Carson City jail after more than a few pints at the Globe Saloon, planting sticks of dynamite burgled from a wind-swept mining shack in Gold Hill just a few days before.

"I could have dug up more if it weren't for the hymn-singing reverend with the guns, goddamn it," the smallest Clancy complained. "Seeing that guy propped up against the house like it was his private latrine, pissing and shitting on the very side of the house where we hid our supplies! I mean Jesus, what kind of people ride around up there, honestly?" the younger Clancy asked his older and bigger brother. None of the Clancys were big enough, or well-behaved enough, to labor alongside other Irish immigrants, who as a group added up to nearly a third of the Storey County population in the fall of 1879.

A man of deep voice though insignificant stature, Paul Clancy rose from his seat at the base of an Ormsby County building and said, a little annoyed, "Probably people just like us, Patrick. They're likely no different."

Paul, Peter and the younger Clancy, Patrick, so named because their mother had run out of biblical names that began with a "P" and had to substitute a saint instead, though not just any saint but an Irish saint, were about to fist and cuff an argument when the "boom" occurred. Not just any "boom," but a big enough boom that it rattled windows all across town.

"You want to tell us again how you needed more dynamite, Patrick?" Paul had asked after the explosion rang his ears.

"No kidding," Peter said, removing his fingers from his ears and shaking his head. "Fucking amount of attention you're trying to get, you stupid leprechaun!"

None of the Clancys did well with being called leprechauns. But Patrick, being the smallest, did the absolute worst. Driving his head into his brother's stomach, Patrick had forced Peter into a ground level wrestling match when the Crestwell brothers ran up.

"Yo, guys!" the oldest Crestwell said to no one in particular. "Was that loud or what?" Both Clem and Remy stopped when they reached the Clancys, hiding on the building's east side so as to catch their breath and keep a lookout for any deputies who might be in pursuit.

"You know what? That man who drop-kicked me at the Globe Saloon was standing right in the middle of the blast, like he belonged there! Big tall guy with a tiny little Bible stuck in his vest and a pack of cards. I damn well clobbered him good."

"It looked like he clobbered you, the way I saw it!" Remy bellowed like a jackass. The side of Clem's hand caught him squarely on the side of the face, uprooting his feet and driving one airborne Crestwell into the still raging pile of Clancys.

"Hey!" everyone in the pile said at once. "Get the hell off me."

The older Clancy, the bigger one though not nearly big enough to be called big, grabbed the left arm of the older Crestwell in a gesture of friendship, and said, looking up at him as he was a very tall man, "Whatever Clem. The point is you're out of there, and we need to get to a place where everyone is safe."

Paul Clancy extracted his youngest brother from the pile first. "You were doing pretty good there, Patrick. Sorry about his calling you a leprechaun." And pulling his middle brother Peter out from underneath the younger Crestwell, stood him up and brushed him off. "You need to treat your brother with more respect, Peter."

Peter hung his head, as he respected traditional family order, though he had no such feelings toward any other rule or regulation. "I'm working on it, Paul."

"I know you are, Peter. I know you are."

Chapter 26

THE CLANCY BROTHERS

They weren't more than a mile out of town, riding the Carson River west toward the Empire City mills, when the two younger Clancys began fighting again, kicking at each other, pushing and trying to make each other fall off of their horses.

The Crestwells had left their boots in the rubble of the explosion, and the Clancys, so as not to let an inappropriate opportunity pass them by, had taken to making fun of the Crestwell brothers' unshod feet.

"Kentucky fried chicken," one of them yelled to Remy, the louder of the two. "That's what your feet will be when we get off the horses and scramble down into the mine. "Southern fried, all greasy and wet. Covered in blood!" he laughed, thinking the Crestwells' misfortune—not having boots, shoes, moccasins or anything to wear on their feet—would provide extraordinary entertainment over the next few weeks. "There's a lot of rungs to climb down to get to the safe house, you dummies. What are you figuring on using for shoes when you get down there?"

Remy Crestwell was no fan of the underground area their Irish friends had devised. They didn't like the darkness. They despised the cold, and they couldn't much stomach the stench, either, as their Comstock cavern retreat had a sulfur hot spring running through it, which kept the mine warm even though it was wet.

The damned leprechaun was right. He and Clem would need some boots, if they were going to be down there for a while. And perhaps the only opportunity to get some, saving taking the Clancys' boots, was to find some losers along the way.

"You're a jackass, you lame brain," Patrick shouted, kicking at Remy, who was riding next to him.

"I got a plan. Don't you worry," Remy brayed.

"You got a plan?" the older Crestwell interrupted. "I'm going to need some boots too, you know."

"I know, Clem. I'm thinking of you."

Clem rubbed his ribs, where the former reverend had kicked him, propelling him through the doorway of the Globe Saloon. The man not only cracked the door frame, he broke one or two of my ribs, he sputtered to himself, remembering he had gotten his hands on him at the jail house after the explosion, but not recalling the result.

"Remy? You remember that guy I tackled at the jail house? A big man with a Confederate slouch turned up in the front?"

"Yup, why?"

"He's the same clown who punched me through the door with his boots at the Old Globe. Then they cuffed us? I'm just wondering, did I mess him up good before I got knocked out?"

"Nah," Remy responded. They looked out for each other, not like the Clancys who seemed to fight constantly, with only the older Clancy to intervene. "He dropped you on your head, brother. Pulled you right down on top of him. You don't remember that?"

"I don't."

"Yup, they hauled him out of there before I pulled you up and started dragging you down the street. Hit you real good. You kissed the floor real hard, brother. Why are you asking?"

"Because I'm hoping to meet that son of a bitch again," Clem said, "you know?"

"Yeah, I know. Hey!" he yelled to one of the Clancys, who was now slapping his back with a tree limb. "Get the fuck away from me, you moron!"

"You talking to me?" Clem's face turned red immediately, turning a sharp eye toward his younger brother, Remy.

"No Clem, I'm talking to Peter-dick here," nodding toward the middle Clancy boy, who was taunting him with a one-inch-thick switch taken from a Cottonwood tree he had grabbed along the river. "You touch me with that again and I'll break your neck, Peter!"

Clem Crestwell relaxed.

Paul Clancy sighed. Even though he was riding ahead, where he didn't need to listen to the bickering between the brothers, he heard it all.

The elder Clancy had happily promised their mother he'd look after them, thinking that things were going pretty well in Placerville after his father's death. But after the mines played out, mom Clancy lost the family business. After she died, "what wasn't easy" turned to "ain't never going to happen again." And it had only gone downhill from there.

"Knock it off, guys, we've got a dozen miles to go before we're up on the Comstock, and I want to make it before dark. What the hell is the matter with you, anyway?"

The question wasn't as much of a question as it was witness to a lack of character. Clancy blood wasn't any better than Crestwell blood, in terms of getting in trouble. But the last couple of months had been more difficult than ever. There seemed to be some reasonable synergy with the two families hooking up. Small notions had become big ideas in no time. But the constant bickering and fighting weighed on Paul Clancy, particularly in the closed-in comfort of their tiny rat hole on the Comstock.

"Mom never intended it this way," he said many times to his brothers. Being a Catholic family, hanging heads and contrite hearts were the instantaneous result. Guilt was good, but it hadn't made things more peaceful and it hadn't put big money in their pants or saddlebags until Henry Nauman came along.

Now he was missing. "I don't know where he is!" the lady at the bar on Ormsby Street said. "All I know is that he left town."

It was about sundown when they found the old silver mine outside Gold Hill. And it was dark when they finally lit the lamps and started heading down the main shaft. Paul Clancy had something troubling on his mind and hadn't shared it with anyone. But he had faith that the five of them could figure the future out, if things were as bad as he imagined.

Chapter 27

UNDERGROUND

Remy Crestwell didn't enjoy living underground. He enjoyed even less the fact that he was living underground with the Clancys, them being Irish and all. The younger Crestwell didn't much like the Irish, despite their number and prominence in the mining districts of Virginia City and Gold Hill. From Remy's point of view, the Irish made good laborers. And Irish women made decent lovers. Still, he figured them to be hard-headed, horribly moody and difficult to get along with. They may have been among the first on the Comstock Lode to find anything of value, if the stories were to be believed. But, as Remy figured, it took an Englishman to make an Irishman productive and, though that attitude wasn't enough to endear him to many of the mine owners, it had gained him a few foreman jobs where he had made good money. But it had gotten him into a few fights as well.

More than the Irish, however, Remy didn't like Virginia City. He much preferred Carson City, despite it being a little too civilized and laid back. Fact was, the Comstock's water supply had been horrible over the years. The flume and pipes from Marlette Lake hadn't solved much, and food—gone were the days of a free lunch, at the saloons he frequented anyway—was scarce or expensive. Sure, things had quieted down in the last four or five years, but folks up that way still seemed to fight with each other just for fun.

He and his brother weren't against a good fistfight. Clem was a natural at it, given that he was a much bigger man than most and didn't seem to mind being hit. But Remy had to scrap, being a man of small stature and large opinion. While he found his friends willing to step up if stepping up didn't mean stepping too far in, by virtue of his very size and attitude, Remy would have to hang onto something in order to see it through. Punch one Irishman in the face and before you turn there are two of them hanging off your back and a third waiting for you to spin around.

Remy woke his older brother by putting his forefinger to his brother's lips. "*Ssshhhh*," he said. "I'm headed to Virginia City for a bit. Cover for me if anyone wakes before I get back."

Clem rubbed his eyes, swiping at his brother's hand. "Where are you going?" he asked. "Why are you awake?"

"I'm going to get us some boots, Clem, just like I said. I can't stand another minute down here without them. I've got shit growing between my toes and if my ankles take another hit on the ladder, I swear I'll cut my legs off below my knees!"

"Yeah," Clem whispered. "You're still bleeding, Remy. I'd help you clean up but we'd have to walk a ways to get some clean water."

"Screw the water," Remy answered. "And screw my legs, too. The point is that we need some boots."

"Well, I'll go with you, then. But I thought you said we didn't have any money," Clem responded. The two had left behind a sizeable and hard-to-account-for roll of bills when they'd fled the Carson City jail the day before. The stash had probably gotten them jailed in the first place. Clem grabbed for his hat and then realized that he had neither boots nor a hat, having left both of them in the jail rubble.

Remy put his hand over his brother's mouth and whispered, "I'm going alone. You need to stay here in case anyone wakes up. Tell them I'm down the tube a ways to relieve myself. Or that I had to get some air."

Clem nodded, hoping that the noise of a horse leaving the mine wouldn't wake the Clancys. He knew that the three of them would be very upset to hear that he was in Virginia City, given that they were supposed to be hiding. Telegraphs and travel being what they were—he'd seen the wires strewn down Virginia Street, and if the telegraph wasn't working there were certainly papers on all of them in Storey County, or maybe even a deputy had wandered up this way looking for them. Catching either of them would mean that all of them would sooner or later be caught, given their preference for talking rather than keeping their mouths shut.

"I like brown," Clem whispered after knocking his brother's dirty hand from his mouth. "Try to find me something that has a left and a right," he added, remembering that his previous pair of boots fit nicely despite their being so beat up that he couldn't strike a match on them without burning his feet. "My feet hurt too," he added.

"I know Clem, but keep it down. It's important that no one knows I'm gone."

Clem laid there a while in the dark, after watching his brother head up the tunnel. He laid there remembering the older Clancy boy's story the night before that the missionary man had moved on and that they'd have a much harder time getting children to work the mine, not that it was a good idea, anyway, given the attitude of some of the Cornish laborers in the area, though he'd seen at least one kid standing outside the Sutro Tunnel at some point. And while he didn't understand what the changes Paul talked about meant, he knew he wasn't going to continue moving all that rock. He deserved a turn at the pick, too, and the children—he figured they needed ten or twenty of them, but maybe thirty would be a good number and it wasn't like anybody needed to know—they could work the wheelbarrows to move the earth and rock. And maybe someday, if there was enough work, he could be a foreman like his brother had been. Someone who could stand there and just make sure the work was done rather than doing any real work himself.

Given how his ribs were still feeling, he figured he was getting older. And that this worn-out mine the Clancys had found might be the future for him and Remy. And that the Clancys weren't too bad, as long as they weren't fighting with each other or picking on him. And that the children wouldn't mind the work, given that they were Indians.

Chapter 28

THE MINE

"Them's indications," Peter Clancy had told his brothers a couple of months before. "The red and yellow rock is what you're looking for. No matter how much other rock is mixed in with it. We set a peg, put up our notice and we're in business," he reasoned, though his brother, Paul, thought the whole idea of finding an open area to mine in Virginia City was like trying to find a Catholic virgin in a Comstock whorehouse.

Just as Paul had imagined, it turned out to be that way. There wasn't any unclaimed land in Virginia City and hadn't been for years. Everything was taken, and what wasn't being worked was likely long played out—until they found the hole just south of Gold Hill. A little bit of wood scattered about was their first clue that they were on to something. The mine's opening was well obscured by a difficult ravine and oddly hidden by layers of sagebrush and mid-afternoon shadows, making the find even more appealing.

It had taken the three of them a long day's work to extricate the dead from the heavy rocks that had piled a few hundred feet within the mine's entrance. But when they pulled the bodies out and moved quite a few rocks around, they discovered a fairly large room with water nearby. With sleeping berths cut into the rock, clearly someone had put some thought into the place. Among the bodies—they discovered a Scotsman judging by the plaid, a couple of Mexicans or "vaqueros" Peter called them, and an Englishman who was found with a leather case attached to his wrist, making him the likely owner—they figured the mine was now un-staked and un-owned. And while not legally theirs, not in the strictest sense of the word, it was certainly theirs for the taking, at least for the time being. And all they needed was some time being.

Working the mine would get them some cash, enough to find something else. To get them "back on track," as Paul constantly reminded them. "The Clancys don't want to be involved in criminal pursuits," he liked to say, though the boys didn't always understand what that meant. Their late mother wouldn't have approved and Paul had promised to keep them out of trouble. And all were agreed, save perhaps "the leprechaun."

Paul never called him that to his face, as the taunt was too much and none of them liked the word anyway. But Patrick had been a fighter all of his years. His mother couldn't control him, and now it was Paul's responsibility to see that the boys made good, despite the Comstock Lode being nearly played out and their dreams becoming more and more scarce.

While the Crestwells were a serious bother, criminals to be sure and Protestant slackers even more so, the elder Clancy wondered if they'd be more trouble than they were worth.

Finding a willing compatriot in Henry Nauman was a good thing. He seemed supportive in keeping the boys' heads above water. While collecting a dozen Indian children was initially a concern to Paul, more or less because they were in the habit of running away, an uncontrolled Indian was as much trouble as an unconverted one. He expected the extra hands would be a big help in moving the ore out of the mine into the hands of bona fide buyers and other speculators.

Nauman's comment that they didn't need to move the ore as much as establish a promising claim was helpful, but a bag of gold in someone's hand was a great deal better than promises on paper. Now Nauman was gone, and the Indians—what were left of them anyway, as the number Nauman said he could get them seemed always to be uncertain—well, it all meant that changes would need to be made. And as small as the details probably were, it all seemed overwhelming.

"Look," he had told the Crestwells and his brothers the night before, "Nauman is gone. I don't know where and I don't know if he's coming back. But we're going to have to figure out how to do this without him." Every one of them said that no one could be sure whether Nauman was indeed gone unless they went to the mission and saw things with their own eyes.

"The mission," Paul Clancy mumbled to himself in the darkness. "The goddamned mission," he repeated. And reminding himself that he didn't want to go anywhere near a place so goddamned as a Protestant mission, he turned onto his right side, fingering his mother's rosary beads until he fell asleep.

His dreams were dark and filled with the sounds of horses.

Chapter 29
BOOTS

Remy bumped into the man as he rounded the corner in the dark on D Street. "Excuse me," he said, smiling and then gazing down at the color of the man's boots, reckoning them to be about the same size and color as those left in the rubble of the Carson City jail. Looking up into the man's eyes, he quick-drew a worn revolver from the right side of his belt and whacked him on the left side of his head with the plow end. "Straight up and straight in," he later boasted to one of the Clancys.

The misfortunate man was large, but crumpled easily under the weight of Remy's nearly three-pound .46 Rimfire Remington hand gun. Wearing riveted blue jeans, a red woolen shirt, and a clean butternut colored canvas jacket—the kind one might wear for an evening out on the town—Remy thought about taking the jacket, too, as he tugged at one of the big man's boots. It didn't take him but a moment to realize that the man was still conscious and beginning to stir.

Dropping his left knee, Remy watched the man's hands shaking as if palsied by the previous pistol strike. When he noticed him struggling to sit up on one elbow, Remy frowned and, stepping over him, dropped onto the man's midsection, straddling him with such a thump that the poor man's chest went immediately flat for lack of air. He raised the gun again above his head, swung two wild arcs and hit him first on the left side of his skull and then on the right. He repeated his blows until the man stopped breathing. It wasn't Remy's first kill, but it was his most vicious.

Leaning forward onto the man's neck with his forearm until he was sure he was dead, the younger Crestwell brother, who many called "Jackass" for his wild living and contentious ways, looked about to see anyone had noticed. And reckoning not, he stood up to begin tugging at the man's left boot again.

"Packer boots," he said to himself. He'd have to teach Clem how to tie the laces as his fingers were too big and his brain not all that nimble. He laughed, but felt good about his selection as they'd be great boots for what they needed. Thick-cut leather and well-waxed, they'd definitely keep out the rattlesnakes and the wet. Remy chuckled to himself and took a second look at the man's flannel-lined canvas coat and, thinking it too large in the still thin light of the early morning, wished the man had been smaller. Remy stood up with a boot in each hand, tied them together, threw them over the saddle horn and was thinking about another score when a second man rounded the corner and yelled "Hey!"

Remy jumped, but not quick enough to dodge the lawman's right fist as it caught the left side of his face and knocked him against the side of a Comstock bawdy house. A fan and frequent attendee of the area's prize fights, Marshal Ash's second punch was a left uppercut, which caught Remy at the jaw line and launched him into a small fence, pinching his head between two white picket boards out front of a grey Southern Colonial style home on Virginia City's famed "Sporting Row." Augustus Ash, an occasional guardian of the night in Virginia City's red light district and elsewhere, then placed a firm boot on Remy Crestwell's private area and waited for him to wake up.

A moment passed. Remy stirred. And Ash asked, laughing, "Something I can help you with, son?"

"Augustus," Remy squeaked, remembering that he had bought the marshal quite a few beers over the years. He pushed at the marshal's boot but was unable to dislodge it from the tender area between his legs. "I wasn't doing nothin' ... " he protested.

"This guy here offered me his boots and then tried to hold me up. I hit him a couple of times on the head to defend myself."

"Was he coming or going?" Ash asked, thinking if the man was going, Crestwell's claim of self-defense wouldn't hold up. But if he was approaching the young Crestwell, then maybe there might be some truth to the story.

"Huh?"

"Yeah, I didn't think so," Ash said, smiling.

He looked at the big man rolled over next to the saloon, and noting that he was indeed beaten and not breathing, made his first solid decision of the day and informed Remy he was under arrest. "That will be an interesting story to tell the judge, I'm sure," he said, looking at the victim's well-calloused hands and obvious girth. "Imagine we'll want to get a committee of his peers up in these parts to sit on the jury."

Remy struggled to sit up, his head still stuck between two boards, the small fence finally giving way allowing a two-foot section of the fence to sit up with him. He sat there for a moment, groaning.

"You'll have to keep me to hang me, marshal."

Ash laughed, as he hadn't seen anything as funny as a man with a fence on his head all night.

"I don't have a problem with that, Remy," he hissed. Some nights he hated his job, and stomping hard again at the space between the tiny Irishman's legs, knocked the jackass out cold.

Chapter 30

SOUND OF HORSES

"I'm thinking that was one of *our* horses," Paul Clancy said to no one in particular as he sat up. He pulled on his boots and began waking his brothers in the underground chamber they were calling home.

The space showed remarkable planning, fitting carefully carved sleeping shelves along two walls. Separated by forty feet of miscellaneous mine tailings, the two sides offered some privacy for miners staying there, not that men working the Virginia City mines generally needed privacy. But for the two families of brothers dwelling there, the space couldn't have been more valuable, or now, more problematic.

Neither the Crestwells or the Clancys were able to hear each other in the small space. Once they laid down for the night, the Crestwells' conversation about heading a mile or so up the road to Virginia City and finding a couple of pair of boots had gone unheard by the Clancys, who were busy with their own conversation about hating those sons of bitches sleeping across from them.

Paul Clancy's sudden awakening was the product of an unusual dream, where he was watching a troublesome herd of horses flee. He was awake during the dream—which he thought was strange—and was feeling oddly aggressive. As he was about to chase some of the horses, he realized that the annoying whinny he was listening to wasn't a part of his dream but was coming from somewhere outside. Pushing himself up from his bedroll, he shouted to his brothers. "Wake those clowns up," he yelled, "and go check on the horses!"

Peter was first on his feet, but Patrick, not to be outdone by his brother, threw a boot across the cavern, hitting Clem Crestwell in the face and waking him up.

"Goddamnit," he shouted. "Would you stop touching my face?" he asked, causing him to stir and calling to mind his brother's touching his mouth earlier that evening. Looking over at his brother's bunk, he sat up and hit his head on the rock above him. "Jesus," he shouted, "Where's Remy?" And then, remembering his brother's instructions, he mumbled something about his brother having "to see a man about a horse," which would have been understood differently if Paul hadn't already woken everybody up talking about horses in the first place.

"I mean, he likely went on a walk," the big man said, throwing off his blanket and climbing over the tailing so as to face Peter and Patrick, who weren't at all entertained by the big guy's fumbling ways.

"You're so stupid," Patrick said. "Which is it, he went to wee or he went to walk?" He laughed, thinking how clever it was to say "wee," given that Remy was so small.

"Maybe he went for a walk and to piss at the same time," Peter said, trying to stifle his laugh so as not to encourage Patrick further. "I mean, he's so full of piss and vinegar!" Patrick erupted into laughter.

Another boot was hurled their way by the elder Clancy, missing the two brothers by mere inches.

"Go find out what's going on!" Paul Clancy bellowed as he hopped across the cavern floor attempting to retrieve his boot. "If that son of a bitch is gone, I'm going to do more than complain. I'm going to start pounding on people, you simple-minded bastards!"

Patrick and Peter looked at their brother. They were surprised because they had rarely heard him lose his temper. "Move!" Paul shouted. They both jumped and ran to the front of the mine, leaving Clem and Paul looking at each other.

"Is there a reason you're still sitting there?" Paul asked.

"I don't like people yelling at me, for one," Clem said, holding his glance so that Paul knew he meant it. "And two," Clem paused, "because I think you ought to know that Remy isn't here. He's gone looking for boots."

Weighted down by concern for everyone's safety and the success of their venture, Paul sat down and leaned his head into his hands. "This isn't good news at all, Clem. That screw-up brother of yours is bound to get caught and start yapping."

Clem Crestwell nodded.

"Where's he gone to?" Paul asked. "He's gone to Virginia City, right?"

Clem nodded again.

"He hasn't gone to buy boots, right?" Paul said, now only a half-dozen inches from Clem's face. Clem shook his head tentatively.

"He's gone to steal them, right?"

Clem looked down. His brow wrinkled as his face turned red. He was embarrassed by Paul's line of questioning.

"Jesus, Mary, Son of God!" Paul shouted, standing straight up. "Boys," he yelled to his brothers, who were scrapping with each other at the front of the mine. "Get your clothes on. We've got some riding to do."

"Clem, you stay here," Paul said. He hoped he didn't need to struggle with him. He was a big boy and it would take a real pounding to make him do what he didn't want to do.

"What for?" Clem bellowed. "It's my brother who is missing. And maybe he's in trouble. Why should I stay here?"

"You need to stay put because I need you to begin packing. We're going to need to get to go to Carson City," he said. "Nauman is either alive or dead. And I want to make sure I know which before we go looking for the children. If we're going to make any money at all, we're going to need to find them."

Chapter 31

STOREY COUNTY JAIL

Ash yanked Remy out of the fence line by bracing one end of it under his boot and bending the other end toward him. The resultant crack of the fence boards woke him up as two of the boards went scraping past his ears. Ash put his foot on the younger Crestwell's chest and told him to roll face down in the dirt. "Place your hands behind you," he commanded. And then, clicking a pair of cuffs behind Remy's back, he picked him up by the cuffs and the collar of his shirt and slammed him into the side of the building.

Remy collapsed into a bed of winter pansies and sat with his eyes wide open, blinking. It had been a long time since he had been handled that way and he hadn't believed that Augustus Ash, a middle-aged U.S. Marshal, was capable of delivering such abuse.

"Sit still. Don't move," Ash said as he walked over to the other side of the alley to check on the man Crestwell had waylaid. "I think he's dead, Remy," the marshal said with a smile. Ash liked to be polite.

"Good breeding consists of concealing how little we think of other people," he had once heard Twain say, when he worked as a reporter for the Territorial Enterprise. Ash had met a great many Nevada residents since becoming the district marshal, particularly in Storey County, where he had mining interests. He was appreciative of the advice and a big fan.

"I do believe that I'm going to need a little help with this one," he said, looking at the dead man and then looking back at Remy. He paused to consider if he should take the cuffs off Remy and have him help, or whether he should lock his prisoner to a piece of fence again so as to find a Virginia City policeman. "Let me ask you," he inquired, "do you mind hanging around here for a few minutes while I go and get someone to help with this unfortunate man?"

"Fuck you," Remy responded.

"Not tonight, thank you." Ash ploughed a boot into Crestwell's head. Remy fell, unconscious, into the flowerbed. The marshal placed a second, larger set of cuffs on the boy's legs before walking down the street to find Virginia City's night man. It was near daybreak, by his reckoning, and he wondered if it was near shift change.

Remy was waking up about the time the Clancy brothers found him on D Street. "Jesus, what happened to you?" Patrick Clancy asked with an uncharacteristic expression of concern.

"Someone watered me, moron, and I sprouted here. What the fuck do you think happened to me? The damn marshal arrested me! But he had to get some help to carry that big pile of shit to the digger."

"Well, what happened to him?" Peter asked, looking over at the man collapsed against the building. He noticed the man was not wearing any shoes.

"I happened to him," Remy replied, shaking his hand and leg irons at Paul, hoping the brothers would take the hint.

"Grabbed those boots from him," Remy said. "Real nice pair, if you don't mind me sayin'. Was about to get me a second pair when the marshal happened by to pay his respects. Assuming you don't have a key, how about grabbing my horse and throwing me over it?"

Paul shook his head, and unable to think of any other option, reached down to pick Remy up when he was surprised to hear a lever-action rifle cycle behind him.

"I'd leave him there if I was you," a gravelly voice said.

"You bet," the elder Clancy replied, without moving an inch. And then, bending straight up, he turned around to face the voice behind him. "Marshal Ash, I presume?"

"Indeed."

"And your deputy, I would guess."

"Former sheriff, in fact, Tom Kelly."

"Very nice to meet both of you."

Suddenly dropping to his knees, Clancy drew his Colt Army from a strong-side holster and thumbed a .45 caliber bullet, winging the former sheriff's chest, spinning him into the wall. Fanning a second and third cartridge, he hit Kelly in the arm, causing him to drop his rifle and dropping him into the already dead man lying at the marshal's feet. The sheriff's well-worn Wesley and Sons firearm tumbled to the ground.

Ash stood there with his mouth open, surprised at how quickly Virginia City's former sheriff and police chief had been injured, and how slow he had been to react.

Paul Clancy turned toward Augustus Ash, and meeting his eyes, said, "I think we'll be going now, if you don't have a problem with that."

"No. No problem," Ash stuttered, looking back at the oldest of the two brothers and knowing that any movement, any movement at all, would surely result in his death and Kelly's.

Peter grabbed the sheriff's guns and gestured toward Ash's firearm. He looked at Patrick, who removed it from its holster. He then pointed to Remy's feet. Taking hold of his hands, Peter grabbed both legs and placed him sideways across the horse. "What the fuck is the matter with you guys? Sit me up, morons," Remy bellowed.

"Careful," said Paul Clancy to Remy, without taking his eyes off of the lawmen. "I might decide to kill a couple of people today, and you just moved up a couple of rungs." Spinning the marshal around, he hit him on the back of the head, crumpling him into a pile of three.

Paul Clancy holstered his sidearm and glanced at his brothers. "Let's get out of here boys. The sun is about up and we've got work to do. We need to find somewhere more amenable to people like us.

"What's a 'menable,' Paul?" asked Patrick. Paul winced and turned toward his horse.

"Amenable is the word, Patrick. It means friendly or agreeable."

"Oh," said Patrick. "Then I think we should go there, too."

Chapter 32

LATE NIGHT CALLERS

Emma heard the knock and expected it to be Ronin, back from his evening walk. Instead, three trail-dusty men stood at the doorway and two more by a half dozen horses tethered lightly to the house corral. By the time she broke away from the window and got to the front door, she was surprised to see that one of the men had already entered her home.

"May I help you?" she asked, afraid to hear the answer but fully prepared to dispatch the men if their presence became a problem. She had been through worse, she figured, and Christ was always by her side.

"The director is not available," she said, searching her visitors' eyes for subtle signs of character and intent. It was a long-practiced habit. Even with the Indians, the windows of the soul are in the eyes, she reminded herself.

"Well, thank you ma'am, that's in fact who we were hoping to see," Paul Clancy said, looking around the living room and peering back into the kitchen. "My apologies, ma'am. I thought this was a public area when I entered. It was not my intent to frighten you."

"It is, sir. It's just a little late."

Emma relaxed. The man seemed like a nice enough individual. She heard the tone in his voice and noticed the crucifix around his neck, hanging slightly askew because of a patterned black silk kerchief. The scarf appeared to have come from some-one's dress, perhaps his mother's or a fiancé's.

"The director isn't available this evening," she repeated. As she spoke, it was if she was listening to her own words. She wondered what her new role would be at the mission, given her husband's sudden and apparently permanent absence. She shook her head to clear her mind; there was so much to consider. She stopped when she realized that her hair was down for the night and that her guest was looking at her strangely.

Still, none of this was their business.

"Is there something I can help you with?" she asked again, looking toward the front corral and watching the men fidget.

"Well ma'am, I'm thinking we need to talk to Mr. Nau-man." The man paused. "I apologize, ma'am. I'm being rude. My name is Paul Clancy. These are my brothers, Peter and Patrick. Your husband and I had business together and I'm wondering where he is?"

Six feet tall, the man was an imposing presence in her house, despite his appearing cultured and Christian. Emma was still a bit nervous and wondered if there was some inference to the man's question, suggesting that whatever business they had was men's business, not just her husband's business. And had she told him that he was her husband? She couldn't remember, but they did know her last name.

She drew her shoulders back and looked at her visitors. This was as much her work as it had been her husband's. It was the Savior's mission, not the mission of men. No man, no men, no five men—she counted them to be sure—would make her feel like a stranger in her own home. There was only one person still com-mitted to the work they'd begun there, or her husband would be present. They were talking about the children, weren't they? Was it possible Henry had other business?

"I frankly don't know where my husband is," the new di-rector of the American Gospel Mission said, stepping forward, tentatively. Not backward, she thought, never backward. "Are you speaking about the children?" she asked.

"Well ma'am," Paul Clancy moved closer to his brothers. "I'm thinking that we need to talk to him." He paused and looked at his brothers as if to ask permission. They nodded, so he began again. "But if he'll be away for a while, I suspect we could talk to you."

Emma looked again at the men out front. No one had un-saddled. Their horses were loaded heavy, and were tethered to the wing-fence. They hadn't entered the corral. Of the five men, only one seemed calm. The man who didn't have any boots on; perhaps the small man standing next to him didn't have shoes on either. She couldn't tell as she pulled the shawl around her. It was begin-ning to get dark.

Everyone seemed as if they were in a hurry to leave.

"You and the boys are welcome to unsaddle your horses, if you like. Supper is over and the food has been put up for the night. I could have one of my men come around to help, and there's still some sourdough on the stove." She waited for their reaction.

Paul Clancy bit his lip as he considered his reply. He need-ed to settle the question of where the Indian children were that Nauman had sold them. He read deeply the hard lines on the woman's face and gazed into her reddened eyes. She reminded him of his mother, though she was much younger than he remembered her. Her lips were curved into a kind, natural smile, though he couldn't imagine them smiling if they dealt with children every day, Indian children at that. He would be surprised if this woman knew anything about her husband's deal. "Rented" was a much better word than "sold," though either in his mind seemed le-gitimate, not that he knew, not that he cared. The point was the children, and he'd be teaching them a trade.

He looked around the front room again and peered into the kitchen. Where were they? Not that he expected them to be here. Were they somewhere else at the mission, maybe in one of the other buildings? Could they be in Carson City or Reno? They were somewhere, he figured. Nauman had already given him some of their names.

Paul Clancy stood there, listening to the woman as she asked what sort of business they had with her husband. He heard his brothers, shuffling their feet on the throw rug by the door. He glanced at the Crestwell brothers, standing by the corral with the horses. They didn't look much better. So he returned to the woman, who so much reminded him of his mother. He asked her the question to which he already knew the answer, the answer he knew he didn't want to hear. The answer, in fact, that he feared, but needed to face if there was any money still to be made, any future still to be had.

"It's the children, ma'am. The point is the children, ma'am. Your husband was going to ... provide us ... with some children," he said.

Emma grabbed the doorframe. Her face flushed. The quick change in her demeanor was obvious to everyone, even the boys standing impatiently at the corral fence. It made her interrogator nervous. She grabbed for a chair as he reached to steady her.

"For the ranch," he explained. "He was going to ... get us children to work the ranch."

And in that singular moment, it all came together in Emma's mind. So many angel voices that her thinking swirled: her husband's strange need for privacy, the mission's missing children, her guest's story about Washoe Indian families, Henry's sudden disappearance. Instinctively, she knew the answer to every question in her head. Her stomach rumbled and turned sour. Stumbling backward, away from the man's hands, she felt suddenly faint and fell down forcefully into a kitchen chair.

"Mr. Clancy, I believe you need to leave," Emma said, catching her breath and holding her chest. The room was spinning. "I have no children for you to employ ... or for you to use in any other way, for that matter."

She took a deep and shaking breath. Unable to focus, she stared at the yellow flowers on the floor, from a vase that had fallen and shattered, when she had grabbed the chair. "These children are residents here. They are ... my students," she said, her voice rising and trembling strangely. "They are ... *my* children, Mr. Clancy. They are my *children,* sir, not your employees. Not your ranch hands ... not your slaves."

She couldn't believe the word "slaves" had come out of her mouth. Mustering every emotional reserve she had, she turned toward her unexpected guests and demanded, "Please leave. Now!" she screamed in an uncharacteristically shrill voice. The uninvited men left her porch, and as soon as they mounted their horses and began to gallop down the mission's driveway, she wished she had waited for Ronin to return. Something terrible was happening to her children. And these men, more than any of the others she had met in their questioning of persons in Carson City, might be at the heart of it.

Chapter 33

RONIN ENTERS THE HOUSE

"What was that all about?" Ronin asked. Pushing the front door open, he immediately spied Emma sitting on the davenport with her head between her hands. She was shaking. It tore at his heart. "What's the matter, Emma?" he said, crouching down, trying to be sensitive. It was a trait he had only begun to practice a few months before, when it became necessary for him to live somewhere that could offer him needed post-surgical support.

While the operation to repair his broken leg had gone "without complication," as the doctor had put it, Quinn had wondered aloud if Emma's more recent bouts with dizziness—likely "reactive," he had called them, thinking of her husband's disappearance—and Ronin's professional interest in helping to solve the mission kidnappings might offer an unexpected "synergism."

The term was an unfamiliar one to Ronin, who thought he may have seen the word in a theological text somewhere. Quinn assured him the word was "medical," and a recent one at that, but Emma said she would feel better if someone with Ronin's experience could watch after things at the mission until the Ormsby County sheriffs could figure out what was going on.

It had been a good move for both of them, allowing Ronin to stay off his feet, except for taking meals with the children or an evening walk alone or with friends. Nearly two months later, he was ready to leave.

Ronin noticed that the front door didn't fully close after he entered. As he knelt there, he made a mental note to see if the door frame had swollen. Given that the air was unseasonably chilly, he didn't know whether to stand and shut the door or remain on his knees so as to comfort his friend.

"What happened?" he asked, standing to pull the door shut. "Who were those men?" Looking out the front window, he could still see the dust of the five horsemen galloping through the mission gate. A beautiful alpenglow on the western most mountains warned that nightfall was near. "Are you hurt?" The questions stumbled from his lips as he made a quick examination of his friend and the front room. There were no immediate signs of struggle. He waited for Emma's reply. The woman was such a mystery to him. Every woman was, for that matter.

"I'm not hurt," Emma sighed. "But I believe I made a big mistake."

"What did you do, Emma? What's happened?"

"I was in my bedroom, laying out my bed clothes, when I heard a knock at the front door. So I came out to see who it was, and instead of deciding whether to open the door—you've been real clear that I shouldn't just open the door, but look to see who it is instead—I found someone already standing inside the house."

"In the house?" he asked, looking to see if he could still see them on the approach road outside the mission fence. "They simply walked in?" Ronin didn't know what to think. While offering shelter or food to a passerby was common in the Carson Valley, to be expected in fact even after nightfall, no rider ever approached a ranch house without first calling out and receiving an audible invitation.

"Well, yes," she said, still shaking. "The man who entered the house said he thought it was a public place and apologized." Emma looked up. "He had men with him. He identified them as his brothers, but I don't know. They remained in the doorway," she said. "There were two others by the corral. Two of them had no shoes."

"Did you know them?"

She shook her head no.

Ronin stomach knotted. He began to feel sick about being so far from the house when the visitors came. He had walked down to the river to sit a spell, having found the night sounds of the Carson Valley to be comforting over the last few weeks.

"Did they hurt you?"

"They did not," Emma said. "The tall man was respectful. And he wore a golden cross, which made me feel safe. But he asked about the children."

Ronin looked perplexed. He looked out the window again. The dust had finally settled along the fence line and the glow, framing the Sierra Mountains to the west, was nearly gone. The moon was slim. Following tracks would be near to impossible.

He looked back at Emma. "I don't understand. They asked about the children. Why would they come to the mission at night and ask about the children?"

Emma swallowed and looked away. She seemed to be crying. "They said they had business with Henry."

"Henry? He's been gone nearly three months. I don't understand."

Ronin felt a profound sadness come over the woman who had cared for him so completely the last few months, and he was now feeling some anxiety of his own.

"Exactly," Emma's voice cracked. "They had business with Henry …"

She folded her hands around the back of her head, as she sometimes did, kneading at her neck muscles, and then lowered her head to her lap. Her friend touched her chin lightly, and then thought better of it. She looked up.

"I understand, but why has this got you so upset, Emma?"

Emma began to cry. Not in an explosive way, but slowly, as if she had come to realize something she had not previously understood. He had only been gone an hour, Ronin figured. How could so much happen in so little time? He sat down beside her and put his left arm around her shoulders, and waited.

She whispered, "Ronin. I don't believe I'm saying this."

"Saying what, Emma? What are you thinking?"

She swallowed hard, and taking a handkerchief from behind her apron, wiped at her right eye. "I wonder if Henry was involved in something so horrible that ..."

"That what, Emma?"

She pulled his arm from around her shoulder, grabbed both of his hands and sat so that she could see him. "I wonder if Henry was ...selling ...the children?"

Ronin immediately understood the implications. He had heard of Chinese children being sold into sexual slavery in San Francisco. He had seen children working in the tiny, rat holes mines in Virginia City, and of others working inside the Sutro Tunnel. As a southerner, he'd seen people put kids to work in all kinds of situations, where a better educated or compassionate person would have hesitated. The possibilities and potential horrors were endless, and in every way, sick, unethical and grotesque. She collapsed into his arms, sobbing. He held her, and his questions, until he could better consider his words.

Chapter 34

HORSEMEN

"What the fuck was that?" Remy Crestwell asked, as Paul Clancy pulled up his reins after the quick gallop from the mission grounds.

"What the fuck was what?" Paul Clancy responded, glaring at him. A smaller man might be found, he thought to himself, but never a bigger mouth. "I nearly killed you in Virginia City, Crestwell. You're not out of hot water with me yet."

Always the peacemaker, Peter Clancy pushed his horse between the two of them. It took him a few moments before he spoke. "I think what Remy is saying is that we don't understand what's happening, Paul. You told us we were heading to Carson City and maybe to Reno. And we rode plumb through Carson City to what, *East Jesus, Nevada,* to see this lady, and now we're riding back again? Can you tell us what the plan is?"

Paul pushed his hat higher up on his head. He took a deep breath and put the gold cross his mother had given him back inside his shirt. "Look, everyone. I've gone over this before, and I'll not tell you again. Fact is, I'd rather dig each of you a fucking Protestant grave before I have to explain this again. Nauman was our contact for children to work that damn mine Peter found us. He had people working for him as well. But I don't know who they are or where the children are that we've already bought. But we're not going to be making any money until we find the children that bastard already sold us ..."

Patrick interrupted, "Paul, you said we were going to somewhere 'menable.' And now we're back on our horses ..."

"The word is 'amenable,' you fucking moron."

Patrick was the youngest. And while the Crestwells were a great deal more bother, there were days when even Patrick got on his nerves. "I'm sorry, Patrick," Paul said, but before the words finished coming out of his mouth he was shouting again.

"Do you understand the fucking situation we're in? We have a gig that will get us out of fighting in the bars and robbing banks. It will get us off the streets, maybe build us a home. It ain't much, but it's a small piece we can call our own. Jesus ..."

The eldest of the three Clancy brothers, the one to whom mother Clancy had entrusted the care of his brothers after his dad's death nearly twenty years before, took a moment. He gritted his teeth, shut his mouth and looked around the small stand of cottonwood trees under which they had stopped a mile or so from the mission entrance. Taking a deep breath and pacing himself, he began again. "You see boys, we've got to find these kids if we're going to have any working capital at all. It may be a compromise to our Catholic ideals ..."

Peter interrupted again. "It ain't, Paul. None of us like Indians."

"... Let me finish. If we're going to have any money at all, to get a spread, to keep our heads above water and the reach of the law, we're going to have to locate these Indian kids, goddamnit, assuming there are kids to be located, I guess."

"Paul?" Remy Crestwell interrupted. "I might know where they are."

Every eye turned to Remy. Everyone was surprised to hear the jackass offer something constructive.

"There's a group of Indians living just north of Reno in one of the valleys heading to Pyramid Lake. Well, my brother and I have had some contacts with them and while they're a feisty bunch, I suspect they might know something about Washoe Indian children who have ...um, wandered away, so to speak ...from their tribe."

Paul Clancy was stunned and fully understood the import of what Remy Crestwell was saying. Not only did Nauman have a hand in providing Indian children to people with money, but Crestwell did as well. And likely, while he had no experience with the Northern Paiutes, a deal might be made that would set them up in a fashion to which his mother would be proud.

"It hasn't been that long since the Pyramid Lake War, Remy. Are you saying we can talk to these 'skins?"

The Clancys had lost their father during the Pyramid Lake War, when some of the Northern Paiutes, Shoshone and Bannock Indian tribes raided Williams Station. The raid was, oddly enough, in retaliation for the kidnapping and rape of two young Paiute girls by the station's proprietors. His father, Paul Sr., had been prospecting in Virginia City at the time and had joined a force of over a hundred men under the command of Major William Ormsby, an honest-to-God Nevadan pioneer in his father's eyes.

"I'll not risk my brothers in this."

"Not to worry, Clancy," Remy responded. "Clem and I have been there many times, tradin'. If we can't find Nauman's Indians children there—a Paiute is no friend to a Washoe—they'll likely know where they are."

Paul Clancy nodded, and then looking at his brothers Patrick and Peter, who couldn't possibly have understood what they were agreeing to by nodding back, said, "Well, let's get moving. It's already nightfall and I want to get there before morning."

Chapter 35

CHRISTMAS DAY

Christmas Day came and went at the mission, marked by Emma's singing in the kitchen and a rousing Christmas day dinner and songfest by the children at the mission.

It had been a long time, seven years he figured, since he had any Christmas responsibilities. While the sentiments were always appreciated by him during the darker time of the year—kindness, hope, charity toward all and so on—he had found similar solace and anticipation in the wintry smell of sage in the Sierra foothills, the unanticipated beauty of the winter's first snow and ice storms, and the slow, trudging goodness of the people who had cared for him when he needed it most, in the Carson Valley.

Most Western folks weren't as seasonally exuberant or excited as those he knew in Pennsylvania or Kansas. The closer folks lived to big, eastern cities, the more inclined they were to celebrate with big city customs. Ronin found the lack of Christmas traditions relaxing.

A stuffed bird and a few carols was about all he could stand from the litany of Christmas gatherings he remembered from his years at St. John's Episcopal Church and seminary before that. The memories now too dim, the pain still too large, the what-might-have-beens, at times though not many times, still too haunting.

The Reverend W. W. Ronin had departed in a winter huff that left a great many of his parishioners confused. Despite his explanations that he no longer believed as he once did, that he wanted to do something more concrete with his life, that he hoped to live as regular men did and anticipated enjoying the exploration and discovery of new environs and habits, the simple folks in his church met his words with blank stares and looks of betrayal. "Don't let the door hit you on the way out," one person said, confusing his own pain in having to wait for a new pastor with his one-time affection for him and his ministry.

It had been nearly seven years.

Ronin gathered his books and clothes and wrapped them in the leather and canvas valise Emma had given him the night before. He hadn't carried such things in a good many years, but Emma believed that her hand-made rollup bag would come in handy once he left the ranch, particularly after he settled things in Reno. He traveled that much.

"I don't know what I'll do," she said, "once you're gone. I hope I'm not being too presumptuous by saying so, William. But I've enjoyed your time here so very much."

Ronin didn't immediately answer, as her candor always took him by surprise.

She was perhaps the most complete woman he had ever met. The way she had blossomed after her husband's disappearance, the manner in which she was beginning to care for the children and the business of the mission, had impressed him over the three months he had enjoyed the valley's hospitality. He enjoyed being close to her. And yet, at other times, she seemed possessed by an irrational spirit. There were times that she was so caught up in religious fervor, he couldn't find a place far enough from Emma to relax.

He turned to her and looking at her intently, decided to tell her his innermost heart.

"I feel the same, Emma, and I don't know what to do with my feelings."

"I want you to head to Reno," she interrupted, a moist tear forming in her left eye underneath the small scar he had come to know and love. She hesitated. "Someone needs to make things right, and if the children are there, I worry about them. I'm angry about what my husband did to them. I want things to be the way they used to be."

She looked down and then toward his leg. "Are you sure you're up to it?"

Ronin nodded. His leg, though still painful, seemed stable enough to walk and ride.

"Things are never as they appear, Emma," the former reverend said, thinking of his own life but also of the missing children. "Our impressions are simply attachments, ghosts of what we want our lives to be or to become."

Ronin pulled his gun belt off the bedpost and began wrapping it around the holster. He looked around the room to see what had become of his rifle.

"Life is what it is. That's my best guess," he said, looking at the woman who had become so much more than a friend, but what? He looked at her and was quiet.

Emma took a step forward, never backward she thought, and put her hands on the ex-preacher's shoulders. "Some moments are better than others, William, and all of them are a part of God's good future," she smiled, "I wish I could convince you of that."

She placed Ronin's saddlebag on the window seat and sat down on a Shaker bench in the bedroom. Her husband had constructed the simple seat when they lived in Ohio. "I made it for us," he said. It seemed like a dozen years ago. Patting the space beside her she said, "Come here and sit for a moment, would you?"

Ronin walked toward the bench but stood an arm's length away.

"Here," she said, patting again at the long red, cotton cushion she had sewn to lend the bench comfort and ornamentation. "Sit next to me. I want to tell you what I am thankful for. It's Christmas, after all."

W. W. Ronin sat, as he was told, and turning toward her, gazed at the beauty of her brown, shoulder-length hair. Looking into her green eyes and trying not to smile, he listened.

"Not to sound like a preacher," she said, "but I am thankful for hope, when hope seems to run out. I am thankful for faith, when it is so difficult to have faith in so many. And I am thankful for ..."

He recognized the construction from the Apostle Paul's writings in his pocket Bible. Faith, hope *and love.*

"Love?" he asked.

She looked at him and then smiled.

"Yes, love. I think love makes everything worthwhile. It changes difficult times and makes them much better. Don't you think so, William?"

"Sometimes," he said. He thought of the moments in his ministry when love didn't change anything. Or the horribly rich days and weeks he had spent as a Confederate soldier—days he didn't choose to remember until recently—moments when he had cradled the dead and the dying, writing letters to their folks back home and wondering about the meaning of life and suffering. He remembered a friendship he had developed with a woman, when he was a Pinkerton. "An inappropriate one," his employer had said before cutting him loose from the case, and later his responsibilities. Love hadn't changed anything. In fact, love had made things more difficult.

"I am thankful for you, W. W. Ronin."

Ronin looked up, and despite his reservations, told her what he thought she already knew. "And I you, Emma."

And the man who had never found real fulfillment in his ministry, who never experienced happiness in his work as a soldier, or as a Pinkerton detective, or as a man who solved difficult problems and sometimes sought and subdued difficult men suddenly wondered if he had found fulfillment in an extraordinary woman.

"I am thankful for you, too, Emma." And with that he kissed her upturned mouth, but not before he kissed the scar above her left eye.

Chapter 36
BREAKFAST

Ronin rose early the next day, happy that he and Emma had shared the words and affection they had the night before. It was strange that they had lived together throughout the autumn months and had never, until last night, spoken so intimately about their hopes, dreams or feelings for each other.

He pulled his shirt from the high-backed chair beside his bed and wondered if he had been too agreeable in lying with her as he had. They had kept their Christian decorum, as he had called it. She and he were both committed to honoring whatever was left of the relationship that Emma had with her husband. But she was so needful, she had said, of the warmth between a man and a woman, and it had been years since he had embraced anyone in so loving a way.

When he had discovered his feelings for Madame Bovary, his Pinkerton client—whatever her real name was, as he found out later that her name and affections were a complex ruse involving dozens of men—he knew his affections for the woman would ultimately lead to his removal. Perhaps it was his acting on them that did. Whatever the case, it hadn't occurred to him until last night that Nauman and Bovary had the same first name, Emma. Maybe it was the pain of being in a relationship again. Maybe because their demeanors were so different, he hadn't made the connection.

Bovary was an aggressive woman, physically speaking. While he had been taught as a pastor to be careful, he had enjoyed private moments with her as a Pinkerton that would have made his former bishop shrink in surprise. They had proven to him that he was a man, though when he had learned of her multiple involvements, he wasn't proud of that fact. The resulting discipline was as it should have been. Business was business, and mixing business with pleasure was rarely what a professional man ought to do.

Sliding the shirt over his head so as to avoid the tedium of buttoning it, he fastened the buttons on each of his sleeves. Dust-sucker would be coming out to the mission around noon. They'd find a couple of trees so as to sight in their rifles and maybe get in some fast draw shooting. It had been a couple of months since he had used a gun. Given the importance of what he was going to do, he didn't want to be careless about it. He pulled on his pants and fashioned his braces a little higher than he would usually wear them, so as to allow him a little more room for his gun belt and cartridges.

Ronin had an usual relationship with guns, rare in the sense that one would expect a detective and bounty hunter to like the tools of his trade. But he had been raised by a Sunday School teacher in Philadelphia, an area favored by folks with pro-foundly religious fervor. If you weren't a Quaker in Philadelphia, he had heard tell, there was a good chance you were a Mason. Either brand had a religious rigor about it, Masonic arguments to the contrary.

History be told, Masons and Quakers weren't as strange to guns as widely believed. Both brands were known to get into fiery scraps when Ronin was growing up, though not with each other. The bloodiest of feuds were often worked out with one end of a gun or another.

Given that he had been raised an Episcopalian, Ronin and his family didn't have particularly pacifist leanings. As a young man, he had gotten into a number of fist fights. And while guns were a matter of economic necessity for some folks and protec-tion for others, his hard-working, church-going family had long enjoyed the privilege of having their meat and protection provided by others less busy or conscionable.

Hunting wasn't a practical necessity for his family, and game was hard to come by in Philadelphia. Industrialization had taken a strong foothold in the Northeast, and local grocery markets appreciated the growing business of providing meat and other staples for people who had money. Who was going to hunt after doing a full day's work and then some in one of Philadelphia's factories? And which among the emerging class of wealthy Philadelphia industrialists would tolerate such activities amidst the city's row houses and brownstones?

Besides, Ronin didn't eat pigeons or squirrels unless circumstances called for it, even when Emma insisted. She was rural and he was city, a difference she didn't always seem to understand.

Pulling on his boots at the mission, his injured leg as good as it was going to get, Ronin remembered a Revolutionary War-era musket hanging over his grandfather's fireplace. He hadn't seen anything similar in his own house growing up, nor did he expect that his father was hiding a firearm. "The war is over," his dad would say from time to time, referring to the wars that had been fought with Great Britain, "and I've got nothing to say about them." Nothing else was ever said, as far as Ronin remembered anyway.

It was as if his father's attitudes toward firearms, criminality, the right to self-defense, the role of civil rebellion and so on didn't exist. For all Ronin knew, the manly side of his father—the part of him that he had come to understand as feeding, planning, nurturing and protecting—didn't seem to exist, either. He was a blank slate, Ronin thought, feeling poorly that he hadn't been able to get to know his father in the way that his older brothers did.

Maybe that's why I turned out to be like this, Ronin thought, half-cocking his single-action revolver and opening the loading gate before inserting six cartridges into his revolver. Ronin did what he did without any real feelings or connections toward his guns. They were simply his tools. Two original 1873

.45 caliber Colt Peacemakers: a seven-and-one-half-inch "Calvary Model" which he generally kept in a holster on the horn of his saddle when it wasn't in a cross draw holster on his waist, and a custom four-inch "Sheriff's" model he handled from his hip. An 1866 "Yellow Boy" Winchester rifle sat in a separate scabbard behind his saddle for shooting intermediate distances. The same neutrality of passion and purpose extended toward the men he hunted, except this time.

Ronin took the shorter of his revolvers out of its holster and grimaced. He hated the thought of someone hurting his dog. While he hadn't enjoyed the warmth of a woman in a long time, he had endured many a cold night cradled up next to his dog, Kuon. He now believed the Crestwell or Clancy brothers were behind the killing of his constant companion, the same with Emma's children and likely whatever children were missing from the Washoe tribe north of Carson City. The two sets of brothers were responsible for an inordinate amount of wrongdoing. He would be part of a posse of people intent on making them pay, and he had heard they were heading to Reno.

Ronin hated people who harmed innocent folk, a strong word for a man who rarely felt poorly about others. If it wasn't for his well-practiced skill with his firearms, his feet and hands, one might have argued he was a Quaker, not an Episcopalian, though in time he had come to regard himself as neither. He laughed so loudly that Emma called from the kitchen to check on him. "Breakfast is ready, if you're ready, William."

Emma's voice had a ring to it he could get used to. "I'll be out in a few minutes," he called back.

Chapter 37

BULLETS FOR BAD GUYS

It was noon when Dustsucker banged on the front door. Ronin walked from the kitchen, where he had been talking and helping Emma with the dishes. He greeted his friend. "Let's do this, buddy," he quipped as he opened the door.

"You're in a good place, if you don't mind me saying," Dustsucker noted. They walked a few hundred feet past the house corral, when Ronin finally responded. "I am, but let's keep our mind on business."

He drew from his cross-draw side, thumbed the first cartridge and fanned the following two, using his first and fourth fingers. The combination sounded like one shot, but the three bottles they had set on the fence broke cleanly. His last three shots were fanned with his left thumb in quick succession, shooting a vertical zipper line up an old fence post before the last of the bottles broke. Thumbing the Colt's hammer back a couple of notches with his right hand and opening the loading gate to remove his spent shells, he paused to watch the smoke clear and wondered what the next morning would bring.

His intention was to load six, not five as was customary, in both of his Colts. He set aside a couple of boxes of .44 caliber rounds for his Yellow Boy. The toggle-bolt action was capable of firing 28 rounds per minute, and more if in the hands of someone practiced who was able to manipulate the lever while keeping the rifle on target. It was the Yellow Boy he was hoping would conduct most of his business when rescuing the children.

Once he found them, that is.

He reloaded his gun and holstered it without flourish or fanfare. He hated fancy gunplay. He didn't think it proper or appropriate for safety's sake. A habit gained in play wasn't helpful when it came to performance. Like the Earps, with whom he had little more than a than a passing acquaintance when some of the Earps lived in Wichita, a six-shooter in the right hands was more than a tool. It might have hammered a few fence posts in its day, or posed handsomely around the red-festooned waist of a well-dressed cowpoke on his way to a sporting house or Sunday meeting. But it had no place twirling on the end of one's fingers unless one was fixing to pound someone with its butt end.

A gun is a tool. "It's what I use. It's what I do," he murmured to himself as he slipped the four-inch Colt out of its holster and leveled it from his hip at the fence posts and other targets he had set up earlier that afternoon. He drew the gun a couple times but did not fire. First his strong side, then his cross-draw. His right again, then his left. They were fine tools. And it didn't matter to him which end he brought to business.

He squared off to the fence, and then placing his right foot forward, cocked and drew his revolver with such speed that the sheer drag of the hammer and movement of his hip caused his gun to clear his holster and put into battery a 40-grain black powder charge. It exploded one of Dustsucker's bottles twenty-some feet away. Tossing it live into his other hand, he drew the Calvary Model from his cross-draw holster and let loose, thumbing nine additional .45 caliber slugs down range in quick succession, shattering glass and splintering wood in a dark and disciplined cloud of holy blue smoke.

"What do you think?" he asked his friend.

"I think we're ready," Dustsucker laughed. "I don't think we've ever been more ready."

"Expect not," Ronin replied. They were headed to Reno. Putting up his guns for supper, he figured there would be hell to pay when they got there.

Chapter 38

LAST SUPPER

"Dusty, I'm glad you're staying for supper." Emma gestured toward the sink. "You boys can wash up there, if you like. The food will be ready soon." Emma had made an early meal for the mission children so that the three of them might be able to speak more privately before morning.

"I'm always happy to be here, ma'am. Your cooking is legendary. And your kindness, well, it's much appreciated."

"You're the one who has been so kind," Emma replied, taking a skillet from the stove and setting it on the table. Dustsucker looked over his right shoulder while washing and licked his lips while grunting with obvious pleasure. Ronin laughed.

Fried chicken was both of their favorites. But for Dustsucker, it was Christmas, particularly when it was accompanied by mashed potatoes and a fine bacon gravy.

"You've visited your friend nearly every day since he's been here," Emma said, noticing her guest's obvious pleasure and joy.

"It was easy to come, ma'am. You keep feeding me! I hardly could have stayed away."

The three of them laughed while pulling out chairs and setting additional food on the table. When it was done, chicken sat alongside the men's favorite gravy, potatoes and winter squash, green onions and corn.

Everyone smiled. Emma folded her hands, a signal Ronin and Dustsucker had gotten used to though never fully embraced.

She began, "Our Father, who art in heaven, hallowed be Thy Name. Thy kingdom come, Thy will be done ..." The two men joined in, missing some words, affirming others. "...on earth, as it is in heaven. Give us this day our daily bread and forgive us our trespasses."

Ronin thought of what he was about to do, and wondered if he'd need anyone's forgiveness, given how ugly the crimes had been. "… as we forgive those who trespass against us. Lead us not into temptation, but deliver us from evil."

Good Catholic that he had been, Dustsucker looked up, thinking the prayer was finished, only to see Emma's eyes still closed. "…for Thine is the kingdom, and the power, and the glory, for ever and ever. Amen." Protestants, Dustsucker thought. He'd never understand them. "Amen," he added, thinking the evening's prayers to be finished.

"Almighty Lord," Emma continued. Ronin looked at Dustsucker and both bowed their heads, wondering if the prayers would ever end and if the chicken would be cold by the time they did. "…and everlasting God, vouchsafe, we beseech Thee to direct, sanctify, and govern both our hearts and bodies in the ways of Thy laws, and in the works of Thy commandments; that through Thy most mighty protection, both here and ever, we may be preserved in body and soul, through our Lord and Savior, Jesus Christ."

Emma opened her eyes, "Amen."

"Amen," Ronin answered. Looking at Emma and realizing she had memorized the second prayer from a century old prayer book from his saddlebags, he leaned forward to kiss their hostess on the forehead.

"That we may be preserved in body and soul," he said. "What a kind thought, Emma, a very kind prayer and very touching of you to remember those words."

"You boys are making an important trip tomorrow. I wish I could be with you …"

Dustsucker and Ronin spoke simultaneously, "No ma'am, it's not safe," one said. The other, "You need to stay here. This is not a trip for women." Emma smiled, not knowing who said what.

She continued. "What I mean to say is, I wish I could be with you, to protect you, to care for you, to make sure that the children are well."

"Ma'am, we don't know that we'll be able to find the children," Dustsucker replied. "It's a big town—not as big as Virginia City, but big enough."

"You'll do your best, Dusty. And God will guide you."

"Yes ma'am, I imagine God will."

Dustsucker glanced at Ronin, who had remained silent throughout, knowing that Emma believed this too was a part of "God's good future," as she called it. And having heard enough, thought it was more productive to grab one of the chicken legs in the pan before his friend got hold of both of them.

"Chicken, Emma?" He pushed the iron skillet in her direction after removing his favorite piece of dark meat. "It sure looks fine."

Emma stuck a fork into a small cracker-covered breast in the pan, her family's secret recipe, she liked to say. "My question to the two of you is this: how will you find these men? I mean, where will you start?"

Ronin took a spoonful of potatoes. While not his favorite, he preferred it to the corn. While appreciating corn's December rareness, the vegetable always seemed like it should be given to cattle. "We're assuming it was Paul Clancy who visited you a couple of nights ago," Ronin said. "And given your description of the big guy by the corral and the two boys on your porch, it's a good possibility that the Crestwells and the Clancys have gotten together."

"They're both known to us," Dustsucker added, meaning local law enforcement. "I had a conversation with Augustus Ash a few days ago. He's the U.S. Marshal out of Virginia City?"

"I've heard of him," Emma said.

"Well, the two sets of brothers were seen in Storey County a couple weeks back. Actually, broke the youngest Clancy out of jail, or rather custody. Augustus took a bit of a beating, so he's hoping we'll take him along. And given ..."

"You're thinking of enlisting his support?" Emma interrupted, knowing Ash's reputation as a lawman was good one. She looked at her friend. "He's no windy, Ronin. He's a good man and would be a big help to both of you, I'm sure. I don't believe anyone has ever had the best of him."

Dusty and Ronin looked up from their food and smiled at each other, Ronin remembering that he had nearly killed the occasionally hapless marshal a few months back when Ash had surprised him while he was sleeping in the foothills outside of Gold Hill. And Dustsucker, because he had just said that one of the Clancy brothers had smacked Ash upside the head. Former Virginia City police chief and sheriff Thomas E. Kelly had been shot as well, though neither of them thought it important to mention that fact.

"Yes, we're going to pick him up on the way," Ronin answered, hoping to put an end to the discussion.

Emma finished placing an appropriate portion of each of the evening's foods on her plate. "Saint Thomas Aquinas said, 'An excessive desire for food is a simple sin resisted.' My mother used to say that at every Sunday afternoon meal," she said to no one in particular. Ronin had heard Emma teach the children a Christian commentary on the thought one night during an evening meal. Eating too soon, too expensively, too much, too eagerly, too daintily, or too wildly were all troublesome variations on the sin of gluttony, she had said. Ronin believed that Aquinas—saint or not, he didn't care—clearly had a problem with eating, given the portly portraitures he had seen at seminary. More so, nothing should get in the way of a good meal.

"I'm sorry, Dusty," Emma said, correcting herself. "I interrupted you. You were saying?"

"Well ma'am, I was simply saying since Ash has an interest in these men—he calls them 'hustlers,' since he has some history with them—I thought it only appropriate to include him, and maybe one other."

"He'll be an able hand," Ronin said, tearing at the chicken with his knife and wondering if Dustsucker had decided to ask Tom Kelly to come along.

The three of them ate quietly, enjoying their meal and discussing what the next day would bring. When Dustsucker went to bed, Ronin lingered in the front room.

"William, may I have a word with you?" Emma asked, putting up the towel from her hands and untying her apron.

"Of course."

"You'll take care of yourself, won't you?"

"I will." He paused. "Why do you ask?"

"As I care too much to let you go, William, and ache too much to ask you not to."

Chapter 39

THE CORRAL

W. W. Ronin mounted his horse as the sun came up around 6 a.m., a few minutes before his friends came to the corral. He wanted some time to himself and figured the day might best begin if he got used to the stirrup leathers before anyone else joined him there.

He saddled his quarterhorse, a sorrel-colored stud named "Jackson," after Stonewall Jackson, the Confederate cavalryman. Jackson was strong, hardy and quick, had a broad chest and what Ronin believed to be amazingly powerful hindquarters. He was taller than most at 16 hands and quite a handful for Ronin, who preferred steel-shorn wheels to horse hooves, even if they were on railroad cars.

Ronin had been driving wagons since he was fifteen, initially as a cook's helper and later as the sole rifleman—the cook's protector, he figured and a good one they said—in Biffle's 19th Tennessee Calvary. Colonel Biffle had died in 1877, when a man named Scott Waters shot him at his Oklahoma ranch. Waters had been Biffle's cook and the killing had taken place during a December cattle drive. Ronin figured that Jackson was his best bet to tracking Waters, but in his mid-thirties, he was beginning to feel a certain tenderness about remaining in Nevada instead. He had moved around too much. Wondering whether he'd ever find a wife or even have children, he hankered to settle down in the Silver State and believed Oklahoma might be too far away to seek Biffle's killer.

Ronin's work as a priest and later as a Pinkerton didn't necessitate any real friendliness with horse breeds. Jackson had been easier to deal with than other horses he had owned since leaving the Pinkertons. He smiled and patted the horse's mane before putting his left leg in the saddle stirrup and grimacing. He much appreciated Jackson's speed and power when chasing down a fugitive or climbing a hill, though neither at this point did much for his leg.

"Whoa, Jackson," he said softly, looking past the cottonwood trees to the sun as it was just beginning to crest the foothills. "Keep it down, my friend. I just want to see how my leg is going to hold up." Jackson came to a halt in the crowded corral. He seemed to understand Ronin's pain and hesitation.

Healing had come more slowly than he had anticipated for his leg, though Emma did what she could to help things along. They had taken to applying a horse liniment to his left leg most evenings. Despite his initial protestations—born, he thought, in large part by his years as a priest and bachelor, but also by the words on its label—he had come to enjoy the attention and missed it when Emma was busy with the children or Ronin had business to attend to.

Emma had known the Sloan family in Zanesfield, Ohio prior to moving west. Earl Sloan had been a friend of her family's and was well known for his veterinary surgeon skills during the war. Growing up, they had come to rely on the Sloan liniment formula as "good for man or beast." Ronin seemed a little bit of both, Emma had argued when Ronin pointed to the words.

Sloan had bought and sold horses during the war and had an uncanny ability to turn a farm horse with a stiffened shoulder or hindquarter into a perfect plough animal again. So much so that folks throughout the Upper Ohio Valley had not only come to call him "the Village Vet," but "Doc Sloan." She didn't think he had ever attended a medical or veterinary school, not that it mattered.

She remembered the liniment when she arrived in Nevada and, corresponding with the doctor and his family, was happy to receive a supply of it from time to time for the needs of the mission animals and children.

Ronin didn't believe that the nostrum had been any more effective for his bad leg than Emma's prayers had been, but given that she had, at least initially, applied it herself to his injured limb and later to his good leg as well—she didn't want the muscles to be "imbalanced," she explained, or for a "well-toned leg to go to waste"—he more than tolerated her ministrations. He even looked forward to them.

But the leg would likely always have some ache to it, he had concluded. Placing his leg up into the left stirrup that morning, he convinced himself that it didn't really matter as long as he could sit upright.

He was sitting tall in the saddle when Dustsucker and Emma came to the corral.

"Well, I guess we're off," Dustsucker said grabbing his horse blanket from the corral gate. "We'll send for you in a couple of days if we find your children. Either way, we'll let you know the results of our investigation, Emma."

"I suspect I'll be way ahead of you," Emma replied. "I've been praying about this trip for a long time," she said. Ronin and Dustsucker looked at each other. They had only recently decided to follow up with their own investigation, after Ormsby County officials had dropped theirs. "I have only good feelings about this trip," she added. "I just hope you'll both be careful."

Emma looked at Ronin with kindly eyes, the kind of look that meant he was special to her, precious, even. But she was still married, he reckoned, while not very married given her abandonment three months prior by the former director of the mission. She was, "still married in the eyes of the Church," he murmured to himself.

"Let's get going Dusty," Ronin said. "Reno is two hard days' ride, given my leg. I want to be there by Tuesday. Tuesday is a good day to change someone's life, don't you think?" he said, grimacing, while adjusting his rifle scabbard from the back of his saddle to the front. He hoped Slade hadn't seen him wince.

"'When the wicked perish, there is joy,' *Proverbs 11:11*," Emma said, looking at both men, smiling and waiting for their reaction.

Ronin was chilled by the thought that a Bible verse should be used to explain the killing of a few men.

"Maybe so," he replied, and then turning toward Dustsucker, said, "Let's get moving."

Emma looked up at Ronin, who had already begun to pull his reins to the right. Catching her eyes, Ronin loosened them, trotting the horse closer toward Emma and the house.

"I hope you'll be careful," she said again. "Anyone who would steal a child can't be a very good person." Ronin thought of her husband, Henry. He couldn't imagine that Henry was a bad person, not if Emma had been married to him.

"People get caught up in things they don't intend to," he replied. "It doesn't make them bad, though it does make some of them unlucky." Some folks needed to die sooner than others, he figured. In the end, it was up to God to sort things out, if there was a God who did such things.

"I'll be careful. And thank you again for everything you've done for me these last few months. I don't know that I could have put things together again as easily as I did without your help."

He was speaking about his infirmity. But Emma took it differently, or more deeply.

"I think you're a good man, Mr. W. W. Ronin, whether you're a preacher or not. What makes you special in my eyes, William, is that you choose to be a man when others don't much bother to think about it."

Dustsucker smiled. It was that same quality in Ronin that appealed most to him.

Chapter 40
RENO

Myron Lake's hotel sat just a few yards away from the Truckee River during a hard spring run-off, and had sat there on the south side of the river since the discovery of gold and silver veins on the Comstock Lode in the late 1850s.

A simple log building at first, the "Lake House," as it was called, was the sentimental favorite for travelers heading to Nevada, or to California if you were coming from the other way. Sitting initially by toll bridge, where Lake earned upwards of $40,000 a year in Truckee River crossings, the town was no longer defined by the crossing—or the ramshackle blend of tents, sheds and saloons that made Reno famous—it was a railroad town now. By design, Myron Lake's properties and businesses were at the center of things.

Slade hadn't been north of the Comstock since Reno's disastrous fire. As Slade understood it, the fire had started in the early morning hours behind the Masonic Lodge on Sierra Street. A strong gale blowing from the west soon sent people screaming from their homes destroying nearly ten city blocks. A couple of the city's deputies, who doubled as firemen, had been involved and talked about the event when visiting in Carson City. Chinese laborers had been pressed into service. Only five lives were lost—a couple of citizens and some transients, none of them his friends—but the post office, the Pollard, the International and Arcade Hotels, a half-dozen clothing and dry goods stores and a couple of groceries had been destroyed in what some folks said were the fiercest gale winds in years.

"The loss was nearly a million dollars, wasn't it?" Ronin asked, thinking the town had been lucky as he had read houses as far as two miles away from the city were lost because of burning timber pieces carried through the air.

"Yup, it was bad," Dustsucker said, riding past some of the newer buildings on Commercial Row. "Someone told me they're going to be using bricks from now on. I don't know that I like the change, but it's better situated against fire than wood, I guess."

Ronin nodded, "You're not much for change, I know."

"Tell you what though," Dustsucker continued, "Virginia City's fire was a hell of a lot worse. Ten times worse, if you ask me."

Ronin looked at his friend, who had lived in Nevada before it was a state and figured he had seen a great many things change. They counted more than a dozen saloons, hotels and restaurants on their way to Lake's three-story building along the river. The Lake House offered travelers and tradesmen a comfortable place to do business away from hustle and bustle of it all, and it had been doing that since its erection in the 1860s. While he didn't much appreciate what he knew of its founder—Lake had been something of a philanderer from his point of view, and a wife-beater if the stories were to be believed—still, Lake's toll bridge and trading post had turned into a something he and Dustsucker had long appreciated. He couldn't think of a single time passing through Reno when he didn't stop.

To tell the truth, Ronin liked the Lake House's amenities. He enjoyed the bar, despite not being a big drinker. The restaurant, or day room as it was called when it wasn't serving breakfast, was pleasant and roomy enough to entertain a large group of guests, though Ronin had few. And oddly enough, for a man who had transformed himself from a professional saint to occasional sinner and saddle tramp, he liked the light. He enjoyed the way it faced the street.

When Dustsucker and Ronin arrived, they walked through the west entrance of the hotel together to register, tying their horses to the balcony's wooden supports. Many a moment he had sat on the second story looking north over the bridge and river. Looking around, he saw a loud, agitated man was drinking in the day room, something that wasn't allowed even on holidays when the house was packed. Staff members were busily trying to talk the man into moving into the saloon. Two days of hard riding didn't make for pleasant friends.

"Brother," Ronin shouted at the man, "how about you take your loud mouth outside?"

"How about you take *your* loud mouth outside," the drunk said. Clever comeback, Ronin thought, turning back to the register underneath where Slade was signing his name. "I'm talking to you!" the man said, placing a hand on Ronin's right shoulder and abruptly pulling him around.

Turning just as quickly, Ronin chipped a left uppercut into the man's liver and, shooting a right jab past his face, grabbed him around the neck, kneeing him in the chest. He was about to throw a second knee to his face when Dustsucker pushed him away, causing him to stumble.

"He's down, Ronin!" He pulled the ex-preacher back toward him and pushed him up against the hotel's front desk "Ronin! Let's just take this guy outside and lay him upside the building. What do you say?" he asked, grabbing both of Ronin's arms. The man was doubled up on the floor, wheezing. "He's not hurting anybody, right?"

Ronin shook his head, struggling to clear his head. "God, I can't believe I'm hitting people already." He rubbed his forehead while taking a slow breath. "You bet. Let's take him outside."

They grabbed the collar and shoulders of the unfortunate victim's insulated jacket and dragged him outside, apologizing to folks along the way about the disturbance while looking back to see if the man was still breathing. Hotel staff appeared relieved.

And when they were finished, they moved to the hotel register and addressed a quiet, smiling, thin man standing behind the register desk.

"My apologies to you, sir," Ronin huffed, as the surge of adrenaline had taken his breath away. Through the first floor windows, they saw the man outside beginning to stir.

"Not needed. Mr. Ronin, isn't it?" Ronin continued to scratch his name into the register. "I've got a room overlooking the street if you ... if you're expecting more trouble ..."

Ronin interrupted. "What makes you say that?" he inquired, looking up at the man, who might have been in his late sixties. He had the kind of wrinkles that made one think he'd spent some serious time prospecting. Large, strong, weathered hands confirmed Ronin's observation. "We're generally peaceful people, the deputy and I. Have we met?" he asked, curious why Sally Curtis wasn't behind the desk.

Sally was a bar maid and manager at the hotel. On occasion that he'd happen by "the big little," as he liked to call Reno, as it was larger than many of the towns he had been to but still quite quaint, Ronin had spent an evening or two talking with Sally about life's deeper mysteries. Anything more than an evening or two and he became uncomfortable. But she helped to pass the evenings when Ronin was in town, never the nights. Sally was a constant source of information when he was tracking a man.

"We have not, sir. I'm the owner's father, just in from Sacramento. My son has put me to work." Both smiled, an awkward smile that said they'd both be working into their sixties, though Ronin had a few more years to go to match the innkeeper's age.

"Well, congratulations to you," Ronin replied. "We'd like to get some supper if it's not too late. Are you still serving in the dayroom?"

"We are not, sir. But there's plenty to go around in the saloon."

He looked at Dustsucker, who was already halfway up the stairs to stow his gear. Dustsucker nodded. "That will be fine," Ronin continued. "Say, do you know if Sally Curtis is working there tonight?"

The man looked up, turning the registration book back into place. "She is, Mr. Ronin. She works there pretty much every night, after she finishes here. Shall I tell her you're in town?"

"I'd rather you didn't. I'd like to surprise her," Ronin called over his left shoulder, lifting the bag and heading up to their room on the second floor. He noted the man they had removed from the hotel's day room was up and headed across the street to the saloon.

"We'll be headed there as soon as we put a few things away."

Chapter 41

RENO SALOON

Ronin settled down into a chair next to the piano player. While he wasn't a big fan of piano music, he had noticed in his travels that few people will shoot a good piano player, or even a bad one if he's attached to his instrument. Folks hadn't spent enough time in church, he figured—otherwise they'd be shooting more musicians. The former reverend smiled as he leaned back in his chair to observe.

Dustsucker had stumbled upon a friend by the door and, tossing his first beer backward, had already signaled the barkeep for a couple more. He seemed to be catching up on old times.

Across the room, a handful of men leaned up against the bar listening to a conversation between a well-oiled codger and a perky but unimpressed barmaid. A dozen or more men were gathered at tables with wives or mistresses enjoying a variety of liberties and libations.

No one seemed particularly agitated. And nobody had paid peculiar attention to them entering the saloon, other than a few who stared at Dustsucker's unusual girth. Given that it wasn't the fat man's first rodeo, he ignored all but the most ignorant of glances his way.

"Jesus, God!" Sally Curtis yelled from across the room. Seated on an out-of-work freighter in such a way as to gently pass the evening, Ronin's long-time female friend began bouncing up and down, clearly pleased by his unexpected appearance at the Lake House Saloon.

She tumbled out of the man's lap at about the same time the man wheezed "stop bouncing" and, bounding across the floor, jumped full up on to the table and slid into the former reverend's lap. "Jesus, Sally. You know I don't want that," he hissed.

"You do want that, William," Sally teased. "You just don't want that now!" Sally laughed, straddling the ex-reverend. She looked into his eyes and, placing a hand on each side of his face, said "I miss you."

"Well, I miss you too," Ronin said, taking her hands and placing them into her lap, which he then noticed was uncomfortably close to his own. Grabbing her around the waist, he lifted her up on to the table and asked, "Can I can get you a chair?"

Sally burped a couple of guffaws, laughing like a female tenor in a Baptist church choir, and shouted to the bar, "Billy get this man a couple of beers. I'm buying!" Every head didn't turn, but nearly every body did as a free beer on a Monday night was rare indeed, not that Sally intended to buy beer for the whole house.

Mondays were generally too slow to see free beer, though Ronin was of the opinion that if such kindnesses were kindled, samples on a slow night might be better than free beer on a busy night to increase the saloon's traffic. At least that was how he'd tended his church.

Though it had been a long time, the bigger religious festivals of the church year, such as Christmas or Easter, caused people to come a far bit to be part of things, sometimes as much as a couple of hours or so. The whole point of growing the Wichita Episcopal mission, it seemed to him, was multiplying such events, though his bishop didn't always see things that way.

He couldn't remember how many religious holidays the ancient Hebrews had—Sally's bloomers being so close to his own wasn't helping his memory, and he hadn't been reading his Bible like he used to—but he figured it was near to a dozen. And throwing free food or liquor at folks to attend church didn't seem entirely inappropriate if people were going to drink and eat anyway.

Ronin kicked a chair out from the table and gently nudged his female friend toward it as the swelling in his pants grew. "I'm moving. I'm moving," she protested, though both of them knew the protesting was in fun.

Sitting in the chair, but still close enough that he could smell her perfume, she smoothed the wrinkles out her dress, what there was of it. "How you doing Ronin?" Sally asked, nodding her head toward the door. "That Dustsucker with you? He's fatter than I remember him," she said.

"Maybe so, Sally. And we're doing fine, though we're mighty hungry and anxious to get started in the morning. Know anything about ..."

Sally interrupted, "And bring a couple of steaks," she yelled, causing Bill the bar man to immediately turn around and head back toward the kitchen. "You're looking for some people?" she asked, pausing to apologize. "I didn't mean to interrupt."

"We are. But first, tell me how you are."

One of the reasons people liked W. W. Ronin was that he was kind. Say what you want to say about religious doctrines and dogmas, the ex-Episcopal preacher typically told his friends when they were curious as to why he had left the church, nobody argues about kindness. If the whole point of religion was compassion for people different than oneself, it didn't make much sense to argue the fine points about being Protestant or Catholic.

"I'm good. Business has been good. We moved everything out of the dayroom to the saloon, except for breakfast," Sally said. "Folks just don't want to eat breakfast around the smell of stale beer and whiskey, though it never bothered me."

"No, I don't guess that they do," he replied. "I've gotten so that I hate to eat indoors, unless it's raining."

"Still figuring out what it means to be a cowboy, aren't you?" Sally interrupted, laughing. God, he loved how she laughed. "What's with the leg, Ronin? I noticed you limping."

"Oh this," he said tapping on his left leg. "I broke it when the back of the Carson City jail blew up. Hear of it?"

"Of course."

"Well, I happened to step through the door a moment or so after the cellblock blew and stepped right into a hole in what used to be the floor. One of the prisoners ploughed into me and the unfortunate upshot was this broken leg."

"Hmmm..." Sally said, trying to remember something. "Seems like I heard that story a day or so ago. From a big guy," she said, picking up her pace. "A real big guy, I remember. And not all that smart, if you ask me."

"It sounds like we've headed in the right direction then." He looked at Sally. He was sorry it had never turned into anything else, though he wondered if he could ever be with a woman who had been with so many. There were moments in his life he wished there was someone other than Dustsucker to partner with. Emma had stirred the same thoughts in him, though he hurt a bit more when he thought of her and didn't quite understand what that meant. "Listen Sally. I'm going to need some time with that big guy by the door tonight over supper. If you're around later, I'd sure like to catch up with you."

"Well, of course," she said. She hesitated a moment before continuing. "Are we talking down here," she asked, gesturing toward the bar, or ..." And looking up toward the rooms, asked carefully, "somewhere else?"

Ronin hesitated. It had been a long time. Picking up his beer, he barely whispered the words, "I'm sorry Sally. I didn't mean to mislead you."

"Nah," she said, "I was just kidding."

He smiled gently, placing his hand upon hers. He wondered what it would be like to hold a real live woman in his arms again, not just lay with one. But hold her in the way a man holds a woman when he wants to possess her. He took a deep breath. Sally noticed and smiled. "I'm talking here, at the table or bar. I've missed you these last couple of months, while I was recuperating at the Gospel Mission in Carson City. And I want to catch up."

"You sweet on Emma?" Sally asked.

"You've met Emma?" he asked, surprised.

"Ronin, I've met everybody in these parts, or know people who have. But don't you worry. Whatever's good with you is good with me, and I'd like it to be good with you."

Ronin smiled and waved to his friend Dustsucker.

"See about those steaks then, would you? We've got some plans to make. And if you happen to see the U.S. Marshal tonight, mind sending him over to the piano as well?"

"No problem."

Sally Curtis got up, straightened her skirt if you could call it that, and walked rhythmically toward the bar. She looked over her shoulders and caught Ronin's glance.

"Hey, I didn't say I wasn't still looking," he shouted after her, tearing his eyes away from her hips and legs.

"Never heard of a man who wasn't still looking," she laughed as she headed back to the kitchen.

Chapter 42

DAYLIGHT

It was almost daylight when Ash knocked on their hotel door. "Dustsucker! Ronin!" Ash looked at his friend Thomas E. Kelly, a former lawman in Virginia City, to see if he heard anything. Kelly shook his head no and tried the door. Ash spoke again, knocking a little more loudly. "You guys up?"

Funny how he couldn't keep a certain district marshal from disturbing his sleep, Ronin thought as he stirred. He wiped the nighttime crud from his eyes. "Give us a minute, would you?" He grabbed his pants from the chair next to the bed and pulled them on, one leg at a time. Slipping his boots on, Ronin walked to the door.

When he was younger he used to experiment with his morning habits. He had learned to comb his hair while sitting in the outhouse, had figured out how to put his shirt and jacket on do it all simultaneously and concluded it all had to do with how they were taken off. He had practiced jumping into his pants for a time, but had ripped a few pairs along the way and had a hard time explaining the value to his mother. It exercised both of his legs, he said, and was a very efficient way to get going in the morning, especially if shoes weren't needed. He wasn't disappointed that his mother didn't see the up-side to the trick, as he had nearly fallen out his bedroom window a couple of times while attempting it.

Fastening his suspenders, he noticed that Dustuscker hadn't moved at all after the knocking and wondered just how lazy his friend actually was, given that this was the first time they had shared an inside room and that inner values were all too often dictated by outer disciplines.

Despite his taking exception to Emma's elaborate commentary on the sin of gluttony, he liked to keep an eye on such things. Even if he wasn't all that religious anymore, whatever that meant, he liked to keep a tidy inner life and expected the people around him to do something of the same. When he'd find himself obsessing over it, he'd remind himself that the seven deadly sins were pretty much an arbitrary list and that what was important to him likely wasn't all that important to another.

He'd argued with Emma once that the seven deadly sins weren't even in the Bible. "If you're serious about finding a list of things one should avoid, you might read the *Book of Proverbs,* he said, pointing about midway in the big book she always had sitting in her front room. "Right after the Psalms," he said, beginning to turn the pages in what he assumed was a heavy family Bible.

"Yes," she'd replied. "Proverbs 6:16 through 19," she added, reciting each verse without error. "A proud look, a lying tongue, hands that shed innocent blood, a heart that devises wicked plots, feet that are swift to run into mischief, a deceitful witness that uttereth lies and him that soweth discord among the brethren."

Despite his years of seminary classes, and years more teaching the Bible to Episcopalians, in the three months he stayed at the mission, Emma always bested him. He wondered why she hadn't been a preacher. The Second Great Awakening had put more than one hundred women on the street, holding meetings from one end of the country to another. He remembered hearing of Harriet Livermore, the daughter of a congressman and the grand-daughter of a senator, who had been heard by more than a thousand people in congress in 1827. He had never aspired to such crowds, but didn't know why Emma hadn't. Emma would have been one of the better preachers he had ever heard, though he was pretty positive he didn't want a preacher for a girlfriend or wife.

Looking at Dustsucker, who still hadn't stirred, he wondered why he was thinking about her. He opened the door.

"Marshal Ash, I presume?" he said. He didn't recognize the man standing next to him.

"Funny, Ronin. Real funny." Ash didn't look happy. "We've been up all night ridin' and you're doing imitations of 'Dr. David Livingstone?' Yep, you're a real funny guy," the marshal said, pushing past him, stopping to stare at Dustsucker, still very much asleep with his mouth hanging open.

Ronin placed his hand on Ash's friend's chest. "And you are?" he asked, stepping back into the doorway.

"I'm sorry Ronin, that's Thomas Kelly, my deputy. Kelly's was police chief and sheriff in Virginia City for a couple of terms. Your boys snagged him with bullet a couple of weeks back and stole his side arm. I thought it might be handy to have him along."

"My apologies, deputy," Ronin said, stepping aside.

"Not needed," Kelly muttered, looking at Slade asleep in the bed. "Don't know that I've ever seen him awake," he said to Ronin, who was still standing by the door. "Known him long?"

"Long enough that we're friends, Kelly. I've yet to get to know you, if you know what I'm saying," Ronin smiled, holding his glance.

"Knock it off boys," Ash said, swatting Slade's feet with his hat. "Kelly is a good family man, and handy with a gun. Nothing else needs to be said."

Ronin smiled again. Turning toward Ash, who was preparing to swat his friend's face given that hitting his feet hadn't done it, he corrected the marshal's earlier accusation. "It was actually Stanley that I was imitating, though I've got to tell you, I'm impressed that you read *The New York Times*."

"Yeah, well we're not all ignorant in these parts," Ash responded, kicking at Slade's bed instead. "A few of us actually read. What the hell is going on with him?" he asked, realizing that his hitting and kicking hadn't stirred his the Ormsby County deputy.

"I suspect he's sleeping," Ronin said.

Ash glared. "Well, wake him up. I want to know what's happening, and then we want to get some sleep. Since you've had all evening to play, I'm hoping you know something worth reporting."

Ronin winced. He didn't like the tone. It took him right back to Wichita.

A half-hour later, the three of them gathered downstairs in the hotel day room for breakfast. Dustsucker was still buttoning up his shirt, having slept in his long underwear. There was a little bit of last night's dinner still on his collar.

"Morning, Tom. Morning Augustus," Dustsucker said yawning. "Sorry to keep you guys up."

Manners came easy to the lawman. Big boys learn to apologize early on, given they tend to bump into things more than smaller people do.

"Good morning, deputy. No, it's me who's sorry. I just needed some coffee, I'm afraid. We're sitting here talking about the time Mryon Lake stood on the bridge there with his six-shooter, still demanding his toll."

"That's a long time ago, Augustus. Were you there?"

"Nah, a constable or two ran him off as I remember. Did you know he was making $2,500 a day with that thing? County closed him down a couple of years ago, though I can't remember when. It didn't go well when they did."

"I heard it was the city," Dustsucker said. "His license ran out, as did his luck with his wife and a bunch of other things. Bridge tolls tallied to about $100,000 a year, some say," he added, unable to sense where the conversation was going.

"Sure beats what I made as a sheriff," Kelly replied.

"Me, too," Ash added, "or the four dollars a day I pay laborers to work my mine."

Ronin gestured toward a server, looking around the room for Sally and recognizing she must have gotten a sleeper to stay the night. An overnight guest probably paid handsomely for the privilege, he thought, having no personal experience with Sally's profession. "Coffee for both of us, please. And some eggs and some …"

"Not some," Dustsucker laughed, knowing that he was interrupting, "a lot of bacon. No bacon? We'll take sausage." He turned to his friends, who were both smiling. "Gotta get my meat," he explained.

"How was your ride?" Ronin asked the marshal.

"It was a horse," he replied, apparently no friend to his mount. "I'm tired, so I want to know about our guys. Are they here?"

"I think so," Dustsucker said. "Ronin heard from the gal at the bar that Clem Crestwell had been in the night before last, talking about the explosion a couple of months back at the Carson City jail. And there was some mention of a house in Washoe City. The older Crestwell doesn't travel without the younger, so we figure Remy is here as well."

"And where the Crestwells are, the Clancys might be also," Ash smiled, touching the back of his head. "This might be a lucky trip after all."

Chapter 43

PLEASANT VALLEY

The next morning, the four riders discovered that a cold white mist had settled into the Washoe Valley, coating cottonwood and pine trees with a delicate frost. It was not unlike the Pennsylvania ice storms Ronin remembered as a kid. He was about to comment when Dustsucker spoke first.

"The Indians call this 'Poco Mist,'" he said. "It means 'death' or something like that."

Ronin looked at Ash, who nodded back. Ronin whispered, "Geez, that's not a good sign." Ash ignored him.

The four raised their kerchiefs to cover their mouths and to force warm air into their lungs. It wasn't that long after Christmas, though Ronin couldn't remember exactly how many days it had been. While he didn't like the cold, the beauty of the valley was something he simply would never get used to. A long yellow narrow plain, compared to places he had ridden in Iowa, Kansas and parts south. Framed by the towering green Sierra mountains on the right and the brownish, tree-shorn Virginia foothills on the left and a shallow blue, frozen lake a few miles ahead, it was beautiful.

"You know, there wasn't a chance this town was going to survive," Ash remarked as they headed out of town.

"Reno?" Ronin asked, his revelry interrupted and not quite understanding the marshal's point.

"Washoe City, Ronin," Slade piped in. "Remember the buildings we passed in the valley, just south of the tall stand of timber?" Ronin nodded, not having realized that they had been looking at a town site when they passed by a couple of broken down fences and some stone buildings a couple of days ago. Winding through Pleasant Valley, they pointed their horses west toward the mountain. Washoe City was just a mile or so away. "There are still a few buildings standing, though we didn't see them."

The sun was beginning to crest the Virginia range when what remained of the town came into view. Clearly, Washoe City had seen better years. A small explosion of activity had occurred in the early sixties. Saw mills were constructed at the foot of the mountains so as to accommodate Virginia City's need for timber. When the trees played out, the town's population took to building smelters, supporting the numerous mining claims in the area. A couple of thousand people lived there at one point.

Dustsucker spoke quietly about the stores, churches, saloons and a newspaper that had literally blown away in the nine or ten years after the county seat had been moved to Reno and a healthy railroad trade had developed between Virginia City and its neighboring cities north and south.

Ronin had once risked his ministerial position by warning the members of his parish about the kind of people who would come with the railroads. But it hadn't occurred to him at the time that it wasn't the passing of rural life that folks needed to worry about. Rather, being passed over by the railroad might be the worst of circumstances a small town might face. Given that ore was now being shipped by rail uninterrupted to factories and cities all over the United States, little towns like Washoe City didn't have a chance.

"We'll unsaddle here," Ash said, pointing to a stone building that appeared to have some occupants. A few other houses and a couple of other buildings, well worn by the ebbing of Nevada's golden age, sat to the east. Ash tethered his horse and headed toward the door. Dustsucker stayed behind as Ronin reached for his rifle. Dustsucker shook his head. "Ash says these folks are friendly, Ronin. The marshal said something about knowing some skins in the valley and stopping there first."

The door opened and out walked an old Indian. Hunched over and wrinkled as if he was weathering a difficult winter, the Washoe man wore a bowler hat, a faded blue corduroy shirt, a woolen vest and manufactured tan pants. Dressed like a white man, he didn't seem any the better for it.

"Howdy, stranger," the old man said smiling. "What brings you to my door?"

"Come on, Happy Hands. You know this isn't your house. We've talked about that." A young boy peered out the window, perhaps 12 years old. The man met his glance and frowned. The boy disappeared.

Happy Hands and his son Little Wolf had lived on the edge of the Washoe Indian colony for years, squatting in empty buildings and living apart from the rest of the tribe. A spouse he couldn't get along with was explanation enough. To be frank, it was none of Ash's business—it was a civil matter, in his mind, and there were too few officers in Washoe County to care about something so common—and the fact is, he liked the man and his boy. He could also understand why some folks would want to live alone.

Dustsucker and Ronin thought they recognized the boy, but as soon as he appeared, he was gone and their attention was focused on the Indian at the door. The two of them caught only every other word or so as Ash was conversing so quietly and quickly. An abrupt nod on both men's parts ended it. Ash pressed a silver coin into the Indian's hands before he turned and walked toward the horses.

"Happy Hands, I get it," Ronin said to his friend.

The marshal smiled briefly. "The Indian says that five white men were here yesterday, but rode out last night toward Reno. One of them was unusually large. He said 'there was little light in him,' meaning I think, that he wasn't the brightest torch in the mine."

"So the Crestwells were here last night?" Ronin asked without waiting for a reply. "Given there were five men, we can safely assume the Clancys are here also."

"Well, I can't say for sure, but it certainly sounds like it," Ash said, putting a foot into his stirrup. "I'm thinking that the two of you should ride back. Happy Hands says there's a rogue band of Paiute north of Reno that we might want to check them out. I'll stay here and see if I can't pick up some tracks, in the event not everyone went to Reno."

Ronin interrupted, "All of the Paiute north of Reno are rogue. That's no help."

Dustsucker weighed in. "Listen Augustus, you're not making any sense at all. There's five of them and just two of you! There's no reason to divide ourselves. You want to do a little detective work, send your deputy to talk to the Paiutes."

"Paul Clancy shot me," Kelly growled in response, "and took a hand gun I've carried for nearly a dozen years. I'm going to see Paul Clancy dead, whether Ash likes it or not. I'm not riding out after any Indians."

Ronin hated hearing grown men talk of killing so easily, particularly a lawman, or someone who used to be a lawman.

"Dustsucker's right," Ronin said, lifting himself up on to his horse. Jackson began pulling toward Reno as if he already knew the outcome of the conversation. "We started this together, we'll finish this together. We can take a quick ride around to see what we can see, and then head back. The point is to catch up to these bastards, because they may know already where the children are."

Dustsucker and Ronin waited for Ash response.

"That may make better sense," the marshal said, spitting at the ground and looking up at his deputy. "Because if Clancy's alone, any one of us might kill him before we learn anything. You good with that Kelly?"

"Yup," Ash's deputy nodded, glaring at Ronin.

"Is there any possibility that we might achieve a lawful arrest instead?" Dustsucker wondered out loud, stating the obvious protocol and sounding a little bit officious.

His question went unanswered.

Chapter 44

SHOOT OUT

They hadn't been back even an hour when the man Ronin had thrown out of the dayroom the evening prior came knocking on their door. Ash startled first and, not recognizing the man, rose to the backside of the door, drawing his gun. Kelly stood up.

"Mr. Ronin! Mr. Dustsucker!" the voice inquired. Opening the door, Ronin pulled the man through the doorway and bounced him on to the bed. "This behavior of yours isn't any more appropriate tonight than it was last night," he began.

"I'm not doing nothin'," the man said, surprised that he had been propelled a second time through a door by someone he was just getting to know. "Really, I'm thinkin' only of you."

"Continue," Dustsucker said as Ronin, noting the man wasn't armed, shut the door and sat down in a leather wingback chair by the room's windows. He wasn't saying anything. Ash and Kelly continued to stand by the door. Everyone was anxious.

"This morning, my gal Sal told me that you were looking for two sets of brothers, one of the brothers a rather big boy."

"My gal, Sal?" Ronin exclaimed, getting out of his chair. Dustsucker shot him a glance that said 'not now.' Ronin shrugged his shoulders and sat back down. "Never mind, please go on."

"She said that one of the men was pretty large and not all that bright. She said also that they were in some sort of trouble." Looking around the room, he added, "I'm just hoping I'm not in trouble, too." He stared directly at the Ash, who was still standing by the door with his gun pointed at him.

What an odd guy, Ronin thought. "We are looking for some men," he said, "three brothers on one side, two of them are kind of unruly. Two brothers on the other side, the smaller of the two is a loud-mouthed jackass. His brother is a big, dopey guy. Both families can be sort of rough."

"You've seen these men?" Ash asked, holstering his gun and walking toward the bed. The man recoiled slightly as if he was afraid he was going to be hit.

"No, I've not seen them. I'm seeing them!" The man pointed anxiously past Ronin, down to the street where five men were heading into the hotel saloon.

Ash and Kelly pushed toward the door but were stopped by Dustsucker, who was still struggling to keep things decent and in order. "Whoa, whoa!" he shouted. The two men stepped back from the door with their hands in the air as Ronin stood.

"What?"

"You boys know very well what I'm talking about," said Dustsucker, pushing at Ash and Kelly. The two stumbled backward. When they regained their balance, their hands were on their hips. "I'm not one to shit in someone's breakfast, if you'll pardon the phrase. I don't have a problem with arresting these men. Two of them took an unauthorized hike from a formerly perfectly good jail. I'm not about to forget that. And the other three ought to be arrested for suspicion of whatever ..."

"Suspicion, my ass," Ash interrupted energetically.

"Now hold on Augustus, I'm not finished. You're the U.S. Marshal, so you can do what you want and call it what you will: conspiracy to commit a felony, interference with a police officer, attempted murder, whatever. I don't care ..."

Dustsucker looked at all three men, and waited until each of them met his eyes. "But I will not sit comfortably with our killing five men in Reno, for whatever reason, without our first talking to a local officer."

"I don't need no officer, Slade," Ash said snarling.

"I know you don't, Augustus, I'm just sayin'..."

"Well, that's the difference between you and me," Ronin interrupted, looking out the window. "Guilty's guilty, my friend. And these boys are itching more than most to meet their maker. Jesus, man! They bought and sold Indians to work in a mine or God knows what." He took a breath. "They broke out of your perfectly good jail, as you call it, winged Kelly here while trying to kill him and they've tried to kill me a couple of times. The Clancys? Who gives a shit? Ash's authority is good enough for me. He needs our help, and no part-time Reno fireman or constable is going to be of much help, anyway. Get out of the way."

Dustsucker stepped aside. An angry ex-priest wasn't someone he wanted to wrestle with, even if he was a couple of hundred pounds lighter. And the marshal was the marshal.

He put hand on his friend's arm. "Ronin, I'm just saying. Let me go over to the courthouse while you guys keep an eye on the saloon doors. I'll grab a couple deputies and head your way. And we'll do it all nice and legal like."

"Good enough," Ronin sighed. "We'll wait a few minutes here by the window while you take whatever professional steps you need to take to make sure we don't kill these sons of bitches."

Dustsucker started headed down the stairs and into the street toward the new courthouse. He fast-walked past buildings that had at one time been a crazy mix of buildings and tens along the Truckee River, with barely a promise that someday a railroad, and the commerce and manufacturing that would come with it, would transform everything.

Wheezing because of the exertion, and anxious that Ronin, Ash and Kelly wouldn't wait long enough for him to return with a couple of Washoe County deputies, he thought about Myron Lake's hope to keep things civilized near the hotel that he had built. Wife-beater or not, he had built a magnificent city, despite the criminals and lesser-do-wells who sometimes lived there.

He was heading up the courthouse steps when Ronin grabbed the doorknob of their room and pulled the door open.

He had counted to ten, before grabbing his gun belt and rifle, about the time it took for the marshal to look at his deputy and wonder why everybody was waiting. A disciplined priest, he had found that counting usually cleared his mind. "Ash," he glared, "are you guys coming with me? Or are you going to stand by the window and grow old?"

"I'm right behind you, friend. I was wondering how long you were going to stand there praying," Augustus Ash responded.

"I wasn't praying," Ronin said, while loading six cartridges into each of his Colts and tucking them into his belt.

"Well, then let's get this done, then."

W. W. Ronin, Marshal Augustus Ash and his deputy Thomas Kelly ran down the hotel's inside staircase, skipping two or three steps at a time. They hit the hotel door at a run and were instantly out on the street just as the saloon doors across the street opened their way.

A huge hulk of a man stood between the double doors, his hands straight out to his side, forming a large, Latin cross.

"What the fuck?" Clem Crestwell shouted. His little brother Remy started hopping like a jumping bean, clearing his older brother's shoulders so as to see what his brother was looking at. It was on the second or third jump that Remy yelled out in a shrill voice, "Hey, ladies!" He began giggling.

Slade, who was already in the courthouse's doorway, turned to see what was happening. "Shit!" Out of breath and at an angle to the saloon, he instantly recognized the Crestwells, and peering past the two of them still standing in the doorway, saw the Clancys there as well. He tried shouting to warn his friends, but all that came out of his mouth were squeaks. He doubled over to catch his breath.

They didn't need warning. Ash grabbed his rifle from his horse, and quick-stepping to his right began to make his way south along the hotel sidewalk in order to clear the hotel windows.

Ronin and Kelly grabbed their Winchesters and began walking straight toward the saloon doorway.

Clem Crestwell broke free of his brother and drew his Remington revolver. "Die, you fucker!" the big man screamed at Ronin, pushing his way through a pack of men caught on the sidewalk in-between. Ronin paused, as there were dozens of people in the street. He lifted his rifle to a high-ready position, but held it there, bobbing his head right and then left, like a boxer on point. With every step, it seemed hapless people were tripping, falling, or being flung into the vomitus of tents, poles, boxes and buildings that had become Myron Lake's community. Angry sounds turned into hurting wails. It was the wailing that kept Ronin's sight fixed on the man. It was the sound of surprised, hurting, wailing men and women, caught in a mix they didn't make, that kept Ronin focused.

The giant man had his eyes fixed too, on the gunslinger with a Bible in his vest who had driven his ass through a doorway and into the wall at his favorite saloon. The angry man who had put his head into the broken cement floor of the Carson City jail when the walls came tumbling down, setting all of the prisoners free. The bounty hunter who had caused him to leave his shoes behind, making him live barefoot for nearly a week in the mud and excrement of the Clancys' underground hideaway. He kept his eyes forward, pushing straight ahead into the street, despite the increasingly broad swath of people still standing between him and his prey.

It took Ronin a few moments to realize that the denser of the two Crestwell brothers had his eyes also fixed on him. Slade caught up to the Crestwells on an irregular patch of rock and grass in the middle of a now very dangerous Reno street.

"Move left," he yelled to the ex-preacher, as a man walking diagonally had at least half a chance of not getting shot by a man heading straight for him.

Ronin pushed a large man on his left out of the way, too focused to see anything around him. Dustsucker stumbled, his belly still full from an otherwise outstanding evening. They had gone out for Basque food. And once he got started—given the rigors of the trail, his appetite and the fact that fine food only made its appearance on his plate every few days or so—he didn't stop, finishing the meal with multiple glasses of whatever. Beer was easy. Wine was better. Whiskey was best. He had probably downed it all.

When Ronin shoved him, and Carson City's finest stumbled sideways, Dustsucker barely caught himself. "What the hell?" he exclaimed, his left hand reaching to grab a hitching post, then a horse trough, and finally a wooden sign reading "Lake's Crossing," set firmly in a grassy knoll the middle of the street. "What the hell?" he yelled to his friend again, though the words were hardly audible above the hurting and angry voices circling around him, and Ronin hadn't heard any of it..

"Die, you fucker!" the big man screamed. Another man stumbled on Ronin's right, Ronin caught a glint of a badge as the man felt to one knee. Kelly, he remembered. A man to Ronin's right was yelling at him, but he couldn't understand any of his words, and he wasn't about to stop.

He tried desperately to clear his head, opening his eyes wide so as to intensify his alertness, as he had done so many times before when engaged in combat as a cavalryman. Suddenly, he knew everything that was happening around him. He could see everything and everyone, and particularly the large, threatening man who was running toward him, shooting.

He tossed his Yellow Boy into his left hand, and grabbing his Colt Peacemaker, thumbed the hammer twice. "Die, you son of a bitch," he yelled, "I thought you were already dead!"

Chapter 45

VIRGINIA STREET

Kneeling in the middle of the street, U.S. Marshal Augustus Ash steadied himself, his Winchester Model 1873 firmly welded to his cheek. He chambered a .44-40 cartridge into his carbine—the same cartridge he used in his Colt sidearm—and quieting his breathing, drew a bead on Clem Crestwell, who was shooting at Ronin from just a few feet away.

His sight picture clear, he fired one 200-grain piece of lead into the man's forehead. Forty grains of black powder blew the slug out of his rifle at over a thousand feet per second, exploding the back of Clem Crestwell's hat, spraying the side of the building with brains and blood. Crestwell, who Ronin had once sidekicked through an oak door frame at the Globe Saloon, the man who Ronin had once pile-driven into the rubble which had become the door of the Carson City jail was now dead, even before he hit the ground.

The marshal levered a second cartridge into his gun. Without removing the rifle from his cheek, he turned his 20-inch carbine toward Patrick Clancy next. The youngest of the brothers, whom he had arrested in Virginia City for beating a man to death in order to rob him of his boots, had let go of his horse. Holding his revolver out to one side, Patrick was motioning his brothers Peter and Paul to take a position north of the saloon doorway behind a stack of barrels, near a street that led to the Methodist church.

Ash's elbow rested on his left knee, his Winchester firmly fitted into the pocket of his shoulder. He bent slightly forward and fired a second and then third round into the younger Crestwell, center of mass. Patrick grabbed his chest and shouted "They killed me!" before falling backward into the building, his eyes fixed and his mouth agape. His brothers stopped in the saloon doorway without realizing they were standing in a tunnel of death.

Ronin re-holstered his Colt and swung his Yellow Boy toward the Clancys, who were now framed by the saloon doorway. Thomas Kelly, to his left, raised his rifle as well, slamming two .44 caliber slugs into the door frame, just missing Paul Clancy's head. Both brothers immediately crouched and returned fire, missing Ronin and Kelly but sending Dustsucker stumbling toward the buildings in order to find cover.

Dustsucker fired two 10-gauge loads of buckshot toward the doorway as he ran, deliberately shooting into the street so as to kick dirt and stones up into the air. A bullet from the doorway tore into his right side, spinning him backward and throwing him onto the wooden sidewalk, then against the Lake's House saloon.

The Clancys were now in a cross-fire. Marshal Ash was still on his knee, aiming from the southwest. And Dustsucker, collapsed against the building to the north, was quickly reloading. Paul Clancy grabbed for his brother Peter with his left hand and fell back into the saloon.

"Holy shit," he said to Peter, who grabbed at a chair as he brother yanked him away from the door and onto the saloon floor. "They've killed Patrick!" he repeated twice. Sobbing, he checked his gun, loading a cartridge from his belt. Hotel patrons scattered out the back and began running a couple of blocks north toward the Methodist church.

Ronin turned to his left, allowing him a quick glance at Ash and Kelly, who were loading their guns. "You okay?" he asked. They nodded.

Pivoting to his right, he located Dustsucker, who was leaning up against the outside of the saloon, obviously hurting and crawling to gain additional cover. "Guess I shouldn't have moved, right?" the portly deputy sheriff yelled to his friend.

"None of us should have left the hotel," Ronin laughed. "We could have just leaned out the window and killed the sons of bitches." He moved to a prone position behind a couple of rocks by the hitching post and horse trough Dustsucker had grabbed earlier. Keeping his eyes focused on the doorway, he scanned the street trying to locate Remy Crestwell, who was now hiding behind the very stack of barrels Patrick had motioned his brothers toward when Ash shot him in the head.

Dustsucker nodded. Grimacing, he reached for his wound with his right hand. He tore his shirt away and satisfied himself that the son of a bitch who had shot him hadn't found a lung or a liver. Then rolling to his side, he leveled the scatter gun again, this time bracing it against his hip. He had it aimed toward the doorway, and beyond it the barrels, when the younger Crestwell stood up.

Thumbing the second hammer, he slip-cocked a lethal load of lead shot that hit the younger brother, shattering Remy's pelvis and severing his femoral artery. Stumbling a good seven feet or so, the younger brother landed in a horse trough and began to scream.

Remy's eyes were as wide as silver dollars, and seeing only death in his immediate future, he threw both arms straight up. One firearm flew to the saloon's second floor balcony, where it bounced harmlessly against a sign which pointed to the hotel and read, "Commodious Rooms, Pleasant Views, Good Table, Travelers and Commercial Gentlemen Welcome." The other firearm spun helplessly around the Crestwell's left forefinger.

"No, no, no!" he stuttered. Dustsucker drew his Colt, cocked and clicked it. He clicked it again. He was out. And as soon as he knew, Crestwell knew. Ronin and Ash looked up as they were reloading.

Remy's eyes narrowed. "You're empty, old man," he laughed, bending at his waist like a belligerent donkey, crimson-colored blood and water splashing everywhere.

"Empty, my ass!," Dustsucker returned, pushing two more 44-caliber cartridges into his gun, slamming the loading gate shut against his pants and rolling the Colt's still warm cylinder on his sleeve as Ronin, Ash and Kelly took aim. "Empty, my ass," he drawled, slap-cocking two loads into the smaller Crestwell brother's chest as multiple other charges exploded into Remy's neck and brain. Both of the brothers now lay dead.

There was silence on the street.

Ronin rolled onto his back to reload. Ash and Kelly were up on their feet, heading toward the saloon. Three men were dead. Two Crestwells and one Clancy. And his wounded friend, Dustsucker was lying on the boardwalk, laughing.

Chapter 46

THE METHODIST CHURCH

Ash hit the front door of the saloon running. Expecting the worst, he ran heavy into the east end of the saloon and, twisting to his right, once through the doors, slammed into the bar. Kelly turned the other way, crouching along a series of tables until he came to the far wall. Both men stilled their breathing and sat there listening.

Hearing nothing and seeing no movement other than their own in the saloon's still-intact front window, Kelly raised his Winchester to his shoulder and signaled to Ash, who immediately rolled into a prone position behind the bar. With nothing to react to, the two stood up and scanned the saloon's interior. It was empty.

"Ronin!" he yelled, "anything on the street?"

"Nothing out here!" answered Ronin, who was considering whether it was safe to stand. He was just beginning to move when he heard Ash yelling from the saloon. "I think I see some movement up toward the church on Sierra Street, but I can't tell you for sure!" he shouted.

He looked over toward Dustsucker, who had propped himself up against the saloon, his handgun and double barrel 10-gauge shotgun sitting on the boardwalk to his right. He was dabbing at a hole in his side that looked like it had just missed his liver.

"We're good in here," Ash yelled back, walking toward the saloon's back door. "Check on our friend!"

Ronin stood up, and brushing the dirt and gravel from his shirt and pants, called out. "Slade, how bad are you hit?"

"Shit, I've been shot worse," Dustsucker replied. Ronin hurried over, and kneeling down beside him, took a look. He met Ash's eyes looking through the saloon glass.

Ronin pulled his friend's hand away from his body and said, "Don't touch it. Let me see." A chunk of flesh was missing from Slade's side. As no exit wound was seen, Ronin wondered if Dustsucker's extra girth had been his friend in this case. He grabbed a kerchief from his pants pocket and applied it directly to the hole with the heel of his hand. Dustsucker winced.

"Hold it here. Press on it hard. I'm going to try to get you some ice to slow the bleeding. Then we're going to get you to a doctor. I'll be right back."

Ronin stood up carefully, attempting to avoid the window glass in the event that a shooter was still inside the saloon. He drew his strong-side 4" Colt, peeked around the door and then entered. Ash and Kelly were standing by the back door, which had been knocked from its hinges. Chairs and tables within the saloon were upended and scattered about. "Looks like everyone left in a hurry," he laughed, nervously. Ronin holstered his gun so as to grab some cartridges from the back of his belt. "Any sign of the Clancys?" When Ash didn't answer, he walked to the back door and repeated the same procedure he did when he came into the saloon, first peeking and then entering the street behind the saloon.

Ash and Kelly joined Ronin outside, behind a stack of barrels and boxes. They looked up the street toward the church. "Worse case, they blended in with everyone else when everyone fled," Ash observed. "Or didn't blend, I guess. But the only cover out this way is up toward the Methodist church. I imagine they could have run there."

Ronin nodded. "That's where I'd run," he said. "Folks feel kind of safe in a church, for some reason."

"Beats me," Ash quipped, "I never did." Ronin smiled. If church folk believed their Bible readings, they wouldn't either.

The Methodist church had been erected less than a dozen years ago, out of wood gleaned from the Sierras. Four million board feet a year were missing from the mountains around Lake Tahoe to provide for such buildings. The Methodists were mighty proud of their church's construction and had already begun to think about placing stained glass in the windows, or moving the building further back on the lot so as to add a brick addition. The ex-reverend wondered if the congregation might ever have imagined that their beautiful new sanctuary could harbor a couple of kidnappers.

"Well, I guess we ought to check it out," Ronin said, shifting his rifle into his left hand and touching both of his guns to make sure they were in place. "Get the Deputy some ice, would you Kelly? We can look for a doctor along the way."

Ronin strode off like a man on a mission, which in a way he was, because the bounty hunter had yet to find the children. With all the killing, he had a sour sense that things would only get worse before they got better.

Kelly nodded, and grabbing a pitcher of beer and a few pieces of ice from a cedar tub behind the bar, walked out the front of saloon toward Dustsucker. A dozen or so people had come out of the hotel but had yet to feel safe enough to cross the street.

"Don't drink all of this at once," he quipped, placing the pitcher of iced beer by Dustsucker's scattergun and six-shooter. The deputy sheriff smiled. "Put the ice on your side, underneath the kerchief. It will help to stop the bleeding," Kelly said, remembering similar experiences in the Gould and Curry Mine when he first got to the Comstock. Ice from a local pond was used to cool bodies and to cater to wounds. There were lots of them in the earlier years. "We're headed up to the church. We'll find a doctor along the way. The looky-loos across the way there should be able to help you as well!" Dustsucker nodded. "But should we see a Clancy or two," Kelly's eyes narrowed, "we might ...well, we might dilly-dally a bit."

Both men looked strained and hesitated for a minute, and then broke out into laughter. Dustsucker hadn't seen Kelly laugh before. "Be careful," he said. The former Storey County sheriff nodded and headed around the building's side.

Ronin and Ash had reached the wooden Methodist church by the time Kelly joined them. Listening first by the front doors, Ronin then peered through the church's windows. Twenty or so men and women who hadn't recently seen the inside of a church sanctuary, judging by the bottles in their hands, were huddled by the front altar. The Clancys didn't seem to be present. No one seemed to be praying.

"Ready?" Ronin asked, returning to the front doors.

"Yup," Ash replied, who looked at Kelly and then waited for Ronin to pull the doors open. The church's newest converts screamed. Ash entered first, his Winchester fitted firmly to his shoulder, his right cheek pressed against the rifle's stock. Bent slightly forward with his finger on the trigger, he turned left as Kelly turned right. Ronin then headed up the center aisle as Ash and Kelly spun around to cover the front doors they had just entered.

The Clancys weren't there.

"People, we're looking for two men," he shouted, lowering his rifle to his chest. "One tall, one not so tall. Both answer to the name of Clancy." Silence. Some of the women were crying. "We just killed one of their brothers," Ronin continued, "and two of their friends. Have any of you seen them?" he asked again. It was hard to be patient. And the U.S. Marshal badges didn't do anything to help.

Ronin didn't generally appreciate patience as a virtue. Not counting to ten, even quickly this time, he stood abruptly and fast-walked to the oldest man in the church. "You the preacher?" he demanded. The tired-looking man nodded as if to say yes.

"Not to be taken too lightly here, reverend. But which way did they go?"

The reverend's eyes looked south toward the valley. And Ronin immediately knew where the Clancys were headed. It wasn't the result of a thorough investigation. He had no corroborating witnesses. No testimony from the men who were fleeing. It was just a solid intuition. They were headed back to Washoe City, to a big house, the mansion set on the hill.

The one place they didn't bother to search.

Chapter 47

INDIAN CHILDREN

Paul Clancy dragged his middle brother up toward the Methodist church. While the people around them understood they were somehow different than them—what, with their waving their arms, shouting out orders and all—nobody stopped to consider who was who while they were fleeing the saloon.

Tables had overturned in the panic to exit. Chairs were tripped over. The back door was twisted off of its hinges when one of the saloon's occupants hit it running. No one wanted to be present when the shooting outside potentially brought victims inside. No one wanted to be there when the bodies began piling up next to the saloon's spittoons.

Paul and Peter had just lost their youngest brother Patrick. All Paul could remember was that the oldest of the Crestwell brothers, Clem, the one without boots or brains, was standing in the doorway yelling when his head exploded all over everyone. His brother Patrick was next. Paul remembered him calling to them, from outside the saloon where he had taken to waiting with the horses. And then the words he'd probably never forget if he lived to see another sun rise, "They killed me!" They killed me. Man, how would his late mother ever forgive him! He was to keep them safe, particularly her youngest.

Peter seemed to be in shock. He didn't seem to understand what was happening. Perhaps he couldn't hear with all the shooting and all? Or maybe he was scared. Whatever the case, Paul had dragged him up the street and into and out of the Methodist church before anyone really suspected that they were the ones everyone was running from.

Paul saw two horses by what he figured was the pastor's residence and decided to take them. Folks seemed happy to see them go when they hurried across the church's courtyard toward the house. They were barely saddled before they kicked the horses into a fast gallop toward Washoe City. It might take a couple of hours to get there, but if Ash and the others had tailed them to Reno, there would be no place in Reno to hide. They needed to get out of town. Maybe in Washoe City they could get their bearings and come up with a plan again. Or maybe they'd just grab the kids and sell them in San Francisco.

Peter was just beginning to realize what had happened when they arrived at Bowers Mansion. Some of the boys took their horses and ran them around back. "What the hell is going on?" a stooped over, bushy haired hand inquired.

"Ash, Kelly and that big deputy from Carson City surprised us in Reno! They've killed Patrick and the Crestwells. And I ..." Paul Clancy stuttered, something he had never done before, "... and I think they're probably headed this way!"

The hands, a half-dozen or so men from both Mexican and Paiute descent, looked at each other. They were sitting on a dozen Indian children in the main barn, as Nauman's supposed contacts in New York, Chicago and San Francisco hadn't materialized. They hadn't moved them to the Gold Hill mine either. They were screwed.

Paul Clancy drew his gun and leveled it at the hands, none of whom were heeled as they had been splitting wood for the mansion's fireplaces and stoves. "Don't anyone think that this is a time to run, boys. I'm not about to have this thing unravel over a few do-gooders. And I won't tolerate a lazy Mexican or Paiute."

He continued, figuring that they had maybe fifteen minutes or an hour, but probably not much more before Washoe constables were at their front door. "Peter, take one of the men and get everyone armed. We're about to do some shooting! And Banderas," he said looking at his most dependable man. "Get the kids,

Larry, and put them in the dining room. I want them where I can see them and use them!"

"Si senor," Banderas replied. A large Mexican man with a penchant for flashy clothing, Banderas had been bouncing around the valley—in Franktown, Washoe City and Galena—for years. When the mills closed and the towns played out, Banderas had hoped to trade on misery of property and mill owners, but ended up robbing them instead. Despite being a cruel and dishonest man, he had an affinity for the Bowers Mansion ruins simply because of the number of years he had lived there, and could likely be counted on if things got worse.

"Everybody else, when you get a rifle take a position. I want people on both roofs, someone behind the outhouse, and the rest of you by the woodpiles and livery. If we have visitors, they're either going to come up the front steps or the rear conservatory. Peter, when you're done giving out the rifles, join me here in the front room."

The elder Clancy brother crumpled into a worn brown leather club chair, sitting by the front room's windows. He could see across the Washoe Valley, where a carpet of gray sagebrush led to snowy foothills supporting Gold Hill and Virginia City. He had a lot of history in these parts.

He thought of his late father, a soldier in the Mexican American War, a Placerville merchant until the silver fever caught him, driving him to prospect along the Comstock Lode. He had likely been to Washoe City, maybe even frequented parties at the very house in which he was sitting.

When Clancy found the place, the mansion was deserted. An unbroken road leading past the house indicated that the house and grounds—approximately one hundred and forty acres, prior to its being auctioned—had been long forgotten. They'd chased a family of rabbits out of the living room when they first came across the place. Saddle tramps who came by from time to time told them that the house had been vacant for years, though they didn't think many. And while it didn't take much to make the place habitable—they initially only tore boards off the windows to gain access—in just a few months' time they had replaced door knobs, hinges and lanterns to make it comfortable. A few weeks later, they moved some furniture in.

A crazy Indian had told him that the house had once been a real marvel. That stables and a natural hot spring made it a popular stopping place for people off the Comstock Lode or out of Carson City on the way to Reno. He had heard that there were nightly parties held there, complete with singers, orchestras and sparkling wine. It pleased him to think that his father might have enjoyed the same space he was sitting in. But it had pleased him more that the wine cellar, accessed by a heavy pine door on the back of the house, had been the perfect place to hide the children when people came by. Fortunately few did, as Scotch broom, boxwood and laurel had grown up to cover most of the windows. Tall stands of white pine and cottonwood trees to the north and south of the house obscured it even more. Nailing the gate shut helped to keep the law away. And the Indians—Washoe mainly, who spent the winter season around the lake nearby—thought the place was haunted.

He doubted that anyone knew they were there.

Still, if the marshal had found them in Reno, maybe it wouldn't take them long to find them in Washoe City and the whole plan—to develop a mine, secure a stake and set-up his brothers for the rest of their lives—would certainly unwind.

He was sitting there thinking about his brother Patrick and how horribly he had died, and then his late mother, and her encouragement that he take care of his brothers—he had promised to keep them safe, to find a better life for them, to turn things around—he was wondering if they could find something less criminal, something less dangerous, when Peter entered the room.

"Paul, do you think they're coming for us here?" He had never seen Peter so shaken. It was clear that he still wasn't fully with it.

"It's a good possibility, Peter. But don't you worry." The words rang hollow. "We'll figure it out."

"Have you given every man a rifle? And are they in place?"

"As many rifles as we had, Paul. But most of the men already had guns in the stable, they said. I put a couple of guys on the porch roof and another on the top roof. Banderas is out back by the shitter. Everyone else has taken cover." But even as Peter was talking, the ranch hands were scattering into the hills. Those who could get their horses quietly had taken them and were headed to parts unknown. The others were happy to take their chance with the coyotes and were already climbing the hill out back to avoid what was sure to come. They had heard of the marshal and his deputy friend, and the man tracker who used to be a priest. They didn't want to be there when they arrived.

Chapter 48

HAPPY HANDS

Ronin insisted on heading past the telegraph office before leaving Reno as he was certain they were about to recover the children, and he wanted Emma to know. Perhaps she'd meet him there, though there was really no time for her to get his message and respond. And his thinking about her in that way—that warm way that made him feel as if he possessed a monkey's mind, or what he imagined a monkey's mind to be other than keeping one's mind on one's business—was ...well it was simply unprofessional, he thought as he climbed back on to his horse.

"You look distracted," Ash said, or asked. It really didn't matter as what was going on in Ronin's head was none of Ash's damn business, Ronin figured.

"I'm fine," Ronin replied. "Did you find a sheriff?"

"Well, actually, I found a sheriff and a doctor. They were running down the street toward our friend, when my horse bumped into them."

"Bumped into both of them?" He liked the visual.

"Yup, knocked the doctor clear over on his ass. Funny as hell!" Ash and Kelly began laughing. Weird.

"We ready to go? Or are you going to sit there and laugh your ass off?" Ronin asked, tying his rifle down so that it wouldn't be lost on their fast gallop to the mansion south of Washoe City.

"Let's go then," Ash shot back. "It'll be dark soon and we'll want to see our way up to that house. I don't want to feel my way, I want to see it."

It was dark when they arrived in Washoe City, but not so dark that they couldn't see, a winter moon illuminating the landscape like a Christmas card. They slowed their pace to a trot so as to rest their horses and headed straight for Happy Hands.

"I've seen you coming," Happy Hands said as he opened the door.

"Cut the crap, Happy Hands. I don't believe in that mumbo jumbo. How is it you didn't tell us about the mansion last night?" Ash demanded.

"Tell you what, marshal?" Happy Hands responded, folding his arms. A young Indian male appeared by his side. Ronin remembered seeing him at the Washoe encampment, when he first heard about the missing children and surmised that he was the same kid he and Dustsucker had seen through the window. Little Wolf, he thought to himself, that was his name.

"Little Wolf," Ronin spoke. The boy nodded, looked at him and then turned back to his listen to his grandfather.

"The big house on the hill? You did not ask me about the house on the hill," Happy Hands said defensively.

"I told you I was looking for Indian children," Ash responded.

"Have you seen children at the Bowers mansion?" Ronin interrupted. Little Wolf shook his head no.

"Only a crazy woman, and the ghost."

"I'm not talking about the woman," Ronin replied, thinking Little Wolf was speaking about Eilley Bowers, the owner who had stayed for a time in a small house on the property's north end after the mansion after her fortune was lost and the mansion was auctioned. For loss of anything else to do, she had turned to fortune-telling and had moved to Virginia City or San Francisco, he wasn't sure which, and was now destitute. "We're talking about children," he said sternly, "real children."

Little Wolf shook his head again and then looked at his grandfather. "There's a cellar door in the back of the mansion that has a lock on it. I've tried to open it many times, but stopped when I heard the Water Babies."

"Water Babies?" Ronin jumped at the thought that something or some people might be hidden in a basement. But he had never heard the term. Kelly was shaking his head.

"Perhaps the lock is on the door because of the Water Babies, Little Wolf," Happy Hands offered. He turned toward Ash and Ronin, who were anxiously waiting. "People who live near the water sometimes hear unusual sounds at night. Like the wail of an injured animal or the whimpering of a small child. The Washoe believe that Water Babies live in springs, lakes and even along these shores," he gestured behind the building he was squatting in, toward the Washoe's winter campground, the shallow lake now an ice pond less than a mile from his door.

"It is one reason I do not live with my people anymore. I have heard many Water Babies in my life and do not wish to hear any more."

"Why's that?" Ash asked.

Happy Hands frowned. "Should you hear a Water Baby, sickness and death may come to you. Doom is just around the corner ..." The Indian looked uncomfortable. Ronin noticed his eyes flitting from side to side, as if to see if he was being watched or listened to. "They are powerful creatures, my friends. They are not to be fooled with. Only a holy man can endure their conversations."

Ronin hadn't heard such malarkey since he had pastored a church and proffered similar ideas. Evidently, he wasn't as friendly with the Washoe as he had imagined. He noticed that Little Wolf also seemed afraid. "Would you take me there?" he asked.

"I will not," said Happy Hands. "But Little Wolf will show you the door to the mansion's basement. Apparently, the Water Babies do not want him," he said while shooting a stern look his way. "It is my advice that you stay clear of the fountain and the pools," he added.

"I always do, grandfather."

"I was speaking to your friends."

"Will do," Ronin replied looking at Ash who was already halfway out the door, dragging Little Wolf with him.

Chapter 49

BOWERS MANSION

They traveled a mile or so south and west, tethering their horses to a small stand of trees on the north side of the mansion's pools. Grabbing their rifles, Ash, Kelly and Ronin climbed a small hill until they could see a large house set against the foothills of the Sierras and framed by a brilliant winter sky. A full moon lit a small path that left the main road to Carson City and disappeared into the pine and cottonwood trees.

"Little Wolf, you've been here before?" Ronin asked. The boy was sweating, but he nodded. "Augustus, I'm thinking we ought to keep the shooting to a minimum, given that there may be children there. And the element of surprise may be real important."

Ronin remembered Ash running through the front door of the Lake's House Saloon that afternoon. A similar move tonight could surely get people killed. "If you don't mind, I'd like to enter the cellar of the house and see what I can see before we start shooting."

Ash was listening.

"And since you're so good with that Winchester of yours, how about you pick off anyone that needs picking off when the time comes?" Though they were effective tools, and Ash had proven to be a real craftsman with them, Ronin hated guns. He hoped to secure the children's safety with as little gunfire as necessary.

Ash nodded again, adding a few cartridges to eight or so in his Winchester and checking his belt for more. "I'll be out front," he said. "Kelly, you take the back. But Ronin, if we see a clear head shot of the person in question," he looked at Little Wolf uncertain that he should talk so plainly, "you know who I'm talking about, I'll take it. And you should come running." Little Wolf stared at him blankly.

Ronin nodded, "Same here."

Pulling the boy to his side, and placing his left hand on the young man's shoulder, Ronin and Little Wolf began a short walk up the road toward the house. They kept their heads down. There were deep hoof prints along the sandy path that looked recent and hard-riding. Climbing up the hill so as to approach the house from the rear, they walked past a couple of headstones under some pine trees.

"A child?" Ronin asked, looking at a name he thought unusual.

Little Wolf shook his head up and down, "Yes," he whispered, "the ghost."

Ronin nodded, remembering the boy's comments to his father. Seeing a cellar door opposite the house corral, he counted six or seven horses in the log livery. He figured the house was occupied. He knelt down with Little Wolf to listen to the night sounds.

The horses were standing still, apparently sleeping. Their soft sighs filled the night air. Two of them lay near the livery entrance. The others formed a large, shadowy mass along the livery's eastern side. A coyote signaled his displeasure with winter temperatures and what looked to be a light dusting of snow higher up the mountain.

Moving closer, Ronin noticed that the cellar doors were unlatched and open. He gestured. Little Wolf's eyes grew wide with anxiety. Pointing to the doors, he started to leave. Then, turning back, he knelt in the pine needles and whispered, "Be careful, my friend. If these are the same men who came to our camp six months ago, they are not good men."

He paused for a moment, as if he was thinking. "And if you hear murmuring…"

"Yeah, I know," Ronin interrupted, "Water Babies." They knelt for a moment nodding at each other, as men sometimes do without saying much. Ronin smiled. And then Little Wolf was gone.

He took a deep breath and sat back against a tree considering his options. A Bible verse came to mind. Ronin was always surprised, given that he had left the Episcopal priesthood seven years ago. *The wicked have laid a snare for me, yet I will not err from your precepts. Your testimonies have I taken as a birthright. And I have inclined mine heart to perform your ways always.*

He shook his head, hoping to clear his mind. The students at seminary had been asked to memorize the longest chapter in the Bible. It was a test of their commitment to become priests in the Protestant Episcopal Church, he thought at the time, as certain students refused to, or were unable. Later, he had come to understand that the scripture—a piece from one of the *Psalms*—was about living and dying. It was a wonder why he still remembered it.

Creeping along a corral at the back of the house, the ex-priest left the split rail fence on a fast run, gliding across the yard noiselessly, only the tips of his feet pushing against the sandy soil. The horses remained sleeping. A stone entrance stood five or six feet out from the northwest corner of the house, like a mudroom partially occluded by juniper trees. Someone had hacked a hole in the bushes that had grown up around a short, stone stairway leading down to the cellar. The door was still moving when he pushed past it, his lever-action Yellow Boy at the low ready.

He stopped along the north wall, breathing heavily. The dark hallway led to a second, narrower hallway, constructed with granite stones set in cement. He felt his way along the wall, surprised by the narrowness of the room, until he came to a large, sturdy rack of bottles and barrels on his left and a larger space opening to his right. Hearing nothing, he lit a match. The air was chilly. Someone had built a small fire on the dirt floor; its coals were still glowing. Soot from a series of fires had darkened the wall's whitewash. He was surprised to see blankets scattered about and knew instantly he was in the right place. Realizing there was only one entrance, he retreated quickly to the outside and signaled Kelly.

He sat by the steps while Kelly made his way down the hill to where he was squatting.

"What's up?"

"They're here."

"Someone's here," Kelly commented, explaining that he had seen a shadow and rifle barrel in a second story window.

"There's no access from the cellar," Ronin said.

"And I don't see a second story access from the back," Kelly responded. "If we're going to enter the house, it's going to have to be from one of the side windows. The back is totally open. They'll see you coming."

Ronin looked at the large wooden arbor or lattice work that sheltered patio space across the back of the mansion. He figured it to be an outdoor kitchen or conservatory at one time, affixed to a library wing or perhaps bedrooms. While ivy and other plants still clung to the structure, most of the roof covering had been cut away or harvested for firewood by the mansion's uninvited guests over the years. Two-well trimmed windows stood straight ahead with a door in-between them. The area was indeed open, even on a cloudy night.

They crept around to the north side of the house, and standing a few feet from the building saw a large, open window leading to a back room. Ronin decided to make his entrance there. Kelly boosted him up into the window frame and remained outside to keep watch on the second story balcony and windows.

Ronin placed his right foot down onto a well-worn, dusty, room-sized carpet that had seen better days. Crouching down low so as to not be seen from the outside, Ronin noticed an unmistakable animal smell. Critters of one sort or another had been using the room as a hostel and toilet. A series of shelves on both the west and north walls suggested the space had once been used as a library.

He inched toward a bedroom door, where he saw a flicker of light, casting long shadows on an opposite wall. A staircase to the second floor appeared to his right. He didn't see or hear movement, but knowing he was exposed, placed his finger in the rifle's trigger guard and kept his weapon at a high ready. He peered through the door's opening with the quick peek, as was his habit, and saw a large kitchen surrounded by cabinets. He could hear children speaking anxiously and an adult voice telling them to be quiet. Someone else shouted, "Sit against the wall! Get behind the table." He stepped into the kitchen and listened.

"Anyone moves, and he's a dead Indian! Do you understand?" the same voice shouted. He counted only two men and was wondering who all the horses belonged to when he was surprised by Peter Clancy suddenly entering the room.

"What the fuck?" the middle Clancy brother yelled. Ronin threw himself into the six-foot-tall man with sheer physical abandon, step-dragging his feet across the floor and hitting him in the jaw with the shiny brass butt end of his nine-pound rifle. A big man, Clancy hardly winced. He struck back, clenching his fingers into a fist he punched hard at Ronin's face while grasping at his revolver with his left hand.

Ronin swung the twenty-four inch heavy black octagonal rifle barrel against Clancy's right arm, parrying his punch downward and knocking him into a corner of the kitchen. Crumpled in the corner, Peter Clancy was momentarily unable to draw his gun.

Hoping to cover the distance without shooting, Ronin skipped his right leg behind his left, capturing a good ten feet of distance, and launched his left boot sideways into the man's jaw, a perfect *chasse marche croise*. The cross-behind sidekick drove Peter Clancy's head into the hard plaster lathe walls, leaving a spider web of cracks in the faded yellow paint. His shoulders slumped as his feet slid out from beneath him, parking him momentarily on top of an empty apple barrel.

Ronin grabbed the gun from his holster and tossed it behind him. The kitchen noise was hard to miss, particularly the gun's bouncing on the mansion's wood flooring. He knew instantly he had made a very loud mistake.

Someone yelled from the front room.

Ronin backed up against the wall and faced the doorway with his rifle. "Yeah ... tripped," he barked back. The silence told him the ruse was unnecessary.

Paul Clancy knew there was an intruder. And while he may be too busy to investigate, the two would surely meet. But where? Ronin wondered, moving back behind the kitchen island for a moment so as to use the counter as a rifle rest.

"Paul Clancy?" he yelled. "I'm here for the children!" He looked to see if there were other ways out of the kitchen and into the main room. There were none.

"I don't want to hurt you. Your brother's fine, he's sitting here unconscious but still breathing." He wondered about moving into the hallway, shooting aggressively toward the front of the house so as to keep from getting shot. But he knew he couldn't adequately identify targets along the way, and that children in the hallway or front room might be hit. The vestibule was a tunnel of death. He didn't want it to be his tomb, or theirs, either.

"Marshal Ash and I only want the children," he yelled.

"Ash can go to hell!" Clancy yelled back.

Damn, too much information. When will I learn? He was a communicator at heart and figured that people wanted to hear what he had in his head, long after they stopped paying him to tell them.

"Ash will never let me get out of this alive," Clancy continued. "I killed his deputy."

"Almost killed him," Ronin responded, pausing momentarily to think. "The man survived, Paul," he yelled. "And I'll protect you. He respects me," he said.

It was weak and he knew it. No one could keep Ash from doing what he wanted to do. He was his own man. And the deputy, as Clancy put it, would soon enter the house as well. Neither the marshal nor the former Virginia City police chief and sheriff would be deterred. But the children? How could he get to the children?

He heard a loud noise as Paul Clancy pulled a table on to its feet and slid it across the floor, barricading the doors at the front of the house, he guessed. Given the screaming, he must have grabbed a child. And then a shot broke the glass at the front of the house. Ronin sprinted immediately into the hallway. He slid into a door at the end of the foyer and stood up against it, breathless. There lay Paul Clancy, the oldest of the Clancy children, dead in the main room with a bullet in his head. Glass was scattered everywhere.

And a little Indian girl stood frozen at his side, crying.

Chapter 50

FIRE WITHIN

Emma Nauman cleared her schedule when she heard the LORD speak to her during her morning devotions. She was to saddle a horse and to head to Reno.

But she had never ridden a horse before, she protested as the LORD told her that the children would soon be found and that she would be needed to care for them. Not for any great distance anyway. She had ridden in a carriage, she said out loud, and she had held the horse's reins at times, when her late or departed husband—she didn't know which—had bidden her to do so in order to do something else. One time, she had taken the reins of a small carriage that belonged to the mission. And while she and Henry had been riding toward the river to spend the day picnicking, the horse had suddenly keeled over and died in the middle of the road.

"A healthy horse doesn't just die in the middle of a road," one of her hands had told her. "It's just not something that happens," he said. He knew horses and also knew she was not comfortable around them without a man close by.

Her husband had hardly been a man, she thought. She hadn't been able to depend on him for much after their daughter's death. But Ronin was a man, a very good man, and he had helped to quiet some of her anxiety over simple things that simply didn't matter. A noise in the night, a child's occasional cough or the tugging of an unfamiliar horse's reins.

She had enjoyed their riding together at the mission while he was recovering. Despite the obvious mending of her friend, she had hoped her time with Ronin would never end. And she wondered, at times, how she might regain those days. Or days like those days, though she thought the LORD would never give permission for such a thing while her husband was alive or dead—she didn't know which.

The LORD wasn't asking much, she thought, "but the distance would be at least a day's ride," she protested gently. "You would have me face my fears?" she asked, hoping the LORD would be as clear in answering that question as he had been in creating the anxiety in the first place, or in telling her that she was to ignore it and saddle up and ride to Reno.

Perhaps one day the LORD would give her direction about Ronin as well.

All she could conclude after asking was that the LORD would never have her do less than her best. And if facing her fears meant that she should ride alone, or live alone, or be alone the rest of her life, she would do it, or at least try.

Early on the third day she rose from her bed and, finding her house man on the back porch eating his breakfast, asked him to saddle "Fire Within," an Appaloosa brought to the mission by one of the Nez Perce children. Tall and narrow-bodied, the horse was her favorite, if she had favorites in the mission stable. And given the horse's friendliness toward her, it might be one she could comfortably sit astride so as to ride to Reno and greet her children.

It was a shame that the LORD had not asked her to take a carriage. A carriage would be better, she mused as she grabbed a horse blanket from a rail on the back porch.

With mottled skin and striped hooves, the Appaloosa was one of the most beautiful of God's creatures, Ronin had told her when she first laid a blanket on it, prior to helping him with his saddle. The Nez Perce people lived in Washington, Oregon and Idaho, he'd said. He had met a few, and while no longer warriors—a fate her friend seemed sad about—the horses were being bred as farm animals, a fate she could hardly imagine for her Appaloosa. It was much too spirited and bright.

"Their horsemanship was second to none," Ronin had said, "their spirituality, even more moving," he told her. "They remind me of you," he once whispered to her in a particularly tender moment by the Carson River, when they were having lunch.

"They have vision, Emma. You have vision, too." He had first held her there, when saying that. He had lightly touched her cheek with his right hand and looked into her eyes.

It had been a very gracious moment, Emma remembered. She sensed that the former minister didn't always share her religious feelings and fervor, but understood how important her spiritual practices and perspectives were to her.

She smiled as her hand helped her up into the saddle and winced slightly when he placed a lever action rifle in the saddle's scabbard. "Be careful, Miss Emma," he said, tapping the horse's hindquarters and sending Fire Within walking toward the front gate.

Would he understand her coming to Reno? she wondered as she gathered the reins closer to her waist, kicking Fire Within into a trot and then a gallop. He would have to, she concluded.. God had told her to come.

Chapter 51

AS GOOD AS IT GETS

U.S. Marshal Augustus Ash had shot through the front glass into the main room when he saw Paul Clancy begin to drag a little girl from the dining room into the hallway. He wasn't about to lose sight of the man, given that he had a rifle in his right hand. So when he began grabbing at the girl, he sighted his Winchester on Paul Clancy's hat, a tall ugly gray thing with a western peak and, dropping the barrel a little bit, pressed the trigger.

It took less than a three and one-half pound pull to send the nearly half-inch lead bullet into his head, dropping him immediately and leaving the girl standing next to him, unharmed.

There was always a risk, he thought. His breathing might be off. The wind might be up. The muzzle or physical sight of his rifle might be damaged. He was always careful and had never shot anybody who didn't need shooting, but there was always the chance he might miss and hurt someone he didn't intend to. And all of that always, always was in his mind when he took aim at someone who needed shooting.

From his place in the grass, it looked as if there was no one else in the front room. He wondered if there were others nearby. He didn't see anyone on the porch. And both roofs appeared clear. The cupola on the roof was still a question, but he figured there'd be shooting by now, if anyone was else was present.

"Ash," Ronin yelled. "I'm coming out the front door! Cover me." Augustus opened both of his eyes to view the front of the house, twenty-five yards away. A fountain of stagnant water stood between them. He kept his right eye on the sight picture while attempting to see with his left. No movement anywhere, nothing, save a winter breeze.

"Come ahead," he said. "I've got you."

Ronin poked his head out the door, and seeing no one, allowed his body to follow, looking to his left and then to his right. "You're good, Ronin. I have the porch in view. Anyone else inside?"

"One mouth breather in the kitchen," he yelled back, "but he's no longer standing. Just these children." He began laughing. And with that, a half-dozen Indian kids pressed their bodies through the front door. Three or four more followed, taking in the night air as if it had been a long time since they had breathed anything other than the stagnant smoke-filled air of the cellar, having apparently kept a small fire going there to keep them warm.

Ash stood up. "My goodness," he exclaimed. "My God, I can't believe it," he said. "You were right! I couldn't imagine anyone doing this," he said, running toward Ronin and the children at his side.

"This is Sophia," Ronin said, remembering the conversation he'd had with Emma Nauman at the mission three or so months prior. "And this is Grace, I think." The child smiled shyly. "And maybe Creighton, Sammy and Bekah," he pointed toward others, trying to remember names that Emma had told him when he had taken the initial incident report at the American Gospel Mission. "I don't know everyone. And they obviously don't know us ... "

The oldest of the children on the porch was perhaps nine. The youngest was maybe three, boys and girls, Paiutes, Washoes and other tribes Ronin didn't recognize.

"My God, what do we do with them?" Ash said, falling to his knees and grabbing to hug the child closest to him as Kelly came around front.

"Everything okay?" he asked, looking at the marshal.

Ronin let out a deep sigh. "As good as it's going to get," he said.

He hated the cruelty of white men, and similar brutality of tribes throughout the area, though things had been better among the Indian nations in recent years. He couldn't believe that the director of an Indian mission would be selling kids for God knows what kind of profit and use. People could be so mean.

"Let's get Peter Crestwell tied up and put on a horse," he said. "There are additional horses in the livery. We'll get the children up on the others and let Happy Hands know what we've found. He can look after the rest?"

"The children?" Ash looked confused.

"The horses," Ronin replied. "The children we're taking back to Carson City."

Chapter 52

A FULL WINTER MOON

It took them only a few moments to get the children saddled and the horses roped together, attaching bridle to bridle, since there weren't enough saddles to go around. While there was lots of anguish and crying, the stillness of the night air helped keep everyone calm.

"I'm taking you to friends," Ronin told the kids, some of whom were riding double because of their age. "Sophia, your horse follows mine. Grace, yours, too, then the others. The marshal and his deputy will bring up the rear."

The little girls nodded. No wonder Emma remembered their names. They were beautiful. All of the children were beautiful, despite the emotional and physical cost of their abduction. All children are beautiful, Ronin thought to himself, especially those who have been wronged and neglected. Ronin grimaced as he mounted his horse, his left leg hurting. He had an issue with anger, to be sure. It hadn't served him well as a priest in the church, and it had at times gotten in the way of his work as a bounty hunter and detective. But if the men responsible for this weren't already dead, he'd live to see them killed. He could think of nothing else.

Peter Clancy was tied across one of the larger horses. It had to be uncomfortable, though Ronin didn't care. The middle child in a trio of terrorists, he put Peter Clancy's horse in front of the marshal to keep him distant from the children. He didn't believe the man would cause any further harm, but the mere proximity of the man to the children he had abused was something to think about and appreciate.

Ash would make sure that "justice removed its bandage from her eyes," long enough anyway to distinguish between the good and the bad. He hadn't thought about Ingersoll in a long time. Ash had mentioned to him that the statue of Lady Justice on the new courthouse in Virginia City didn't have a blindfold. "Good," he had said, as they shared a beer. Ingersoll had been widely depreciated as one of "America's leading infidels." Still, he was a better preacher than most Christians, Ronin had decided, if you could call him that.

Goodness was as goodness did, Ronin believed. Goodness wasn't as goodness believed. It needed to have some edge to it if it was to be taken seriously. And if justice didn't distinguish between the good and the bad in *this* situation, he certainly would. He could hardly wait to find out what Nevada's criminal court system was going to do, given that he had witnessed good folks have such a terrible grasp at times on how to fix bad things.

They rode out the well-trodden drive in front of the mansion, the hoof marks of the Clancys, the Crestwells, and God knew who else still sitting deeply in the sand ground from the mountain's granite. The soil prompted him to wonder how deep the scars ran in the psyches of the children they had just rescued.

A light snow began to fall as their horses walked the quiet mile to Happy Hands' home. After a time, the steady rhythm of the horses prompted him to think. Nothing was permanent. The contentment of the Indian children at the mission, the Indian encampment at Washoe Lake, where the Washoe wintered but never summered, Happy Hands' house in God only knows whose home, abandoned when Washoe City failed, years after the Washoe people began wondering what would come of them as their own culture withered. Even the mansion. The Bowers had made a real nice home there a dozen years back. He counted sixteen bedrooms while searching the place for additional hands or accomplices—some of which had been added, he suspected, in an effort to survive the master's death and subsequent financial woes.

No, nothing was permanent.

His own life, as a pastor in Wichita, Kansas, was another example. He hadn't found in the church the something he was searching for. And the five years he had spent at war—the best years of his life his mother later said, given his age—had added up to nothing but toil and misery. A half-million dead, he recalled, counting soldiers alone. Who could say what the total of human suffering had been?

"There is nothing better for a man than to rejoice and to do good," the Good Book said, though he couldn't remember exactly where, and while it didn't seem like much, the guidance was probably adequate enough. In the end, what is there except to drink, to eat and to enjoy one's friends?

The winter moon illumined the hitching posts when they arrived. Frozen short and stubby, they cast a long shadow on the house's front porch. Ronin swung his right leg over the horse's head, wincing a bit because of the pain in his left leg, and began to tether his horse when the front door opened.

It was Emma. Standing there in the doorway, such a beautiful woman! She looked at him. He looked at her. They both looked at the children. And she began crying. "O God!" she exclaimed, tears running down her cheeks. "O God!" she repeated, running to the end of the porch and out on to the road. "This is the day that God has made!" she sobbed. Ronin remembered the verse well, as he used to repeat it as a part of his morning devotions.

She hugged every one of the children before taking time to untie the first, the second, and so on until the very last one was free and standing in the street alongside of her. And she looked into every child's eyes—she was amazing, absolutely amazing, Ronin thought—hugging, kissing, and running her hands over them, until she collapsed to the ground, still trying to hug each and every one of them. Ronin helped her stand.

Happy Hands stood silently on the porch, an earth-colored blanket wrapped around his shoulders. Ronin couldn't tell what the man was thinking, leaning against one of the house's roof supports. Was he embarrassed? How could he not have known that the children were hidden so close to his front door? And what superstition had kept any of the Washoe tribe from discovering their presence in the valley?

He waited to speak until Emma stood next to him shooing the children into the house. "Emma, I don't know what to say ..." he stumbled, feeling as if he should apologize. He had no reason to. But his heart had been torn by the children, and by their mistress, if he was honest enough to admit it.

"I do," she replied, looking at her man. Her man, she thought. I hardly know this man. Ex-priest. Bounty hunter. Pinkerton. Who is he? "I know what to say, Mr. Ronin," looking up into his eyes. "Thank you so much for what you've done," she said, leaning toward him and sliding into his arms.

They embraced for a long time, she continuing to whisper endearments and appreciation into his embarrassed ears. Long enough that the marshal and his deputy, having tied off the horses, untied their bedrolls and, grabbing their rifles and saddlebags, stood there wondering how to get everyone into the house.

"If you guys don't mind," he sputtered, "I'd like to slip past you and see how the kids are doing."

They laughed, and looking at each other and then at the marshal, who had played such a magnificent role in the children's return, said, "We need to thank you, too!" The three of them stood on the porch for a moment, telling stories and grasping each other's arms and shoulders. It was a story they would tell for years to come.

Entering the house, Happy Hands had the children sitting on the floor and he was finishing a story. Blankets were set out around the fireplace, and a roaring fire framed Happy Hands as he spoke.

"The rabbit did not know where it was." He was a natural story teller, Ronin thought, understanding for the first time why he was named Happy Hands, as his hands didn't stop moving while he was telling the tale.

"The rabbit's ears were far back on its head! Like this," he said, laughing. And putting his hands behind his head, he wiggled them until they locked beneath his ponytail, his elbows flapping like he was a chicken.

"And he thumped his leg, like this!" He nearly doubled up in laughter, as the children were laughing as well. A red man had never seen such attention from white children. Stomping his left leg on the wooden floor of the cabin, he began jumping up and down.

"Do you hear the rabbit's foot thumping?" he asked, laughing hysterically. And the children nodded, wiping tears and the crusts of a hundred basement fires from their eyes.

He began muttering to himself and turning round and round in a circle as if he, or rather the rabbit, didn't know what to do. Acting confused, he fell to the ground whimpering. The children slowly quieted.

"And then," he said, looking at each of the adults. "Then," he said, waiting for all of the children to catch up to where he was in the story, the room silent as there was a point to be made. "And then their friends came, finding the rabbit unharmed ..." He slowed the story's pace. "... and happy to be found." He whispered as if he, or the rabbit, was worn-out by the experience and journey while moving as close to the children as the hearth of the fireplace would permit. He looked into each child's eyes, to make sure that they understood.

"And then," he said, looking appreciatively toward Ronin, who was just as interested in the story's ending as the children were. "... his rabbit friends came to him. And looking at him, took a deep breath before they said, 'You were not lost, Mr. Rabbit! You were just …not …yet … found."

The kids' eyes were wide and wet, and the adults too throughout the evening, and into the night.

Chapter 53

NEXT MORNING

A quick breakfast was made the following morning. Deer jerky, or rabbit—nobody was asking—and flat bread were served around the fire. Everyone was anxious to get a start for the mission in Carson City.

Ash indicated that he'd be happy to ride to Reno instead, so as to check on Deputy Slade. And Emma promised to make a full report in either Slade's office, given the mission's location, or Ash's in Virginia City, in that he was the arresting officer.

Ronin was outside, saddling the horses, when the marshal approached Emma.

"Emma," he stuttered. "I don't know you, so I have no reason to ask. And certainly you don't need to answer," he continued, holding his hat in his hand as he was beginning to go out the door in what he hoped would be an easy ride.

"But I'm wondering, and I need to say, Ronin hasn't put me up to this ... "

"Yes, marshal?" Emma smiled.

"Well, do you think there might ever be anything between the two of you?" he asked, putting his hat on with a "There, I've said it" kind of look. Thinking of the occasions he had witnessed Ronin thinking about something other than the business at hand, he had a pretty good idea what was going on in the ex-preacher's mind though he couldn't read the missionary lady. He waited by the door for her answer.

Sophia looked up, wondering what the marshal was talking about and, thinking that Miss Emma was married, looked more than curious and a little bit uncomfortable.

"Mr. Ash," she said, taking off her apron. "We've got a lot of riding ahead of us to get to where God is going, I suspect." She smoothed Sophia's hair and began to re-braid one of her pigtails. "How do I say this?" she added, pausing for a minute to gather her thoughts. "Let me put it this way. I'd be surprised if God didn't have Mr. Ronin in our lives for a good, long time."

Sophia looked down, content with the answer and continuing to put the extra jerky and bread into a sack she had found on the kitchen table. They would need nibbles for the journey, she figured, and food had been so scarce she wasn't about to leave any extra breakfast items behind.

Ash nodded, though he didn't much understand Emma's reply. He typically didn't listen to preachers on the Comstock, though one had insisted on baptizing him with beer once in a barroom fight. He didn't know what constituted a duly-authorized church baptism, but doubted that the Virginia City hoopleheads and hobnobbers who presided had any real authority to do so, the pastor not withstanding. Adjusting his hat and exiting the door to the house, he remembered why he much preferred the straight-talking women on D Street in Virginia City's Red Light District to the God-fearing ones in Carson City or Reno.

Emma continued to braid Sophia's hair once the food was securely packed in the cloth sack she was carrying. She hadn't imagined any of this taking place in her life. The American Gospel Mission she understood because God had given her that dream clear back in 1867, when she and her husband still worked a West Virginia farm outside of Steubenville, Ohio. But she hadn't expected anything that had followed. Least of which, her husband's death or disappearance, the kidnapping of the children, the killings that were necessary to get them back, or Ronin's presence in her life. It had all been a surprise. Surely, she didn't know what the rest of her life would hold.

God moved in mysterious ways, she thought as she tied the last of the braids and patted Sophia's back, signaling her to get up, gather her belongings and begin helping the other children to do the same.

Maybe there would be something to Ronin and her in time. But there was a lot to work to do beforehand, she figured. "Work out your salvation," she said to herself in a sing-song way, quoting the Apostle Paul's speech in the *Epistle to the Philippians,* chapter two, verse two. One of her favorite Bible verses, she hit a high note with the words, "with fear and trembling." She smiled to herself as she gathered up a few of her belongings. She didn't much feel fear or trembling. She felt excitement and that seemed good.

Emma and the children excited the building, horse blankets from the house on the hill under their arms. Happy Hands and his son Little Wolf followed, leaving their animal pelt blankets still unfolded by the fire.

"Let's get going," Ronin shouted as he climbed into the saddle. He immediately swung his right leg back off of the saddle, when he realized the children would need help getting on their horses. "I mean, it's going to be a while. We should head back straight away so as to get there before dark."

Emma looked at him quietly while tying gear to her horse.

"I hate the dark," Ronin explained.

Emma met his eyes and smiled, "We all do."

Chapter 54

BACK TO CARSON CITY

The sun was shining. The snow was still up on the mountain. Last night's flurries had amounted to nothing, except to coat the trees with a gentle frost. Ronin filled his lungs with the crisp winter air. One of the most beautiful things about Nevada was that the best parts of winter pretty much last all year around.

He loved the look of the mountains around him, the Sierras to his right, and the Virginia City range a few miles to his left. The snow sometimes lasted until June on the mountains, even through July at times. And the smell of sage in the valley, hell, in valleys all over Nevada, was practically year-round, especially after a lengthy rain. It would be springtime soon, he thought as he glanced over at Emma, who was riding beside him. She smiled.

"Thinking pleasant thoughts?" she asked.

"Most of the time," he responded, "certainly today."

"I sure appreciate you," she said.

Ronin didn't know what to say.

"I'm not talking about what you do, William. I'm talking about who you are. Your kindness. Your concern for others. Your willingness to make someone else's business your own."

He smiled, remembering Emma's concern that she hadn't seen him working in the last few months, not since he broke his leg in the Carson City jail. He certainly wasn't earning money helping her and the Indian children, she had said. How did he do it? It had been seven years since he had left the priesthood. And

Ronin had continued to be the very same man out of the church that he had been inside of it, though one important thing was different. He was his own man now. He had been owned by other men then.

"It's who I am, Emma. It doesn't always serve me well," he had said the night before, thinking of the times he went without and trying to speak to Emma's concern. "I've had some pretty lean times," he confessed. "I'm not on anyone's payroll, so it gets pretty hard."

She wanted to know how hard his life was, what inner demons he wrestled with, what he liked and didn't like, if there was any possibility that they would ever be together. A crazy thought to be sure, given her responsibilities at the mission. But who knew?

"Would you ever think of settling down at the mission?" she had asked tentatively, knowing that it sounded forward, but hoping that Ronin would excuse its tone.

He hadn't anticipated her asking.

He sat quietly in the saddle as the horses plodded along and wondered if his response had been adequate. "Oh, I imagine," he had said. "I imagine there might be a time when I'd look to settle down," he had replied, watching her eyes as he had spoke. "But I don't tend to think that far ahead. I like to focus on the now. It keeps the questions at bay."

Emma looked confused last night, as if he hadn't answered the question. It was not an unfamiliar look, he thought, as Ronin's speech sometimes meandered before getting down to a solid yes or no. He decided to try again.

"I figure I've got a couple more years of adventure in me before I think about becoming someone's man again."

Emma smiled, glad that he had brought it up again. "I didn't mean ..." she paused. "I didn't mean a marriage, Mr. Ronin, not that there would be anything wrong with that." She couldn't believe she was speaking so frankly. "Last night, I was talking about a job, William. I was asking about your working at the mission," though she couldn't be sure she actually meant that, then or now.

"I'm so embarrassed," she added quickly, biting her lip.

"I've enjoyed being with you, Miss Emma," he smiled. He liked the sound of the name the children had given their new directress. She put her hand toward him. He reached toward her. They rode hand in hand for a while together, until they noticed the children looking.

They rounded a bend he remembered seeing the first time he had passed along Washoe Lake, alongside the Virginia mountains. The foothills used to be heavily wooded. Seven years later most of the trees were gone. The Comstock mining binge had ruined the quiet Nevada settlements Ronin had originally been attracted to when he moved west. The powerful muse that tempted men to do horrible, despicable things to each other in search of silver and gold had left a real imprint on everyone and everything.

"Have you ever been up this way before?" he asked. Ronin noticed how wide her eyes had gotten the night before when he shared the story of what had happened in Carson City, Reno and also in Old Washoe, though she had heard the shooting. The gunplay, the discovery that her husband was selling children and that other men were buying them for God knows what left her speechless and badly shaken. He had noticed that she had tossed and turned throughout the night.

"I'm very much upset by all of this," she said, ignoring the scenery and their discussion of a job at the mission. "It's as if white people haven't learned anything over the years. First, we enslave the Africans. Then we do the same to the Indians and the Chinese," she said. "Have I been so sheltered and parochial that I didn't know people were capable of doing this to each other?"

"I mean," she stuttered, holding her breath. "I knew there were Chinese people working on the railroads," she said. "And I'd heard of the Asian shanty towns in San Francisco. Laundries, railroad workers, prostitutes and so on, these things aren't new to me. But I had no idea *we* were employing them, that *we* were benefiting from them, that so much of our trade and lifestyle was based on them. I mean, look at what has happened at my mission."

Ronin didn't understand what she was getting at.

"I thought these were choices that people made, Indian tribes, families, who didn't have enough food to feed their children throughout the winter, people who wanted to work in the mines, or on the railroad, or whatever. I figured they wanted that, that they chose that. I had no idea that so much of this was the product of what other people wanted."

Ronin nodded.

"And, I'll never understand the choices those men made, selling my children."

"No," Ronin said, "nor will I."

They rode silently for a while, Ronin thinking about the fierce abolitionist in him that he had kept secret all of the years he fought for the Confederacy in the Civil War, and the years he had taught religious ideals and doctrines. There were so many more important things he thought to say and to do than to stir people up about things they often disagreed over. He had kept his mouth shut, for fear of his own safety when he fought alongside of Southern soldiers in Biffle's 19th Tennessee Cavalry. He had done the same in the church, he had finally decided before leaving his parish. Every Sunday was a popularity contest that determined whether he got paid or not, even if they paid him in beef, potatoes and corn.

"People sometimes do cruel things to each other," he said, breaking the silence. "And some people aren't what they seem to be," he added. "We were all God's creatures, more or less, in God's sight." More recently he had decided, mostly less.

"Lincoln's war should have settled the question of how human beings should treat each other," Emma said. "There's a place for you, Ronin."

He nodded, as they rode silently for a while, Ronin and the new directress of the American Gospel Mission in Carson City, his first, honest-to-goodness, real female friend, a string of Indian ponies and children trailing behind them.

Chapter 55

THE MISSION

A couple days later, Deputy Sheriff Marcus T. Slade returned to Carson City, having taken a stagecoach from Reno to Virginia City and then on to the capital where a deputy took him by carriage out to his room at the Warm Springs Hotel.

Slade figured it was good to be home, whatever home is. Word was that his favorite hotel was going to become a prison. While the prison was necessary given Carson City's need for a larger and more durable structure after the explosive demise of the jailhouse, it made him sad to think that the place he thought of as home would soon be housing for the area's criminals and miscreants.

In legislative session, the hotel jumped with excitement. Senators and assemblymen sat alongside shopkeepers, prospectors and lawmen. Regular folk ignored a better quality of booze in Nevada's capital city for a higher quality of blather and buzz just a little ways out. The trade was worth it. Life wouldn't be the same without the Warm Springs Hotel.

As Dustsucker's right side was feeling pretty good since the gunfight in Reno—he'd had some good care in that town—he asked one of the hotel ne'er do wells to saddle his horse for a short ride to the American Gospel Mission. He looked forward to a good meal and figured that the embarrassment of being the first person down in a gunfight wouldn't sit too terribly high on everyone's dinner agendas. Emma's appearance at the sheriff's office the day before, where she planted a big kiss on his left cheek as an official American Gospel Mission thank-you, hadn't helped his status any, though it was sure nice and caused him ever so briefly to reexamine his priorities and wonder.

The bear-sized hug and smile he had given her in return had gotten him a dinner invitation. Though he liked the man, he was disappointed to see Ronin sitting at the table when he came in.

"Well partner, it sure is good to see you," Ronin said. "I missed you when I took Emma to the capital to make her report. I should have stopped in, but time got away from us. I'm sorry."

Dustsucker nodded, though no nod or apology was needed. Seeing Ronin at the dinner table made the furtive thought that he and Emma might someday hit it off seem even more fleeting. Ronin and he were friends and a fat man, he figured, wasn't going to catch an attractive woman if Ronin was around, even if she was a missionary.

"W., I've been thinking. I'm going to have to move to another hotel in a couple of days," he said so as to change the topic. I wondered if you needed a roommate."

"Wish it were so," Ronin responded, thinking that his room was too small and that he liked to keep things tidy. "We'd have a happy time together I imagine, if we could keep from getting shot that is. I'm sorry," he said, watching his friend's reaction. "I didn't mean to bring that up." He smiled mischievously.

Dustsucker looked at his friend and frowned. "Yup, I've taken a whole lot of derision these last couple of days, William. I was hoping not to hear any more of it tonight ..."

"I'm sorry," Ronin said, trying to be more serious. "Does your side still hurt?"

"Nah, it just hurts to laugh. It pulls at the stitches."

He laughed anyway, before grabbing his side with both of his hands and grimacing, something his heart and eyes were not used to doing. Emma entered the room with a large bowl of Mexican stew, but not before the spicy aroma put everyone on notice.

"You okay?" she exclaimed, finding Slade doubled up at the table, grabbing his side and in tears. He nodded, waiting for Emma to look away before he put his sleeve up to his eyes to blot away the tears.

"He's just in pain," Ronin said wryly, feeling a certain smugness that he had nudged his deputy friend a few inches toward normal, "and he's weeping that he's going to have to move."

"Move?" Emma asked. "You like that place!"

Ronin explained, "Sounds like the Warm Springs Hotel is shutting down. They're building a prison out that way and need the land."

"Too bad," Emma replied. "You can always bunk at the mission," Emma said. Ronin and Slade's eyes met. Slade smiled.

The Mexican stew smelled wonderful. Onion, garlic, cayenne pepper and green chilies from the mission garden made everyone's eyes water. The unusual mix of black beans, corn, chicken and tomatoes caused everyone's mouths to do the same.

Dustsucker tore off a piece of bread and, dipping into the main bowl, suddenly stopped and apologized that he hadn't even waited for Emma to sit, let alone to ladle out individual portions. Maybe he ought to settle at the mission, he thought briefly. Staying there might teach him a thing or two, better manners for one. He drew the bread up to his face as if to appreciate its scent and hoped that no one noticed.

"Well, there's some chance the legislature will leave things alone, I guess. But the state has already signed a lease to house prisoners there. And there's talk of tearing it down to build something grander."

"Just what we need," Ronin said, getting up to pull out Emma's chair. "A nicer, more comfortable place to house people who shouldn't even live in these parts."

"Gotta put them somewhere," Dustsucker replied.

"Maybe so," he replied, "maybe not." He hated thinking the obvious thing was the only thing to think. "You back to work, Marcus?"

Dustucker didn't remember Ronin ever addressing him by his first name.

"Not yet, my friend. Soon. How about you? What are you going to do?"

Emma hesitated for a moment and then continued ladling out the stew into the kiln-fired bowls some of the children had made a few months prior. A new pottery teacher had taken up residence at the school. And while not quite the man her preacher friend was, she hoped his presence would add to the mission's security and safety. It was good to have a man around, even if it wasn't the man she wanted or needed.

The bowls had a nice green patina to them and, if sold, might contribute to the school's financial needs, Emma explained as she dished out individual portions. Donations were down since the kidnappings, as religious folks generally don't like hearing about difficulty or change. Emma pointed out that she'd have to work hard to regain trust among some of the mission's contributors, or find a whole new list of people willing to support the mission's work in Nevada.

"Frankly, I don't know what I'm going to do," Ronin answered, wondering about the tension in Emma's voice. "I had a letter waiting at Saint Peter's Episcopal Church, of all places, when I returned. One of their people walked it over. Been sent there because someone thought I was the parish priest," he laughed. "Funny what people think."

"A lot of us still think of you as a good man," Emma responded. Ronin ignored the inference that a godly man was a good man, or that a good man was necessarily a godly man. He'd known men on both sides of the cloth who were good and quite a few who were not so. "Well, it seems there's a situation up at Lake Tahoe that might bear some looking into."

"Lake Bigler?" Dustsucker asked. Emma looked confused.

"Exactly," Ronin responded. "People at the lake are talking about a couple of drownings or what might turn out to be murders. Happy Hands mentioned it when we saw him the other night, so I was surprised to read the same thing in this letter."

"So you're not leaving?" Emma interrupted, then was immediately embarrassed as her tone seemed inappropriate for a woman still married in the eyes of the LORD.

"Don't think so, Emma. Or at least not yet," Ronin said, without acknowledging the fact that Emma was looking downward as if something was floating in her stew. Her face was flushed, her hands sitting in her lap. Dustsucker noticed too, but figured he had no chance of attracting the woman's attention so long as Ronin was around.

"Fact is, I'm interested. Something has happened up at Cave Rock, other than the usual mumbo-jumbo, or whatever the Washoe shamans do when they go there. The lake doesn't give up its dead, I'm told. But I'm hoping it will give up this one."

Dustsucker hadn't heard about the deaths, but he had been otherwise occupied. And Ronin had a much better connection to the local Indians than he did.

"And get this. Not only are there Water Babies in the Lake …" Everyone groaned. "The Washoe apparently have been sinking baskets of corn and pine nuts into the lake to keep additional killings from occurring. It's a total mad house up there. Indians praying. White men posting guards at the hotels and lumber mills. Churches holding special meetings. Even the settlers are upset."

Emma let go of the words, "Oh God" as she placed a bowl of the stew in front of her friend. "What next?"

"It gets better, Dusty," he said, moving the bowl a little bit closer and placing a cloth napkin into his lap. Slade's bowl was almost empty. "The Washoe say there's a creature that lives at the base of the rock who preys on people who don't do their duty."

"And you believe that, Mr. Ronin?" Emma exclaimed, not at all sure why she was so upset, save that a minister, even an ex-minister, shouldn't repeat such nonsense. She didn't like the idea that Ronin might get mixed up in something that might get him hurt or worse.

"Not hardly, Emma," Ronin replied.

"I'm not about to risk anything," he said, picking up his spoon. "But if there's an unsolved murder at Cave Rock, I'm intrigued. And if there's a creature there that eats people who don't do the right thing? Well, I figure..." His friends looked at him and waited. "...well, I figure he might want a little bit of help."

AUTHOR'S NOTE

This is my first novel. Everything in it is fiction, except for those characters, places and events that are not. I've had too much fun writing this book to count it a serious piece of literature or history. Having said that, I have attempted to stay accurate to the time and locale the book describes, the Comstock Lode, starting in the fall of 1879, even to the extent of making sure travel times, dates, certain characters and other details fit within what I understand the history to be.

An important exception to that fact is my treatment of the Warm Springs Hotel, just east of Carson City. While a prison was eventually built on that site, the transition from hotel to prison took place fifteen years previous. That exception and others were made for the sake of the story.

After previewing *East Jesus, Nevada*, a friend of mine called it an "existential Western." I'm hoping it, and the books that follow in the Ronin series of Westerns, do more than flirt with both terms. The second in the series, *Lady of the Lake*, puts Ronin, Dustsucker, Emma and other characters at Lake Tahoe to solve the murders of a couple Washoe Indians. The history, geography and Washoe mythology, if one will excuse the latter term, were important to me during its writing. The third book in the series, *The Pinkerton Years*, portrays the former Reverend W. W. Ronin's years with the Pinkerton Detective Agency following the defeat of the Confederacy in 1865. The book shares an honest history of the Pinkerton Agency, as well as Ronin's reasons for leaving the Episcopal priesthood in order to live a grander adventure in the American West. It does so in the context of a more contemporary story of divination and spiritualism, popular practices on the Comstock in the mid-to-late 19th century.

If reading about W. W. Ronin helps you live a more meaningful life, with all of life's questions and issues, I'll be happy. If it helps you understand the complex and exciting history of these very formative years in Nevada, I'm happy too. A list of my books and other publications are located at www.greggtownsley.com. I look forward to hearing from you there.

I want to offer a couple notes of acknowledgement. First of all, to my wife Nancy, who is my constant friend, lover and muse. Nancy's efforts to appreciate the man I am becoming, or perhaps have always been, have provided a considerable source of grace and encouragement through the months it took me to complete this work. I have no words to describe what a gift it is for me to live with such an amazing woman and writer. Nancy's writing and editorial work are seen weekly as part of the Pamplin Media Group's publications in Portland, Oregon. Should you want to comment on it, or leave a message as to what she should have corrected in her first edit of my book, contact her at www.nancytownsley.com!

Appreciation too to my two "beta-readers," Cathy Parr and Bill Greb, who asked every Monday for the most recent grist. My weekly goal, to write between 3,000 and 5,000 words, was often not enough to quell their enthusiasm for the first two books in this series. Thank you. Your eagerness for more inspired me to finish.

And to my bold and erudite friend Julie Larson, who acted without compensation as a second or final and furious editor to this work, and who insists that few sentences, let alone paragraphs, should start with the conjunction "and," what can I say? You made me a better writer and person. And Jon Larson, you don't make a bad W. W. Ronin at all, even if you are a little bit older than I picture Ronin to be.

I also can't ignore a cadre of good friends and technical consultants in Carson City, Virginia City, Reno and elsewhere who helped me with research and travel to make this book an interesting and, for the most part, accurate historical read. Particular thanks to Joe Curtis, of Mark Twain Books and the Silver State National Peace Officers Museum in Virginia City. And of course the amazing people at the Nevada Historical Society in Reno. Your efforts made this book a great deal more accurate and interesting.

To my son Joshua, who provided a beautiful series of photos for use in Olivia Passieux's cover design, you've got my back. As always, son, I hope you know I have yours.

Truth be told, my late son Jared started me on this project. An odd and compelling Christmas present in December 2010 set me on a new and healthier course in my life, the gift's most profound contribution being the question, "What would you do if you knew could not fail?"

Jared Samuel Townsley lived that question. A member of the elite climbing fraternity the Mazamas, a mountaineering club founded in 1894, and having summited Oregon's Mount Hood more than a dozen times, Jared was lost to us in February of 2012 during a solo climb.

Jared was a talented athlete and climber. We never reach our goals if we never set goals to reach. More than 30 years after his birth, he reminded me of that. This book — and the bliss I'm living writing other books in the W. W. Ronin series of Westerns — is dedicated to his memory.

ABOUT THE AUTHOR

Gregg Edwards Townsley is a reflective, free-thinking ex-pastor, martial artist, writer and western fast draw enthusiast living in St. Helens, Oregon. No stranger to the places his characters inhabit—Reno, Carson City, Virginia City and Lake Tahoe—he raised his children in northern Nevada, from 1984 through 1993, as pastor and head of staff of the First Presbyterian Church in Carson City.

Gregg enjoys hearing from his readers, posting updates and background to his work on his website and blog at: **www.greggtownsley.com**. You can find him on Facebook: **www.facebook.com/GreggEdwardsTownsley**, or subscribe to his Twitter updates at **http://twitter.com/greggtownsley**.

The author encourages your review of this book and his others at www.amazon.com.